SOLOMON

Vodka & Milk

They: Want You Dead

Printed in the United States of America

Rights Department, 144 North 7th Street, #255
Brooklyn N.Y. 11249

First Edition:

Book and Jacket Design: PiXiLL Designs

Cataloging in Publication data is on file with the library of Congress

ISBN 9780997146219 (Trade Paperback)

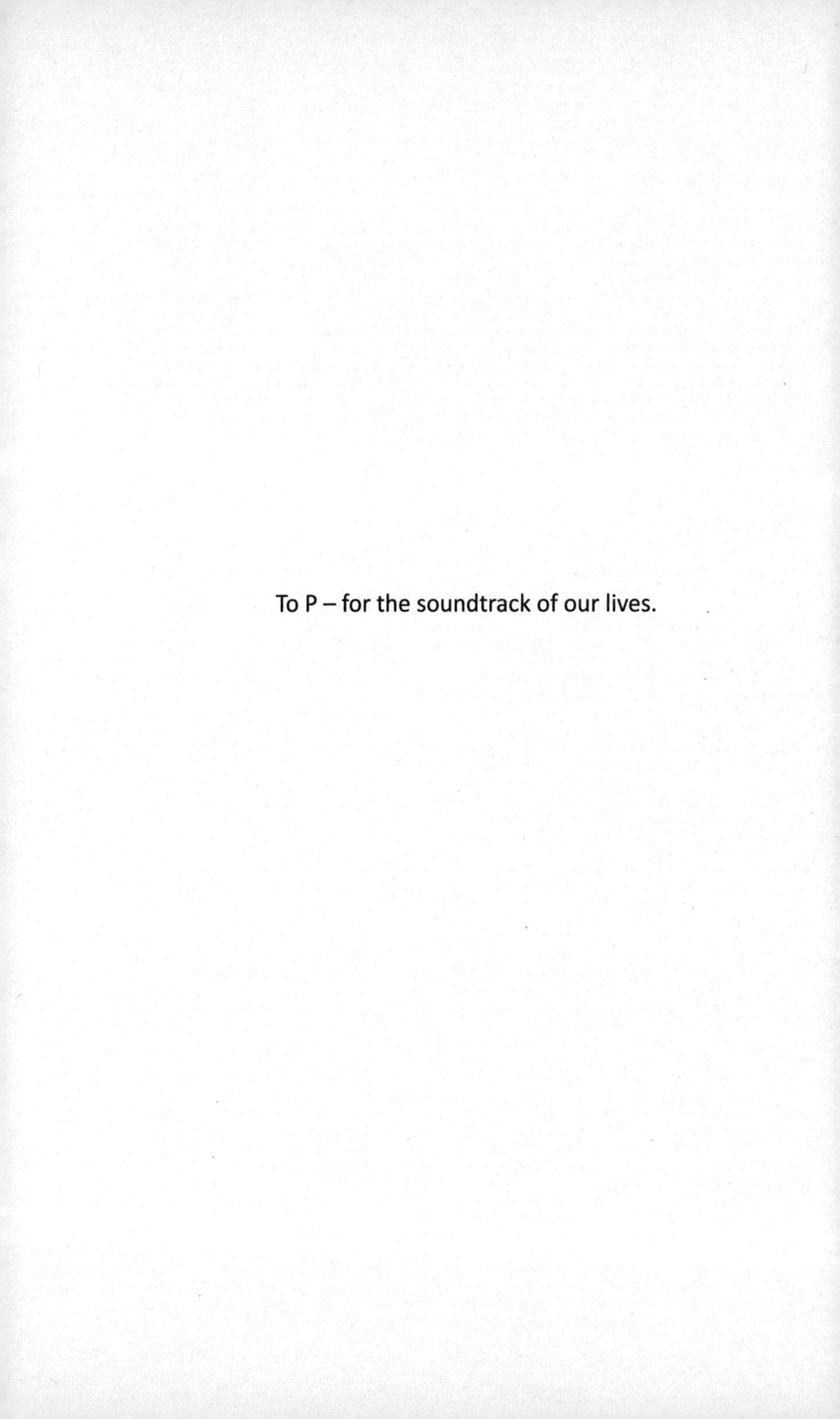

To P – for the soundtrack of our lives.

chapter one

THEY: WANT YOU DEAD

The siren woke her up.

"Shit!" said Howie, his eyes on the rear view mirror. "Shit, no. Not today. Not now."

They hadn't been on the road long. She glanced at the clock on the dash—11:14 a.m. They only left the airport ten minutes ago and were now on the highway into Richmond, Virginia.

Howie was pulling the SUV towards the shoulder, still cursing. She could see his hands shaking.

Melissa Jones twisted around in her seat as the siren blared again. There were two officers in the car behind them, their faces impossible to make out in the haze of the flashing red and blue lights.

"Were you speeding?" Melissa asked.

"Shit no, I ain't crazy." Howie brought the car to a halt by the metal barrier at the side of the road. Vehicles shot by them on the road, causing the SUV to rock as they passed by. He already had the glove compartment open, his hand searching for his documents.

"Just stay calm, okay?" he told her, checking through a small bundle of papers to make sure he had everything he needed. Howie's words made her feel more nervous. It was just a traffic stop, why was he so jumpy? "Keep your hands where the cops can see them, okay? No sudden moves. Don't argue, don't talk back, don't say anything unless they ask you, you got me?"

She nodded. His nervousness was having an effect on her. She tried to calm her breathing. The cops had stopped her before, or at least they'd pulled her dad over when she was in the car. It seemed to happen a lot, and Dad always sighed and said, "Here we go again." But he'd never appeared to be scared for his life. Howie was sweating, shifting in his seat. He looked like he wanted to bolt.

The cops were taking their time, probably running Howie's plates through their computer. Howie checked through his papers for the third time.

"Shit," he said. Awkwardly, he reached into his back pocket and took out his wallet. It took a moment for him to find his driver's license, which he added to the stack of documents. He handed the wallet to her. She moved to put the wallet in her lap but he shook his head. "Keep your hands visible."

"Okay," she said. "It's going to be okay, Howie. Try to relax."

"Sure, I'll relax," he said, wiping sweat from his brow. "Crap, we should record this."

"Record it? Really?"

Howie had his phone out and was opening a live streaming app. He spoke into the camera.

"Okay, this is Howie Do coming to you from I-95 in Richmond, VA. Just been pulled over by a couple of cops. You are my witness." He handed the phone to Melissa.

"You want me to record this?" Melissa said reluctantly.

"Hell yeah."

"I don't know if that's a good idea…"

"Periscope it. Live broadcast on your channel. Just in case

they take the phone away."

The slamming of two car doors interrupted Howie. Melissa glanced in the side mirror and saw two cops, both male, both white, both with hands on their holsters, approaching the SUV. One hung back while the other approached the driver's side.

Howie lowered the window, his hands on the wheel, one still clutching his pile of papers. Melissa did her best to cover him and the cop with the phone camera.

"This your vehicle?" the cop by Howie's window asked.

"Yes, sir."

"You got license and registration?"

"Yes, sir, it's all here. I'm going to hand it to you now, okay?"

Howie slowly and deliberately held out the stack of papers to the officer, who didn't take them.

"You armed?"

"Yes, sir. My concealed permit is right here."

The cop took a step backwards, away from the open window.

"Step out of the vehicle, sir."

Melissa thought he might protest. Instead, Howie opened his car door and stepped out. She had to twist around in her seat now to keep the camera on them.

"Is your companion armed also?"

"No," said Howie.

"Ma'am, step out of the vehicle please." This instruction came from the second cop, his voice muffled through Melissa's window. Her heart hammering, Melissa opened her door and stepped out, phone still in her hand but held to her side so it wasn't obvious it was recording. The roar of a passing truck made it hard to hear what Howie's cop said next, but to her surprise he now had his hands on the hood of the car and the cop was searching him.

Melissa's cop directed her to do the same. She placed her hands on the hood, the phone still in her right, its camera facing back towards her. She tried to remain calm as his hands patted her shoulders and underarms and then travelled down her body. To her relief, he didn't grope her. It was still uncomfortable, and when he was done he didn't say she could take her hands off the car.

She glanced over at Howie, also still facing her. The cop was taking longer to search him. He flashed her a weak smile, but he was clearly scared. She tried to angle the phone in her hand towards her boyfriend so that the camera could see what was happening to him.

The cop found and removed Howie's gun, then checked to see if it was loaded. After that he pushed it into his belt and snatched the papers out of Howie's hand, who was still pressed to the metal hood. As he did so, one of the documents slipped out and fell to the ground. Instinctively, Howie bent to pick it up.

The cops reacted like a bomb had gone off. Both drew their weapons. Both shouted at him to stand still.

Howie froze. Melissa couldn't see his face as it was below the hood of the car, but he saw his back. The cops weren't looking at her so she raised the phone camera.

"I'm just getting my permit," Howie said, his voice hard to hear with the traffic thundering past.

"Do not move!" the cop screamed. His gun was pointing straight at Howie.

Time seemed to slow down. The cars rushing by now seemed to be taking their time. Each whoosh, whoosh, whoosh accompanied by a flash from the gun. Melissa heard only the first shot. At least three more followed. Howie dropped out of sight behind the car. Her hand flew to her mouth. She might have screamed but as she was slammed into the car hood, it knocked the breath from her lungs. The phone fell from her hand as she dropped to the ground. The cop kicked her arm as she lay there. She was distantly aware of the pain. She tried to beg them to stop. For some reason the only word she could get out was the one that made him stop kicking her.

The cop bent over, his face looming and angry.

"What did you say?"

"Canadian," she wheezed.

"You got a passport?"

She managed to reach a trembling hand into her jacket pocket. Her passport fell out onto the asphalt. The cop picked it up, flicked through it and showed it to his partner.

"Shit," he said.

chapter two

THEY: WANT YOU DEAD

Melissa paced her cell with her hands in her hair and tears in her eyes. Whenever anyone passed she would call out to them, asking if they knew what had happened to her boyfriend. They ignored her.

She had little idea of how long she'd been in there. They'd taken her phone and she didn't have any other way to tell the time, so she paced up and down behind the bars, chewed her fingernails and demanded answers from any person she saw. Her ribs and arm ached from where the cop kicked her. They hadn't even given her water. She needed to pee but refused to use the highly public metal toilet in the corner of the cell. Nobody offered her a phone call or provided a lawyer.

But she didn't care about her own condition. She only wanted to know if her boyfriend was alive or dead.

Eventually an officer in uniform took her out of her cell and escorted her to an interview room. Melissa wasn't handcuffed, but the woman tugged on her injured arm and refused to say a word.

She sat in silence for some time, the female cop in the corner still not talking.

"Where's my boyfriend?" she asked. The woman ignored

her. "Can I use the washroom please?" No response. "The bathroom? The restroom? Whatever the fuck you call it?"

Still nothing.

"I'm going to pee right here all over your chair," Melissa warned her. The officer seemed to come to a decision. She strode over, pulled Melissa to her feet by her injured arm, then hurried her from the room to the washroom.

The officer stood outside the cubicle while Melissa did her business, then escorted her back to the room once she'd washed her hands.

Another cop was waiting when she returned. He was white with grey hair and a heavily lined face, like he did a lot of frowning.

"Where's my boyfriend?" Melissa said as she sat down opposite the cop.

"Name?"

"You know my name. You have my passport. Where's Howie?"

"Name?"

"Melissa Jones."

"Nationality?"

"Canadian. Can you please tell me…?"

"Age?"

"Nineteen."

"Reason for being in the US?"

"I'm not answering any more questions until you tell me how my boyfriend is."

Melissa folded her arms and stared at him, daring him to ask something else.

The cop cleared his throat. "I'm sorry to inform you that Mr. Howard Douglas died in the ambulance on the way to hospital."

The bottom fell out of Melissa's world. She stared blankly at the policeman for an age, her eyes filling with tears. She drew her knees up to her chin and hugged her legs, rocking slightly as she chanted, "no no no," over and over again.

"What happens next, Miss Jones, is up to you. You can either walk out of here, get your things from the hotel and take the next flight back to Toronto, or we can charge you with resisting arrest and have you deported. The choice is yours."

"Why? Why did he shoot him? Why did Howie have to die? I don't understand." Melissa could no longer see through the tears. Her wailing voice sounded muffled and dead in the small interview room, which echoed what was in her heart.

"Mr. Douglas was shot by an officer who believed his life was in danger. It was self defense, Miss Jones."

"He wasn't in danger! He had Howie's gun."

"The officer believed Mr. Douglas had a second firearm."

"That's bullshit. He murdered him. Why isn't he locked in a cell?"

The female officer behind Melissa placed a box of tissues on the table before her. Melissa smacked the box across the room. The man opposite her didn't flinch.

"Miss Jones, I *strongly* advise you not to use words like 'murder'. If you want to see Canada again…"

"Are you threatening me now?" Melissa roared at him. "If I don't do as you say there's going to be an accident and I'll end up dead too? Is that it?"

"Miss Jones," the officer said. "Do we need to put you in cuffs?"

Melissa fell quiet. Despite her distress, she was fully aware she was sitting in a police station in a foreign nation, and she could get in serious trouble if she pushed her protest too hard. She *did* want to go home. She did want to go back to Toronto, to her family, to her friends. Here she knew nobody, and nobody was likely to step up and defend her. Without

Howie she was completely alone. There was her agent in L.A., but she hadn't known her long and didn't honestly know if their professional relationship extended to getting her client out of jail. She knew she had to play along. She knew she had to help them cover up the awful thing they had done. Perhaps once safely back in Toronto she could make a fuss, talk to the media, use her channel to tell her fans what really happened.

"Fine," she said. "I'll play along. I won't say anything to anyone if you let me fly home."

"Good. Thank you, Miss Jones. I'm glad you've seen reason."

"Besides," Melissa added. "I don't need to say anything. Howie's fans will have seen the video of the shooting by now."

"Howie's… fans?"

Melissa laughed humorlessly. "You have no idea who you killed, do you?"

"Should we?"

"You've never heard of *This is Howie Do*? The YouTube channel? He has four million subscribers and every one of them is going to be pissed as fuck with you."

"We're prepared for some demonstrations as a result of this unfortunate incident."

"Oh this is going to be like nothing you've seen before. And when my fans hear about it –"

"Your fans?"

"Yeah, I don't have as many subs as Howie did, but I have a pretty big following too. You guys need to spend more time taking an interest in what your teens are watching. Even if I say nothing, Howie ain't gonna go quietly."

The officer sat stony-faced.

"Just remember," he said, unmoved by Melissa's outburst, "get your stuff from the hotel, go to the airport, say nothing to anybody. Do you understand?"

Melissa stood up. She wasn't going to give him the satisfaction of seeing her cry again. She stared at him defiantly as the lady cop opened the door to the room. Without a word, she turned and marched out, her head held high.

She took some time in the washroom cleaning herself up. Her escort waited outside for her this time. Then she led Melissa to the entrance and gave her back her things, including her cell phone.

"Can I have my luggage from Howie's car?" Melissa almost choked when she said his name.

"Not today. The car is impounded at another location. Check back tomorrow."

Melissa didn't argue. She put on her jacket and placed her items in the pockets.

"For what it's worth," the lady officer said to her before she left the station, "I'm really sorry about what happened."

Melissa smiled weakly. It wasn't much, it wasn't nearly enough, but it was something.

Outside on the street, a storm of reporters accosted her. Questions flew thick and fast as she fought her way through the throng to the waiting taxi.

"No comment," she said at least a dozen times. It took well over a minute to travel just a dozen meters to the road. She had to battle to open the cab door against the crush of cameras and microphones. Eventually she managed to squeeze herself into the back seat and close the door, deadening the cacophony.

"Where to?" asked the driver, looking with concern at the crush of people pressed up against the side of his cab.

Melissa checked her phone. Her agent had booked a flight for her to Toronto leaving tomorrow afternoon, and a hotel for the night. She was exhausted, so maybe it was a good thing she wasn't catching a flight right away. She wondered if she'd be able to sleep.

She told the driver where to go and carefully, he pulled the cab onto the road.

chapter three

THEY: WANT YOU DEAD

State Senator Tim Barns took the glass of whisky and raised it with a forced smile.

"Congratulations, *Senator*," said the man who had poured him the drink.

Lionel Granger was, in Tim's private opinion, one of the most repulsive men he had ever met. He was grey, slightly overweight and balding. His suit was immaculately tailored and very expensive, and everything about his office screamed opulence, from the marble desktop to the Henkel Harris chairs.

"I owe it all to you, Lionel," Tim replied, trying not to grimace. It wasn't true. He'd put in a shitload of work himself, and had a small army of staffers who had worked similar long hours to help get him elected. Still, brown-nosing his biggest campaign donor was the expected thing to do, and Tim knew how to play the game.

"Nonsense, my dear Tim. The people love you. You're a natural and I know you'll be the best senator Virginia has ever seen. One day you might be much, much more."

It was all bullshit of course. But Tim played along.

"Well I can't say I don't have ambitions, Mr. Granger, but for now I'm happy to serve the people of this state in any way I can."

Granger raised his glass again, and Tim followed suit. They drank. It was damn good whisky, so that was a positive.

Truth be told, Tim had dreaded this meeting ever since Granger first offered to help finance his campaign almost a year ago. Without Granger's dollars, Tim would never have become such a well-known presence in Richmond, and it would have taken a miracle to unseat the incumbent. But Granger helped him pull off a miracle, and now it was payback time. The wealthy owner of a national chain of big box retail stores had not voiced the conditions of his backing, but he'd made it clear that all he wanted was the ear of a young, popular senator clued in to how the next generation felt. Tim wasn't naïve enough to expect no demands at all, but he hoped Granger would keep his word and just provide some suggestions and engage in a dialogue with him.

"Tim, please, take a seat."

Tim sat down in one of the enormously expensive chairs in front of the unlit fireplace. Granger took the vacant chair next to him.

"I've become very fond of you over the last year, Tim. I like your energy and I like the platform you ran on. The people voted for you because they want real change, and they believe you're the man to give it to them."

"I'm just one senator," Tim replied, eager to remind Granger that his sphere of influence was still very limited.

"For now. Play your cards right and you could be Virginia's next governor. That's what I see for you, and I'm willing to carry on putting up the cash to help you get there."

"Well I greatly appreciate that, Lionel." It had taken him six months and constant reminders from the old man to stop calling him Mr. Granger. Tim still didn't feel comfortable using the man's first name. They were not friends. They did not hang out at the weekends or go fishing together. Their occasional rounds of golf and meetings in Granger's over-the-top office were always pleasantries followed by business. Up until now, that business was about the logistics and strategy of getting Tim into the state senate. Now, Tim feared, Granger was going to want a much larger say in policy.

"So Tim," Lionel said, still smiling. "I love your platform and the voters love it too. I know you've been working hard since you were sworn in and you've started bringing other senators around to your way of thinking. That's really good."

"Right, well I think there's a national movement now to cut down on private companies using state prisoners as cheap labor. Following the federal ruling last year, I don't think it will be hard to get folks on board. I've drafted a bill and it's doing the rounds. I'm hopeful we can get it passed in the near future. Then we can start working on the House. I'm meeting with the governor in two weeks to get his take on it."

"That's great, really great. I have just one small request."

Tim gritted his teeth. "Sure, Lionel, name it."

"Well, as you know, Ambley's never uses inmates to manufacture our store brand goods, but we do stock a lot of brands that do. Since we started talking about this, I've been pushing them to stop doing it, but it's going to take time and I need to get other retailers on board. This goes national of course, because most of the brands we stock aren't manufactured in Virginia."

"I understand that, Lionel, but I want Virginia to be a leader here. If we pass this bill, I'm sure other states will follow our lead."

"Indeed, indeed, and that's what I want to happen too. But it's taking time, and I want the brands we stock to understand that this is the way forward before there are laws on the books forcing them to comply. So what I'm asking for, Tim, is for you to slow it down a bit. I never for one moment thought you'd make so much progress so fast, and I think we need to put the brakes on just a bit."

Tim put down his drink. "With respect, Lionel, now is the time. We need to follow the Feds on this. Other states are moving in the same direction and I don't want Virginia left behind."

Granger held up a hand. "Of course, of course. I'm not asking for a big delay. Just a few months, until I've made some more headway. Is that all right with you?"

Tim tried to keep his voice level. Momentum was everything. Stalling now could mean all his work so far on this issue would have to start again from scratch as legislator's minds drifted to other topics. But he smiled back and said, "Of course, Lionel. Shouldn't be a problem. We want to get this right, after all."

"Good man. Now, onto voting rights for former felons."

Tim sighed without showing it externally. Granger was going to move through all three of the campaign promises that had gotten him elected and he was going to meddle with all of them. After tackling reinstatement of voting rights for former felons he would start on police reform. Tim might as well be the same man as his predecessor. He distantly wondered if Granger gave two shits which senator he was talking to as long as he got his way.

The conversation continued for another half hour, and by the end of it Granger had asked Tim to stall or gut the vast majority of the policies he promised to pursue when he ran. It wasn't hard to understand how state and federal politics achieved so little, with so much money on the line and so many big name donors providing *opinions*.

Granger stood up.

"Well thanks for coming, Tim. I really appreciate you taking the time to come here."

Tim stood also and shook Granger's proffered hand.

"Of course, any time."

"You will take on board my, er, suggestions, right?"

Tim shuffled awkwardly. "Well it is rather a lot to process. I can't make any promises."

Granger's smile didn't move. It was so fixed it was almost creepy. He still had hold of Tim's hand, his grip firm.

"Oh I think you should do more than consider what I've said. I mean, you've kept yourself remarkably scandal-free thus far. It would be a shame if such a spotless record became tarnished."

Tim blinked.

"Are you threatening me?"

Granger's expression was one of shock. "Goodness me, no, I wouldn't dream of such a thing. I just want to be sure we have an understanding."

Tim nodded. His hand was finally released.

"Right, well I'll pay your *suggestions* as much mind as I think they deserve. Have a good day, Lionel."

Tim left the office. He didn't stop to talk to anyone, and he barely breathed before he was outside on the street. He had to lean against a wall for a moment until his head stopped swimming.

Shit! What was he going to do? Could he rely on persuading fellow senators to support his bills without having to spend money on advertising to drum up public support? He'd just have to try, given that the alternative was none of his bills reaching the senate floor at all. Tim wondered how many of his predecessors, heck, how many members of the current Senate, received similar *suggestions* from Granger in exchange for financial support.

Well, dammit, he wasn't going to be one of them. Enough Virginian's knew who Tim was now that he could fundraise from other wealthy folks, perhaps even a grassroots funding campaign, if he needed money. The next election was a long way off – the last thing he wanted to do was stall all his plans until that time, or even indefinitely. He also had the uneasy feeling that his next meeting with Granger would be less about stalling what Tim wanted to do, and more about pushing what Granger wanted to achieve. Tim couldn't crumble at the first hurdle. He had to stand tall and send the message that he wasn't going to be intimidated. He might spend his entire political career in the pockets of lobbyists and donors if he didn't make clear now he was incorruptible.

Screw Granger and his agenda. Tim didn't need his money.

As he headed towards his car, Tim felt an aching in his gut. This kind of bullshit wasn't the reason for his getting into politics. He wasn't naïve enough to be surprised by it, but he hoped to have a few years doing what he loved before the inevitable outside corruption started to seep in. Such a pessimistic view, he mused.

These thoughts made him more determined to resist as long as he still had fight in him. And he would start by ignoring Granger's suggestions and doing what he damn well intended to do in the first place.

chapter four

THEY WANT YOU DEAD

It had been an exhausting day. Scratch that, Melissa thought, the worst day of her life.

Melissa kicked off her shoes and rubbed her aching feet. She was bone tired and her bruises throbbed. She popped the lid from a bottle of painkillers she'd bought from the little store in the lobby, and swallowed two pills with a bottle of water.

There was no pill she could take to ease the deep loneliness gnawing at her. At least, no pill she could buy legally without a prescription. Going to bed without Howie lying next to her was nothing new because they lived in different countries and spent far too much time apart. It was easy to convince herself, for a short time, that he was just somewhere else tonight, that he was thinking about her and sending her sexy text messages. She picked up her phone to divert her attention from the cavernous hole in her heart. She saw dozens of texts and voicemails, thousands of Instagram messages and more tweets than any sane person could ever read. She resisted the urge to turn off her phone and try to sleep. She doubted she'd get much rest anyway, and people she cared about were worried about her.

So she worked her way through her texts, given that they

came from people who knew her best. She answered the one from Shania, her best friend and technical guru who ran her channel, wrote her apps and managed all her accounts. Shania was a genius and a friend for the ages. Melissa's mom had texted her too, so Melissa replied that she was safe, feeling sad but okay, and would be home tomorrow. She didn't mention her bruises. What could her mom do about those? She had enough to worry about.

The reply came back almost immediately. Why had she not responded sooner? Her mom was sick, perhaps terminally so, and it ate at Melissa that she might be the cause of extra stress. Melissa briefly explained that she'd been at the police station since the incident and couldn't reply until now.

Shania was the next to message her.

Saw the video. Are you hurt?

Oh God, the video. Melissa stared at the words. In all of this, she had completely forgotten the broadcast from Howie's phone. She should find it and watch it, to remind herself of what happened.

Did she really want to be reminded? The images already burned in her mind. She would have to watch it eventually, but not tonight.

She replied to Shania, sent another five texts in response to her mother's frantic messaging, then turned her attention to her followers.

Melissa Jones's channel had millions of subscribers, many of whom were avid viewers. She talked about fashion, celebrities, life and her own experiences with her mother's many illnesses. A couple of her posts went viral, her subscriber numbers shot up, and it snowballed from there. She had no idea why her channel was so popular, but she did her best to post regular updates and respond to her fans. Of course there were haters too, but Melissa had a thick skin and didn't let them get to her. That's why she was able to screen out the vile comments without absorbing what they said.

Howie Do deserved what he got…

Donate to Officer Hagley's defense fund…

Hagley did us all a favor today…

Maybe Jones will shut the fuck up now…

Melissa let them all slide past her like she always did with the inevitable hatred surfacing in the wake of everything she posted. Usually her real fans drowned out the shit. Not today.

Thick skin sister, she told herself.

But the trauma of today was unlike anything she'd experienced before. She knew she would have to post something about it. In the past she'd taken on causes, but they were for other people's benefit. She was far too close to this to handle it at the moment. She wasn't about to launch a fight for justice or anything like that. She wasn't strong enough yet. She wanted time to grieve, and then she would talk to her followers.

One last text went to her agent, thanking her for arranging the hotel and flight, and promising to be in touch soon. Jasmine was a dynamo, a true angel on Earth who had taken Melissa under her wing and fought tooth-and-nail to get her and Howie an astonishing deal with a major US network. It had all been so exciting, until this morning when it all came crashing down.

She missed Howie so much. The thought of him caused physical pain in her chest. She curled up exhausted and wanting to sleep but with her eyes remaining stubbornly wide open. She had boyfriends before, but none of them were like Howie. He understood her on an emotional level, on a sexual level, and on an intellectual level. He was so smart. Nobody realized how smart he was. Most of her boyfriends had been man-child idiots attracted by her body and her rising fame.

Howie loved her body, oh God his passion for her left her breathless, but he loved her mind too.

What would she do without him? How could she carry on alone? Now that she knew what was possible when you truly make a connection with someone special, how could she live without it?

A new text popped up on her phone from a number she didn't recognize.

Hey Melissa. This is Howie's brother, Wilson. You holding up?

She wanted to put the phone down, to just shut it all out. But that wasn't fair to Wilson. She'd never met Howie's brother; she was supposed to meet him and his folks today. He would understand if she didn't reply right away. It was nice of him to check on her though.

Doing OK. Thanks for texting. Tired. Can we talk tomorrow?

His response came back quickly.

Sure. Get some rest. TTYL.

And with that, her battery died and her phone went dark. Taking this as her cue to turn in, she plugged in her phone and grabbed the toothbrush and toothpaste she'd bought at the same time as the painkillers.

There was a commotion coming from the street outside. She moved to the window, trying to ignore her painful arm. Parting the curtain she saw nothing unusual, but more noise drew her attention to much further along the street. Her head pressed against the window, she struggled to see far enough down the road to find out what was causing the noise.

Then they came into view. Hundreds of them, marching along the main street, waving banners and chanting. She wondered what they were marching for, as this was clearly a protest.

She had seen before on the news people holding signs at such demonstrations that read things like, '#icantbreathe', or

'Hands Up, Don't Shoot!', or 'Black Lives Matter', but it had always been an abstract thing. BLM existed in Toronto too, she'd seen them at Gay Pride and other events, but this was something else. This was a reaction to something. What?

As they drew closer and filled the street from side to side, Melissa was able to read some of the signs. Most were as expected, similar to what she'd seen before. She could make out what they were chanting now too.

Her mouth fell open.

"Justice for Howie!" they called. "Howie Do, killed by you!"

Melissa sat at her window and watched the march for some time, tears rolling down her face. It went on for a while, and eventually she could cry no more. Her eyes were growing heavy, and the weariness she felt seeped into her bones.

She stood up and drew the curtain, wondering if she'd be able to sleep with so much noise outside. She stripped down to her underwear and checked herself in the mirror. There was an ugly bruise on her side, which hurt if she touched it but thankfully caused her no discomfort otherwise. Her arm was a different story. Clearly it wasn't broken or she'd be screaming if she touched it with her other hand. Nevertheless, the bruising on her upper arm was extensive. Her arm bone ached where the officer kicked her. Clearly the damage was deep, but she felt no desire to go to hospital.

She climbed into bed and laid down on her good side. The noisy protest and the pain in her arm kept her awake for a time, as did the images flashing through her head of a day straight from hell. Thankfully the pain was easier to ignore now that the pills had kicked in. She concentrated on saying a prayer, clearing her mind of her troubles one by one. Eventually she fell into a merciful sleep.

"Hey Penny, it's Tim."

"Hey Tim."

"Hey. Sorry to call you so late."

"Oh that's okay. I was watching the protests on TV."

"What protests?"

"Some rapper was shot by police this morning and his girlfriend beaten up. You didn't hear about it?"

"No, I've been in meetings all day. You're supposed to tell me about this stuff."

"Sorry, I thought you knew. How was your meeting with Granger?"

"Not great. He wants to me to stall all my bills."

"Really? Why?"

"I'll tell you all about it tomorrow. I need you to start thinking about who else we can tap for donations and support."

"Granger's not paying any more?"

"I can't do what he wants me to do, Penny. I can't sabotage all our work because the moneyman says so. I'd be no better than the guys we defeated to get here."

"No chance of a compromise? Delay some bills and not others?"

"He made it pretty clear I gotta do what he says or no more funding."

"Shit."

"Yeah. So, anyway, I figured it was time to cut ties. Nothing official or public, just line up alternative backers and quietly ignore Granger."

"He's not going to like that."

"No, he's not. But other than stop donating, what else can he do?"

"This is one of those, I-can't-talk-you-out-of-it situations, isn't it, Tim?"

"'Fraid so."

"Fine, I'll think about it. It won't be easy."

"If it was easy, it wouldn't be fun."

"Uh huh. Well I'm going back to scaring myself shitless with the news okay?"

"Sure, thanks Pen. Have a good night."

"You too."

Tim hung up the phone and turned on the local news. Sure enough, a protest was in full swing down East Main Street, a mile or so away from his house and heading his way. He watched the images of rapper Howie Do and his girlfriend, Canadian YouTube star, Melissa Jones, and watched the video of the shooting, his hand over his mouth in shock. He knew immediately he had to get involved. It might piss off Lionel Granger and his ilk, but Tim didn't give a shit.

He picked up his phone and called the governor, the state's Attorney General and Virginia's Senate majority leader. None of them answered – it was getting late that was true, but still, it was annoying. Protestors flooding into Richmond's streets and the top brass weren't answering their phones? Perhaps they weren't answering to *him*. He tried calling Richmond's police chief, but as expected, his phone went immediately to voicemail and the mailbox was full. That was no surprise. The guy had his hands full tonight.

Tim stood and went to his front door. Opening it up, he could hear distant sounds of chanting and shouting coming from the direction of East Main Street. He grabbed his jacket, his keys and his phone and headed out to join the protest.

chapter five

THEY: WANT YOU DEAD

The knock on the door woke Melissa. Bleary-eyed, she stared at the clock. It was 8:00 a.m. The knocking came again, so she dragged herself from the bed.

"Just a minute!" she called.

She wrapped a hotel robe around her and winced at the pain in her arm. The pills had long since worn off and her bruises were agony. She shuffled over to the door and opened it to find a porter with two suitcases.

"Good morning, Madam, I believe these belong to you?"

It was her luggage. It could only have been here thanks to Saint Jasmine.

"Thank you," she said. She picked up her purse and scrabbled for a generous tip as the porter brought her suitcases into the room.

She closed the door behind him after he left. She stared at them, hardly daring to believe they were real. What a relief! She hadn't looked forward to returning to the police station this morning to get them.

Images and memories crashed into her mind like baseball bats striking her. She dropped to her knees. The cell. The interview room. The officers. The demonstration. The traffic stop. The gunfire. Her boyfriend, his body twisting with the

She couldn't breathe. Couldn't move. Couldn't think of anything else.

Howie was dead. He wasn't coming back. He wasn't going to knock on her hotel door and surprise her. She would never again feel his body against her skin. She would never hold his hand or kiss his mouth. She would never talk to him, laugh with him, be with him.

He was gone.

Murdered by those fucks!

Anger replaced the suffocation of loss. Hot, burning anger that gripped her stomach and clenched her teeth. She seethed, tears forming a puddle at her feet, fists pounding the floor. She screamed, raged at the injustice. She yelled at God for taking him from her. She roared at the universe for being so cruel.

She had never felt so helpless.

She lay on the floor sobbing for some time. Even when there were no tears left, she couldn't bring herself to move. Her breathing was ragged and her dry sobs came in heaves.

Eventually, all that was left was numbness.

She dragged herself to her feet and went to the washroom. She showered and dressed in clean clothes, then picked up her phone to find dozens of new texts waiting for her. She flicked through them dispassionately, sentiment after sentiment having no effect on the deadness of her soul.

One caught her eye and she stopped. She stared at it for a minute, trying to process what it said. It was from Howie's brother, Wilson.

Meet me at Tremelos at 9 a.m.

Well that was kind of forward. What if she didn't want to? What if she just wanted to get the hell out of this fucked up country and go home right now? What if seeing her dead boyfriend's brother was just too painful a concept for her to cope with? What if the noisy protestors outside had kept her awake half the night and she wanted to crawl back under the covers and go back to sleep?

She could answer all of these questions positively, but she knew full well that Howie would want her to go see his brother. He had spoken of Wilson often, even in the short time she'd known him. It was clear that Howie loved his brother and would do anything for him. Wilson must be hurting just as much as she was, and it was totally fair for him to want answers from the woman who was there when Howie died.

She decided, for Howie, she would go.

The streets were quiet that morning. The rush to get to work was over, and there was a host of city workers clearing up the debris after last night's protest. No storefronts were damaged, but litter was everywhere and there were numerous broken signs abandoned in the gutter.

Justice For Howie!

Put Hagley Away!

And of course, *Black Lives Matter!*

She'd heard of the movement, of course. Toronto had its own chapter, though police violence against black people in Canada was generally rarer than in the States. Still there were disproportionate numbers of traffic stops, minor drug convictions and stop and searches in Toronto, or carding as it was known. Melissa loved Canada, loved the opportunities presented to her and the social safety net of healthcare and welfare, but the country was not without its racial divide and its ugly underbelly of bigotry.

She entered the café expecting to have to look around for Wilson, but she spotted him straight away. He was so like Howie, yet different in some ways. His nose was a little narrower, his forehead a little broader, his chin a little rounder, yet he was so obviously Howie's brother that Melissa found herself moving towards him with her hand outstretched before he'd even noticed her approaching.

He put down his coffee and shook her hand, smiling with sad eyes. He invited her to sit. Neither needed to introduce themselves.

"How you holding up?" Wilson asked, his voice filled with compassion and empathy.

Melissa sighed. "I'm doing okay. It hasn't hit me fully yet, you know?"

"Yeah I know. I got the same thing. I woke up this morning thinking, I should call Howie today. Not spoken to him in a week and that's a long time for us. Guess you kept him busy."

The words weren't accusatory or tinged with jealousy. There was a glint of amusement in his eye that reminded Melissa so starkly of Howie that for a moment she struggled to breathe.

"You all right?"

"Yeah, yeah I'm okay. You look a lot like him."

Wilson patted the table awkwardly. "Oh yeah, I didn't think of that. Sorry. Must be hard for you."

"No, it's fine. It's not your fault you look like your brother."

"Shit no it ain't!" he said in mock protest.

Melissa smiled slightly, then let it fade. "I keep thinking I'll get a text from him any moment, you know? I think he'll call soon, and then I remember. I guess I just can't believe he's gone."

"It sucks, man. Fucking sucks. I figured losing my brother to cancer, or in a flood, or some act of God shit, well that's one thing. Can't control that. But this bullshit? Motherfucking cops looking for someone to shoot. Fuck."

Melissa sat in awkward silence following his outburst. She

felt the same way, but he'd raised his voice and there were people with kids too young to be in school nearby. Wilson followed her glance and took in the family that sat nearby, the mother glaring at him and the father trying to distract their toddler from the bad black man and his nasty words.

"I'm sorry," Wilson said, without any trace of anger. "Cop shot my brother. Not having the best day."

The couple looked abashed at this, almost guilty. Like so many white folk when confronted with violence perpetrated on black people by "their" people, they retreated into awkward reverence.

Wilson turned back to Melissa with a mischievous grin. Despite all that had happened, Melissa found herself happy to be in his company. Even at such a shitty time, Wilson displayed so much of Howie's easy-going it-don't-bother-me attitude that she couldn't help but feel comfortable with him.

His expression turned serious. "Listen, I guess you're wondering why I asked you to be here."

"Sure," said Melissa. "I'm just gonna get a coffee, okay? Didn't sleep much last night."

"Oh shit, where are my manners? You stay here, let me get you something."

"That's nice of you, Wilson. I'll have a latte with sugar."

"Coming right up."

Wilson walked over to the counter and joined a short line up to place the order. Melissa didn't know how to feel. She had to remind herself that she didn't know Wilson – it was far too easy to believe he was exactly like his brother and therefore worthy of her trust. He could be here to find out if she planned to make a claim on Howie's estate. He might even be here to find out if Melissa had planned for the cops to ambush them and kill Howie to get out of the relationship. Okay, her imagination was running away with itself there. The point was, she didn't know him. All she had to go on was the character and word of his brother. Surely that was enough? It was hard not to be paranoid and suspicious after what happened yesterday.

Her thoughts had gotten stuck on Howie and a rising tide of crushing sadness threatened to overwhelm her. Thankfully at that moment Wilson returned, bringing her back to the present.

He placed two coffees on the table and sat down opposite her.

"I expect you want to know what happened to your brother," Melissa said to him after a moment. She dreaded having to recount the awful story to anybody, wondering if she could hold it together long enough to finish, but she felt Wilson deserved to know the truth.

"I wouldn't make you do that. I saw the video. I know what happened."

"Oh." Melissa was secretly grateful she wouldn't have to return to that moment.

"I'm here to recruit you."

Visions of weird cults and their loony leaders appeared in her mind.

"Er, recruit me for what?"

"Yesterday I got a promotion. Black Lives Matter made me an official spokesperson."

"Because of Howie?"

"Because of Howie. I spoke at the rally after the protest march last night. Did you see me?"

Melissa shook her head. "I saw the march from my window, but I didn't join it. I was too tired. I was probably asleep by the time you spoke."

"I was pretty good, if I do say so myself." He smiled at his mock arrogance. His humor was infectious. Melissa found herself admiring his spirit in the face of tragedy.

"I'm sure you were amazing."

"You know what would be more amazing?"

"No."

"If you marched with us tonight. If you spoke to the protestors. If you did interviews on behalf of BLM. I've seen your channel, Melissa, and you're damn convincing. You have millions of followers and a voice that needs to be heard."

"Oh no, I have to catch my flight this–"

"That piece-of-shit policeman needs to go to jail, and he'll get off if we don't keep the pressure on. We need to march and protest and shout from the fucking rooftops until justice is served…"

"Really, I've got to go home–"

"Tell Howie's story. Tell them all how he they gunned him down even though he was unarmed. Tell them what the cops did to my brother! Please!"

Melissa stood up so fast her chair fell over. People were already staring at them as Wilson grew louder, but now everyone in the café was quiet.

"I think I'd better go," she said, picking up her chair.

Wilson stared into his coffee. In a flat voice he said, "You owe it to Howie."

Melissa leaned forward with her fists on the table. She didn't care that everyone was staring. Rage and frustration and grief built in her chest and her eyes were now wet with tears.

"I don't appreciate you telling me what I owe my dead boyfriend," she said. "Of course I want justice for Howie, but I'm not in a place right now where I can parade in front of the fucking cameras and tell everyone all about the shitty thing that happened yesterday so I can be a trending topic for half an hour and boost my public image. I'm not looking for ways to exploit Howie's death for my own personal gain, never mind yours. It was nice to meet you and thanks for the never mind yours. It was nice to meet you and thanks for the coffee."

She grabbed her bag, wincing as she swung it over her shoulder and it bounced against her bruised arm. She apologized to the open-mouthed couple with the kid for her language, and stormed out of the café.

She headed for her hotel. She planned on packing and heading out to the airport early. Her flight didn't leave for six hours but she didn't care. She would sit at the gate and wait. She didn't want to spend another moment in this city if she could avoid it. What right did that asshole have to lecture her on her obligations? Who was he to tell her how she should be acting? There was no wrong way to deal with what happened. There was no checklist to follow or textbook on the subject that she was aware of. She was out of bed, she was dressed and she had plans to leave the country – surely this was an achievement when the alternative was curling up on the floor in a ball and crying so hard and so long she would eventually be nothing but a pile of dust on the carpet.

Maybe she shouldn't have stormed out on him. He was going through trauma too; this was his way of coping. Throwing himself into a movement, with a clear goal and a mouthpiece to spread the word, was a worthy use of his rage – better than violence surely. She could understand why he believed she should follow the same path. But she refused to feel guilty for telling him where to go. She had a right to deal with this tragedy in her own way, and no obligation to follow a course laid out by someone she barely knew.

A black SUV suddenly screeched to a halt in front of her, mounting the pavement. She jumped back in shock, thinking that the driver must have made a mistake. When the doors opened and two masked men jumped out, she realized this was no accident. She screamed and turned to run, but it was already too late. The men were upon her, grabbing her arms and pulling her towards the vehicle. Passers-by stopped and gaped at what was happening. She cried out to them to help her, but then she was inside the vehicle and the driver reversed back out onto the road, then zoomed off at high speed.

Something sharp stabbed her neck and she cried out, struggling to get away. Very quickly she felt drowsy. As consciousness slipped away she heard someone tell her, "… told you not to talk to anyone…"

chapter six

THEY: WANT YOU DEAD

You need to go home right now.

Tim Barns stared at the text message on his phone, scratching his head. He didn't recognize the number of the sender. It was clearly meant for someone else. He clicked the reply button.

I think you have the wrong person.

"Tim, here's the list you asked for."

Tim looked up from his phone. Penny stood before his desk, waving a piece of paper at him. "You asked me not to send it electronically so I handwrote it. I feel so old school."

"Thanks, Penny," Tim said, taking the list. As he did so, his fingers brushed against hers. She seemed embarrassed for a moment, then she smiled.

"Anything else you need?"

"No, no this is great. Thank you. Go home early if you like. You've done great work today."

"Thanks, Tim. Um, actually me and the guys are going to Echelon later for a drink. Would you like to come?"

She smiled at him, and Tim didn't miss the implied reason for asking him.

"Some other time maybe? I want to go through this list before I go home."

"Okay sure. Maybe next time." She gave him a little wave then left his office.

Dear Penny. Fiercely loyal and dependable, always keeping him organized. She was lovely, and Tim certainly found her attractive, but she was at least ten years younger than him and he felt she should be with someone her own age. He had also not given up hope that Claire might come back. Sometimes he missed her more than he'd ever missed anyone or anything. Other times it was a relief to go home and not be scared to say anything for fear of triggering an argument. They had been married five years before she left, three months ago. She hadn't asked for a divorce; said she wanted to work things out. He owed her time to reevaluate and decide what she wanted. He still loved her, still cared about her, but was no longer sure he wanted to spend the rest of his life with her. When she walked out, he was surprised to discover that he felt just as relieved as he was upset.

His phone beeped again. Another text.

Tim, I'm a friend. Trust me. Go home now.

He frowned. Not a wrong number then. He found himself peering outside his office where his staff sat, trying to catch one of them pranking him.

This isn't funny.

He waited for the response. It was deeply unsettling. If he went home would someone be waiting for him? Should he call the police?

The mystery messenger read his mind.

Don't call the cops. They work for Granger. Go home. Tell no one where you're going.

Tim stared at it. Then he packed up his laptop, grabbed his jacket and left his office.

"Going home early?" Penny asked on his way out.

"No, I have to meet a potential donor," he lied.

"Oh, okay. Good luck!"

Tim arrived home some twenty minutes later to find his front door ajar. He crept inside, putting down his laptop case in the hallway and pushing the door closed behind him. Then he stood and listened. Sounds issued from the door to the basement, which was also slightly open. He took his phone from his pocket, intending to call the police. Then he reread the last message sent from his mystery contact.

Don't call the cops. They work for Granger.

He put his phone away and slipped off his shoes. He crept along the hallway, being careful to plant his feet at the edges of the floor nearest the wall, where the floorboards would be less likely to creak. He overshot the door to the basement, heading for his study at the back of the house.

A crash came from downstairs; Tim froze. After a moment of hearing no footsteps on the stairs, he kept going until he was in his office. Carefully taking his keys from his pocket, he found the right one and unlocked a large bureau against the far wall. Inside one of the draws was his prized Richmond Braves baseball bat, signed by a great many players from the seventies. He hated the thought of damaging one of his most valued possessions, but he couldn't think of anything else he might use as an effective weapon.

Holding the bat in both hands, Tim returned to the basement entrance.

Here, he hesitated. Should he just leave? Nothing down there was worth risking his life over. Perhaps he should get out now, wait for the intruder to be done, and then… well he didn't know what he might do. Find a hotel for the night? Call the police anyway? Nuke the site from orbit?

What was that? Was there someone down else down there? Tim swore he heard the muffled cries of someone obviously restrained in between the crashing caused by the known intruder. That settled it, now he couldn't leave.

As quietly and quickly as possible, Tim descended the stairs. The wall continued all the way down to the foot of the stairs, which worked to his advantage – if the stairs were open to the basement, his feet would have visible to the intruder long before he could have ducked his head down low enough to see.

His back to the wall, he raised the bat and made ready to leap out. He peered around first and then ducked back. There was a woman, young, black, terrified, tied to a chair in the center of the room. Her captor, a huge man with a mask on, was bustling around in the far corner of the dimly lit basement. The only light came from the small windows up at ground level. He was not facing the stairs, so Tim stepped out. He raised the bat and crept forward, intending to slam the intruder's head with it.

Unfortunately the woman noticed him and drew a sharp intake of breath. The big guy turned and took in both him and his baseball bat instantly. Tim cried out and nearly dropped the bat as the big man crashed into him, far too close to get in a good swing. And then Tim was sprawled on the floor with the wind knocked out of him. The intruder had already disappeared up the stairs. Tim tried to stand but his legs didn't work and he couldn't breathe. Footsteps pounded across the hall above his head and then the front door slammed.

Praying the guy was really gone, Tim got painfully to his feet and dropped the bat. He stumbled over to the woman and pulled off her gag.

"Oh my God, help me!" she cried, frantic with terror, pulling at her bonds.

Coughing and nursing his bruised ribs, Tim attempted to loosen the ropes holding her to the chair. They were far too tight, so he stumbled over to a shelf where his tool kit sat open. He pulled out a box cutter and crouched down behind the chair.

"Get me out, please!"

"It's okay," Tim reassured her. "He's gone. I'll get you out. What's your name?"

"Melissa," she said. "Melissa Jones."

"Well then Melissa Jones, just sit tight for a moment and I'll get you out."

Tim worked furiously to cut through the ropes. They were thick and took some sawing.

"I just want to go home," sobbed Melissa, exhausted and almost delirious.

"Who was that man?" Tim asked her.

"Don't know," she blurted. "Never… saw his face."

"Did he say anything to you? Why did he bring you here?"

"…Said I… shouldn't talk to anyone…"

At last Tim was through the ropes and Melissa's hands were free. It was easier to undo the ropes tying her legs, and a few moments later he was helping her to stand. Her legs gave way and she fell into his arms.

"Sorry," she said weakly.

"It's okay, you've been through a lot."

Tim took her over to the old sofa beside the far wall. He sat her down and went over to the kitchenette to get her a glass of water. She drank greedily from the glass, draining it quickly, and handed it back to him.

"I know you, don't I?" Tim said, looking into her eyes.

She was breathing heavily, her eyes puffy and damp from her ordeal.

"I've… probably been on the news a lot."

"You're Melissa Jones, right? Girlfriend of…" Tim trailed off. He didn't want to upset her more.

She nodded, struggling to bring her breathing under control.

"My name is Tim Barns. I'm a Virginia State Senator. I think I know why you were kidnapped, and I can guess why they were planning to leave you in my basement for me to find later this evening."

He sat down beside her and put an arm around her. She sobbed into his shoulder. He could hardly blame her after the couple of days she'd just lived through.

Tim's mind raced. If Granger was behind this, and it seemed likely, then he really wasn't fucking about. He must know Tim planned to cut him off. Was this a warning shot or a plan to discredit him completely? Who had sent the warning?

The front door upstairs burst open followed by stomping boots and shouting.

"Police!" yelled someone. Tim stood up, motioning for Melissa to stay seated.

He walked to the foot of the stairs and called up, "Down here!" Then he walked back to Melissa, sat down beside her and put his arm around her again.

Officers swarmed into the basement, all wearing SWAT gear and carrying guns. Tim stood up and raised his hands. They milled about in confusion for a moment, checking for the presence of anyone else down there. This was probably not the scene they had expected. Tim shielded Melissa with his body. He doubted a room full of armed police would do much to comfort her given what she'd been through.

One of the officers approached Tim.

"We got a report of a kidnapping," he said.

"I'm sure you did. The kidnapping is over. I disturbed the man who kidnapped Melissa and was attempting to leave her restrained in my basement."

"Is this true, ma'am?" the officer asked Melissa.

To Tim's surprise, Melissa stood and placed herself between the guns and Tim, reversing the position he had taken to protect her.

"Yes," she said, in a clear voice everyone in the basement could hear. "Senator Barns chased off my kidnappers and rescued me."

"So that we're clear," said the officer, "Senator Barns did not kidnap you and restrain you in his basement?"

"That's correct," she said. Tim was impressed. A moment ago she was sobbing onto his shoulder. He had expected to have to defend himself without her backing up his story. Here she was proclaiming his innocence, despite the trauma she had been through. Tim doubted he could be this strong if someone inflicted a similar ordeal on him.

"You'll both have to come to the station with us to make statements."

Tim stepped forward, putting his arm around Melissa's shoulder. "Of course, I'd be happy to speak with your chief and make a statement. Please, Miss Jones has been through a lot. Do you have a trauma counsellor present?"

"We'll take her to one right away."

"Thank you. Shall we go?"

Tim and Melissa were led up the steps, through the hallway and out into the cool evening air. A crowd of reporters and photographers surged forward, but the police held them back. Tim waved to them to demonstrate that he was not in handcuffs. Melissa stayed close to him, but when they reached the street they were separated and placed in different squad cars.

He sat in the back and the cops closed the door. Once out of sight of the press, he put his head in his hands and breathed deeply. If it hadn't been for that tipoff, he might have arrived home to find the police waiting for him. They would have led him out in handcuffs for all the press to see. Then he'd be fighting to clear his name. It seemed he had sprung the trap much earlier than planned and the result was no credible case against him. He hoped there wouldn't be a second trap waiting for him in case the first failed.

chapter seven

THEY: WANT YOU DEAD

For the second time in as many days, Melissa was in the police station. Given her history with the place and the people in it, she did not feel comfortable. At least this time they weren't keeping her locked in a cell or beating her up on the floor.

Also she had her phone back, and they allowed her to use it. The police had pulled it from a shelf in Tim Barns's basement. Presumably her kidnapper intended to plant the phone and other items of hers around the house to further implicate the Senator. She guessed someone would tell the police where she was and they'd come and rescue her from Tim's basement long after she'd been left alone there. Tim would come home into the middle of a crime scene and they'd arrest him immediately. Since she would never have met or spoken to him, she would have no way of knowing whether or not he was involved in her kidnapping. The poor guy could have ended up in jail.

Melissa resented being a pawn in someone else's game to discredit a state senator. She had no clue who was behind it, nor what Barns had done to piss them off. She did know that using her as the victim sent her a clear message: get out of the country now. She wanted to comply. The irony was that if they hadn't kidnapped her, she'd be back in Toronto by now. She responded to Jasmine's deluge of messages by explaining what had happened and that she was safe, relatively speaking. Her agent offered to rebook her flight for the next day. Melissa told her to hold off for now.

Okay, you let me know when you're ready to go home. I've booked the same hotel for tonight.

Melissa texted back her thanks. Next she texted a bunch of assurances to her frantic mother, telling her to please not worry and concentrate on getting herself better.

Shania was next, her best friend keen to know she was okay but far more practical than her mother. Shania was usually the voice of reason in Melissa's life.

Next she checked a local news site and was unsurprised to see Barns's face next to hers all over the main pages. All called the incident bizarre, and the tone ranged from assuming Barns was having an affair with her to asking why she was found in the senator's basement and did she know some dark secret of his. If his dark secret was that he had a messy basement then Melissa was happy to reveal it.

Only one paper, the *Richmond Times-Dispatch*, carried a picture of Tim being led from his home with his cuff-free hands in the air, and bothered to follow up with the police to discover they had pressed no charges and that her kidnappers were still at large.

The numbers of tweets, comments and messages on her various accounts were now off the scale. She'd never had so much publicity. Normally she would love the attention, but right now she'd trade it all for one more day with Howie.

She scanned a selection of public opinion.

Jones will do anything for publicity #attentionwhore So will Barns. Bet they cooked up the whole thing.

#blacklivesmatter is all talk and marching with no real action. Why can't they keep @MelissasMoment safe?

Oh sure, @MelissasMoment just HAPPENED to wind up tied up in @StateSenTimBarns basement. What's wrong with this picture?

Now we know why Barns wife left him

**HUGS* to @MelissasMoment. After what she went through her head is still held high.*

Damn girl! That's a rough couple of days you've gotten there.

Tonight we march on Richmond again. Spineless @MelissasMoment would rather hide away and cry. #marchwithus #blacklivesmatter #justiceforhowie

That last Tweet really bothered Melissa. She was used to wild conspiracy theories and personal attacks. She could dismiss threats of death and rape, and insults about her looks, her race and her family. But to call her a coward filled her with rage. Yeah it was just one comment from some guy who didn't know her, probably had never heard of her before yesterday and clearly cared more about his cause than the people affected by violence, but it made her blood boil.

The door opened and in walked the female officer who had escorted her from the station the day before. Pleased to see at least one person who held some sympathy for her predicament, Melissa asked the officers name.

"Mulligan, Miss Jones. Officer Mulligan. Can I get you some coffee?"

"Thanks, but I'd rather leave."

"Won't be long now. I have to check a couple of things with you and then you're free to go. Ten minutes tops, is that okay?"

"Sure."

"Okay, I'll be right back with my notes and that coffee."

It didn't take long for Mulligan to return. The coffee was too hot and very bitter, but Melissa drank it anyway.

"I just wanted to confirm you didn't see any faces of the men who kidnapped you."

"That's right."

"So there's no point in looking through this." She placed a heavy binder of suspect photographs to one side. "I do need to ask you the nature of your relationship with Senator Barns."

Melissa blinked.

"I don't have a relationship with him," she said. "First time I met him was in his basement when he surprised the kidnapper and then cut me loose."

"Oh, well, it's just that the officers present saw you stand up for him. They assumed you two were…"

Melissa shook her head. "No no, nothing like that. I just didn't want him to get in trouble. It was pretty obvious someone set him up and I wanted to make sure he wasn't arrested after he saved me."

"That's very brave of you."

Melissa didn't reply. Officer Mulligan smiled at her.

"Now, when the men bundled you into the car, one of them said something to you. Can you confirm what it was?"

"He said I was told not to tell anyone."

"About what?"

"About what happened with Howie I guess, I'm not really sure."

"And who told you not to tell anyone?"

Melissa just stared at her.

"Oh," said Mulligan, looking flustered. "I'm… I'm sorry about that."

"Was I kidnapped by police officers?" Melissa demanded.

"No, no I don't think so."

"Then how did they know what the police told me not to talk to anyone about Howie?"

"I… don't know." The officer seemed distressed, much more upset than the victim sitting in front of her.

"Can I go now?"

"Er, yes. Yes that should be fine. I'll process your release.

Do you want police protection?"

"Do you think I want police protection?"

"Well, probably not but I have to ask."

"Quite frankly I'd rather take my chances with the kidnappers. Nothing personal." She added, "You've been nice to me. Thanks."

Mulligan nodded weakly.

"Let's get you out of here," she said.

There was no taxi waiting for her this time, but the press was out in force. She had to get to the rank further down the street, which meant pushing through the photographers and microphones and questions firing at her from all sides. Nobody had warned her to keep quiet before she left this time, presumably because they felt the kidnapping made that point already.

Melissa was having none of it. She stopped, ignoring the pushing throng of people thrusting mikes in her face.

"Where's the *Times-Dispatch*?" she asked.

A female reporter raised her hand, in which she grasped her press pass.

"Harriet Fletcher, *Times-Dispatch*. Hi Miss Jones, thanks for talking to me. Can you confirm that you were found by Senator Tim Barns earlier this evening, tied up in his basement?"

"That's correct," she answered. "He rescued me."

"Rescued you from whom?"

"I don't know," Melissa replied. "Some men grabbed me off the street. They kept me in the back of a van for hours and then took me to what turned out to be Senator Barns's basement. If the Senator hadn't returned home earlier than expected, I don't know what would have happened. He arrived."

"Have you ever met Senator Tim Barns before today?"

"Never. I'm from Canada so I don't know much about US politicians. I'd never even heard of him before today."

"Will you be staying in Richmond or heading home now?"

"I don't know, I haven't decided."

"One more question, Miss Jones. Do you have any idea why you were tied up in Senator Barns's basement?"

"I have no idea. Thanks, I'd like to get on."

Fletcher thanked her and she and her photographer stepped aside. The others continued to push in close, however, photographers snapping pictures and shouting at her to look up and to "smile", which pissed her off. She didn't feel much like smiling, the insensitive jerks. She was finding it hard to breathe. She couldn't see where she was going and it was hard to walk.

Suddenly there was a new man to her left. He carried no microphone or camera. He was large, black and wearing a #blacklivesmatter t-shirt. Then there was another to her right. Both were big enough to hold back the press to give her space to walk. Another three or four, some men, some women, all black people wearing the same shirts, moved in to surround her. They didn't say anything, they didn't try to steer her in any direction, they simply held back the crush and followed her lead. Melissa thanked them as she reached the first in a line of taxis.

"Wilson would love you to join us on our march later this evening," one of the women said.

"Did he send you guys to protect me?"

"Yes."

"Thank him for me, and thank you!" She meant it. "Please tell Wilson that I still don't feel ready to march, but it's nice that he's thinking of me."

She got in the taxi and gave the name of her hotel, then

She got in the taxi and gave the name of her hotel, then left them all on the street.

chapter eight

THEY WANT YOU DEAD

Melissa sat alone in her hotel room again, enjoying the peace and quiet. She took another painkiller as her arm was starting to bother her again.

It was obvious to her that Wilson had sent those people to protect her from the press in order to convince her she should join the protest. Would it be so bad if she did? Clearly the cops in this town were screwed up. Whether it was them behind the kidnapping or not, clearly the men who bundled her into the van were aware of the warning they gave her the first time she left the police station. What was that about?

She took out her phone and answered a text from her mom, who was now checking in with her every ten minutes, and going into a blind panic if she didn't respond immediately. It was a message from Shania that caught her eye.

Saw the protest last night. Did you join in?

No, Melissa responded. *I was too tired and sad.*

You're joining tonight though, right? There's going to be another one.

I don't know, Shan. Howie's brother asked me to, but I just don't feel up to it.

You got kidnapped, Mel! Aren't you pissed?

Melissa smiled. *Mad as fuck, but how does protesting help?*

I went on a march last year in Toronto, remember? Against high tuition fees.

Yeah I was sick so I missed it.

And how did you feel?

Bummed. I wanted to go. I regret not going.

Yeah, and now you have another opportunity to make a statement about something even more important.

Melissa got the point.

Thanks Shan! Love ya!

Be awesome gal!

"I'm a Virginia State Senator. Of course I have enemies."

Agent Clark clicked his tongue in a manner that was already becoming irritating to Tim Barns.

"Your… sarcasm is not helpful," he said in that slow drone of his. Tim felt uncomfortable whenever he spoke, like an angry wasp had landed on his face and he couldn't move but he couldn't relax either.

These two FBI agents, Clark and Ortega, arrived at Tim's door about ten minutes ago, and since then had demanded he tell the whole story of Melissa Jones's kidnapping twice. There wasn't that much to tell, so they'd switched to asking him who might be motivated to frame him.

"Senator Barns," Agent Ortega began. She smiled at him in an attempt to put him at ease. She was clearly used to people's reaction to her partner's manner. "Obviously a man in your position has made enemies, but not all of those enemies are willing to kidnap someone and tie them up in your basement in an attempt to frame you. Is there anyone you can think of who you recently made an enemy of?"

Tim wasn't an idiot. These agents might well operate at a level well above Lionel Granger's sphere of influence, but any attempt on Tim's part to implicate the old fucker was not going to be met with a reasoned, measured response. What came next, a dead hooker in his bed? Threats against his ex-wife? An *accidental* electrical fire in his home? Tim was no coward, but he wasn't an idiot either. He wasn't about to let Granger intimidate him into capitulation, but neither was he going to do anything so obvious it would immediately bring about retribution. Tim knew now what Granger was capable of. He was a dangerous man to be sure, and not one to piss off unless one was absolutely sure it wasn't going to backfire.

"There's nobody I can think of, no."

"What was your… relationship with Miss Jones prior to the… incident in your basement?"

Why did everyone assume he already knew this woman?

"We'd never met before. I had seen her on the news regarding her boyfriend's shooting, but we'd never crossed paths before."

Clark didn't seem satisfied with this, but Tim didn't care. He wanted these two out of his house before they blundered into this situation and caused him more problems.

Ortega gave that smile again, half apologetic and half placating.

"Have you spoken to Miss Jones since the incident?" she asked.

"Nope. She went her way and I went mine. I don't know why she's gotten caught up in this. I feel terrible about everything that's happened to her over the past couple of days, but beyond that we've not had any contact."

"The man that… was in your basement. Can you… describe him to us?"

Tim stared at Clark for a moment. "I already gave my description to the police."

"I know but… we'd like to hear it."

Tim sighed. "Fine. Well, he was big, over two hundred pounds for sure. He had a mask on, and gloves, but I think

That's about all I can tell you."

Ortega stood up. "Well we won't take any more of your time, Senator Barns."

Clark seemed reluctant to leave, but Ortega pressed ahead anyway.

Tim saw them out and then returned to his TV. Watching the news, he saw that the protestors were out on the streets again. He reached for his jacket and keys. He should be out there marching with them. Then one of the demonstrators caught his eye. It was Melissa, marching arm in arm with Howie's brother, Wilson, and other members of Black Lives Matter, right at the head of the protest. If Tim was going to try to build a case against Granger, it would be smart to understand Melissa's side of the story. Perhaps he should talk to her.

He switched off the TV, grabbed his backpack and headed out to join the protest.

chapter nine

THEY WANT YOU DEAD

Melissa Jones felt empowered. She felt *alive*. For the first time since Howie's death, she was in the right place, doing the right thing, with the right people. She and Winston had been ushered to the front of the march, where they now held *Justice For Howie* signs that someone handed to them. Leading a couple of thousand people along Franklin Street was something Melissa planned to tell her grandchildren all about one day. She had seen images of protests in Washington, Dallas, Charlotte, Chicago, from all over the country – she *knew* she was part of something nationwide, and she knew that this round of protests followed Richmond's lead, and she was at the head of the march. She knew full well the sad truth that before long they'd add Howie's death to the national statistics, mentioned only as part of a list of names in the reporting of the latest tragedy. She knew that at any moment, an innocent, unarmed black man on his way to the convenience store might be gunned down by police convinced he posed some sort of threat, and that some other city would become the de facto protest leader, with Richmond merely a follower, a supporter, a sympathizer.

But for tonight, right now, the world's eyes were on

protesting: parents with small children, the predominantly black members of the BLM movement, but also many white people and Asian people marching with their black brothers and sisters. She saw old people, one guy in a wheelchair, and so many young people, people her own age who held up makeshift signs, Howie's vinyl album covers, or simply marched with fists in the air. These were not just lefty students who always tried to get in on a good old civil rights march. Many of these young adults were fans in mourning, people with no idea how to express their grief over the loss of such a promising and talented artist taken from them so cruelly. They would never again get to hear new work from Howie Do, and it had galvanized them to get involved—to not just voice their pain, but also to shout out against injustice and police brutality.

It was life affirming. Melissa did not smile, she did not whoop; this was not a moment of celebration. The pain of Howie's loss and the agony of a community under siege all across the most powerful nation on Earth – it could not fail to move her. As a black woman, even in Canada, being in public and feeling in a position of strength, unity and acceptance was something she was not overly familiar with. Here she felt like she marched with *her* people, regardless of their nationality, age, race or gender.

Wilson had told her when they reached Monument Avenue, the protestors would gather to hear from various speakers. He asked her if she would like to speak.

To her surprise, she had said yes.

She hadn't even hesitated. And now, despite the adrenalin and the tidal wave of support behind her, at the back of her mind she wondered what she would say. Her YouTube channel was one thing: she was used to talking without a script about being Canadian, about being a woman, about being black, about being a young adult, about politics, about being black, about being a young adult, about politics, about fashion, about whatever came to her that day that she felt opinionated about. But public speaking? The last time she'd spoken in front of people was at a school presentation a year ago. It had gone okay, but she'd spoken to a quiet room of three hundred people. This was significantly more, and they would be loud and vocal, and the media would be watching. What if she said something to upset them? What if she accidentally said something un-American without even realizing it? What if they turned on her?

She forced herself to relax, to experience the moment as it happened rather than dwell on mistakes she had not even made yet. The chanting of, "Justice For Howie!" and "Black Lives Matter" rang in her ears. She would speak from her heart, she would not try to plan what she would say. She did not have to speak for long. She would tell them about Howie, who he was in private, and what he meant to her, and maybe about a Canadian's observation of America's struggle, and how she too faced a similar – but usually less brutal – struggle in her own country. And that would be enough.

The police presence was surprisingly low key. She had seen a few officers, likely those already on patrol of the city when the marching began. This struck her as odd, given that this was not the first night of protests. She had not heard of significant violence from the previous night's demonstration, so perhaps the police did not feel a large presence was necessary.

And then she saw them.

At the front of the march, Melissa could see what many behind her could not. They were still a couple of intersections away, but even at this distant the sight of them made her nervous. Instinctively she stopped, but Howie took her arm and gently moved her forward, not wanting her to be trampled by the mass of people walking behind her. The did not falter. Melissa admired their courage.

They weren't close yet, but the unmistakable bulk of something like a tank but with no gun turret blocked the road ahead. Row upon row of armed police stood in ranks ahead of it. They carried batons, shields and guns slung over their shoulders. They stood silently, waiting for the marchers to approach. Police cars and vans lined the street beyond them, their lights flashing, illuminating the silent army in blue and red.

Someone had decided that this protest wasn't going to continue along Franklin Street.

Wilson was consulting with other leaders of the march now, still heading towards the wall of armed resistance. For a moment, he and the others dropped back a little so Melissa was alone, at the head of the march, stuck out on her own like the figurehead of a massive ship. The tide of support and security melted instantly. The atmosphere had shifted and, for a moment, she walked alone towards the horde of oppressors, marching to her certain doom in the name of justice and civil disobedience.

Wilson was back at her side in a moment and the isolation evaporated. Still it left Melissa rattled. She was sweating and her breathing had quickened. Her pulse was racing and she was light-headed. She allowed Wilson to steer her to the right, heading north onto a side street, away from the police lines.

They followed a wide arc, and without question the masses behind them followed. As the protest turned, people on the western edge of the march started to see Franklin Street ahead and the imposing sight of the police lines. There were gasps and cries from marchers on the left behind Melissa. She glanced back and saw some people break off from the main group, running south to get away from the police and the protestors. Some of them carried small children, and

Melissa could hardly blame them. She resisted the urge to run after them. Suppressing her instincts, she knew that if she ran too it would incite chaos. The front of the march breaking off in different directions would cause a stampede, and panicked people would get hurt.

So she stayed the course, lockstep with Wilson and his allies. The leaders of the march had now fully turned the corner, and the police lines slipped out of Melissa's view. Not before she saw them mobilize, however. If they were on the move, that meant they might engage the protestors in the middle of the pack as the march slowly turned the corner. She glanced at Wilson who had clearly seen the same thing, because he was furiously discussing options with the other march leaders as they continued to walk. She had noticed a distinct quickening of their pace, and a drop off in the number of protestors around her still chanting slogans. Everyone around her had sensed that the mood had changed and the situation was now potentially dangerous. It terrified her; she wanted to be anywhere but here. What had been life affirming now had become life threatening. She wondered how long it would take for the survival instincts of the protest leaders to filter back through the throng behind them. She saw Wilson and others on their phones, texting messages presumably to other BLM members escorting protestors further back, the majority of them still marching on Franklin Street in the direction of the police lines now closing in.

Melissa turned her attention to the road ahead. This street was narrower than Franklin but there was still plenty of space for the protestors. They were heading north to the next major east-west street – Melissa didn't know Richmond well enough to identify the street names – presumably to lead the protestors to a wide open space, perhaps a park, where they could amass and organize a peaceful dispersal. Melissa was just guessing, but that's what she would do.

To her horror, from around the next corner, at least a hundred police officers in full riot gear appeared. They ran in coordinated fashion, quickly forming a blockade across the exit from this street they were marching on. More officers moved in behind them to reinforce the line. The sound of something large rumbling into position signaled yet more heavy-police presence on the way.

Now it was Wilson's turn to halt. Other leaders raised their bullhorns and commanded the people behind to stop. They had no place to go.

Suddenly a group of protestors pushed forward from behind Melissa and surged out ahead of the stopped protest. These men were different from anyone else Melissa had noticed thus far. They wore masks over their faces, and carried sticks and other makeshift weapons.

Wilson and the other BLM leaders reacted immediately, rushing forwards to try to stop these newcomers surging forward. They didn't move fast enough. Instead the police saw a few armed demonstrators rushing them, backed by dozens more potential assailants.

The response was immediate. Police rushed forwards to engage the masked men. Tear gas canisters landed at the feet of the protestors, causing panic and mayhem. Officers with bullhorns shouted warning. They beat down any and all opposition.

Melissa stood in the middle of it all, unsure where to run or what to do. An officer brutally attacked a young black man to her right, and she looked on in horror as his blood ran in the street. She didn't know what to do. She was utterly powerless.

Her eyes streamed with tears. The gas was taking hold of her. She coughed, then wretched, doubling over. Her whole face and throat burned with an intensity she had never felt before, like she'd eaten the hottest chili pepper on Earth and before, like she'd eaten the hottest chili pepper on Earth and then rubbed it in her eyes for good measure. She couldn't breathe, she could barely stand. She couldn't see what was going on through the clouds of gas and the tears in her eyes. She screwed her eyes shut and rubbed at them to try to stop the burning, all the while coughing up her lungs onto the asphalt.

She crashed into someone and sprawled to the ground. Her exposed skin prickled in the poisonous air, but this was nothing compared to her throat, nose, lungs and eyes. Mucus, tears and sweat poured from her, more fluids than she thought she could possibly produce. And the coughing was so intense she couldn't stand up. She rubbed her face but this seemed to make it worse, though it was hard to tell if the rubbing was the cause or prolonged exposure. She couldn't see and she couldn't escape the gas. She crawled on her hands and knees, bumping into other people despite trying to avoid them by the sounds of their coughing. Her own retching made it almost impossible to hear where others were located, and of course she couldn't see anything at all. The pain was beyond anything she could cope with and she started screaming, except that no sound issued from her searing throat. She couldn't breathe. Was she dying? Could tear gas kill?

She was aware of hands beneath her armpits, scooping her up and dragging her away. Were they arresting her? She didn't care. Anything was better than this. They lowered her to the ground, sitting up with her back against a wall. She wanted to die, for it to end. Instead there was suddenly a bottle of water in her hands and a cool breeze on her face. It was like seeing sunlight after years of living underground. She fumbled with the lid of the bottle, desperate to get to the water. Her rescuer – she assumed – helped her remove the lid and she drank greedily. Meanwhile, her rescuer poured more water over her face and into her eyes. The pain and the burning didn't go away, but they abated slightly. She finished the bottle and let it drop from her fingers. Someone was speaking to her. Saying something about moving further away, not being safe yet.

She allowed her rescuer to pull her to her feet. Shakily, she half-stumbled, half-lurched along beside her rescuer, leaning heavily on him or her. Screams and crying and coughing surrounded her, assaulting her ears and disorienting her more, if that was possible.

She felt far from normal, but the pain had subsided enough for her to croak some words and open her eyes. She tried to speak but the blurry face before her made shushing noises and handed her another bottle of water. She removed the lid of this one without a struggle and drank more. Her breathing was improving now, and she no longer felt like she wanted to die.

Slowly, through the haze of tears, a concerned face swam into view. He alternated between examining Melissa and looking up and down the street.

He turned back to her and took off the scarf he had wrapped around his face to lessen the effects of the gas. His eyes were swollen and tears covered his cheeks, but he seemed to have avoided the worst of the gas attack.

Melissa had never been gladder to see a friendly face.

Senator Tim Barns coughed twice and smiled at her.

chapter ten

THEY: WANT YOU DEAD

Tim helped Melissa through his front door and took her straight to the kitchen sink. He took a clean dishcloth and ran it under water, then used it to wipe her eyes, returning the cloth to the water several times. She was still coughing, but had recovered sufficiently to breathe normally and speak to him in one word answers.

When she confirmed her eyesight was more or less restored, he guided her to the sofa and they sat down together.

"Thank you," she said, for what must have been the hundredth time.

"Once again, it's nothing. I saw you in the cloud of gas unable to get out, so I came in to get you."

"You always bring a..." She coughed several times, holding the wet towel to her face for a moment before recovering. "Do you always bring a mask and bottles of water to a protest?"

Tim smiled. "It's not my first rodeo. Every time there's a BLM march I join it – even before I became a senator – and sometimes things can go south real quickly."

"Well aren't you Mr. Socially Responsible."

"It's important, right? I think it's just as important for

white guys like me to stand up and say, this isn't okay. If people see a few white faces in the mix, they might think, well hey, this isn't just black folks bitching again, there may be more to this. It's sad to have to think that way but there it is."

"How many marches you been on?"

Tim stood up and grabbed a bottle of red wine, a corkscrew and two glasses from a side table.

"I've lost count, to be honest."

"Have there been that many?"

"Too many." He opened the bottle and proffered it to her.

"I'm usually a white wine drinker, but I sure could use something. So yeah, why not?"

"I can get white if you like."

"No, no, this is fine."

"It's what inspired me to get into politics," Tim continued, pouring her drink. "I saw this same shit happening over and over, saw cops get off for shooting people, saw the effect it was having on communities in my own city, saw the mistrust of the police boiling over again and again… Something had to change."

"So you're going to change it all?"

"Ha, no." He took a drink from his own glass. The fruity red helped soothe his own burning throat. "But if I can start a conversation at the right levels, it helps right? I got elected on police reform, prison reform and busting the school to prison pipeline."

"The what now?"

"Police in schools disciplining kids, so they leave school with a record or possibly a jail sentence instead of a couple of detentions and a high school diploma."

"That's terrible!"

"Yeah and black kids are three times more likely than white kids to end up with a juvenile record. So anyway, I ran

"So you're using the plight of black Virginians to further your political career?"

Tim laughed. Melissa hung her head. "Sorry," she said. "That came out pretty harsh."

"It was very cynical, yeah. And you're half right. This is what I want to do. I get a lot of satisfaction from it. I'm not gonna lie and say I'd dedicate my life to these causes if I wasn't getting paid for it!"

They laughed together. Melissa took a sip of her drink. Her eyes were still a little teary and she sniffed now and then, but she seemed to have recovered quite well. She took in a lot more gas than Tim did, and he was still feeling the effects. It bothered him greatly: there was no need for the police to deploy the gas.

"I hope all those people got away," Melissa said, her eyes downcast.

"What happened at the front, Melissa?"

She closed her eyes, clearly reliving the trauma and shuddering at the images flashing before her.

"The police forced us to turn off Franklin, then we went north and they marched out to block us again. I don't know why, we were peaceful, at least where I was. And then these guys ran out past Wilson, past all of us."

"What guys?"

"Oh shit! Wilson. I should call him and make sure he's okay." She pulled out her phone but Tim put a hand out to slow her down.

"Tell me about the guys?"

"I don't know, maybe about a dozen of them. I didn't see them before, but they ran at the police. They had masks and baseball bats and other weapons. That's when everything went crazy."

"Agitators," said Tim.

"Huh?"

"Huh?"

"Agitators. Sometimes they're hired by someone with an agenda, or they're troublemakers looking to find more trouble. Either way they're not interested in protesting anything. They're looking for violence. Any chance to cause mayhem, they'll do it."

"Someone hired them to start a fight?"

"More than possible."

"Shit. Who?"

Tim had a damn good idea who. He wasn't ready to talk about it just yet though. He waited a few minutes while she sent some text messages from her phone. He regarded her during that time. She was short, slim and very pretty. Her hair was naturally curly and her eyes were dark, deep pools. She was clearly smart, a little wiser than her years, and Tim was impressed by how she was keeping it together. After everything she'd been through in such a short space of time, she was remarkably calm and still caring for the wellbeing of others.

He missed having female company about the place. He wasn't about to make a move on Melissa. She was attractive, certainly, but too young for him. Plus the press would have a field day if they started dating. He doubted she would be interested in a thirty-something senator from a different country anyway. Still it was nice to have her here. The house felt more *complete* than it had since Claire left him. He'd thrown himself into his work to such a degree that he hadn't stopped to consider his own loneliness. Maybe he should take a breath, let the whole Granger thing slide and take some time to start dating again. He shouldn't wait until he was fat and balding. He was still eligible.

But no. He had to keep pushing. The time to push his agenda was now. If he paused, or let Granger intimidate him, his bills would fail and he likely wouldn't be able to marriage; he wasn't going to squander his efforts now.

Melissa lowered her phone.

"I can't get hold of Wilson. Maybe the police have him. Can we check?"

"We can go down to the station first thing in the morning. Let the dust settle for now. We should stay off the streets."

"But he might be hurt."

"In which case he'll be in the hospital. I'll make some enquiries first thing and we can go find him. It's been a very long day, Melissa, and we should both get some sleep. I have a spare room you're welcome to use. I'll put out a towel and some blankets. My ex left some clothes behind so I put them in the closet in the spare room. I should really have thrown them out but never gotten around to it. Help yourself to anything."

Melissa nodded, grateful. Tim was glad she felt comfortable enough to stay here. It was the least he could do for her. She never asked the police to shoot her boyfriend, for her to be arrested, to be kidnapped and tied up in someone's basement, to be tear gassed. Most other people would be a bawling wreck by now.

Tim's phone buzzed. He pulled it out and unlocked it with his fingerprint.

We need to talk.

He frowned. The message was from the same number as the warning to return home when Melissa was tied up in the basement.

I can meet you in the morning.

Now.

Tim sighed. He could tell this person to go away, but they had saved his career with that tip off.

"What's up?" Melissa asked.

"I have to go meet someone. It's the mystery person who tipped me off about you in my basement. If it weren't for tipped me off about you in my basement. If it weren't for them, I'd have come home after your kidnapper left and the police would have arrested me."

"And you want to find out who it is?"

"Of course. They want to meet right now. Will you be okay here?"

Melissa put down her nearly empty glass and stood up.

"I'm coming with you."

"No, I don't think that's a good idea."

"Why not? I don't really want to be on my own. I feel a lot safer with you, even out on the streets."

"I'm flattered but really, it's…"

"Shush. Where are we going?"

The café was deserted, partly because it was late but mostly because the earlier violence meant there were few people on the streets voluntarily. Tim wondered if this was such a good idea. He was quietly glad Melissa had insisted on going with him because he didn't fancy being there alone. The only other person in the place was a solitary waitress, who delivered them coffee all the while keeping an eye on the door. She'd clearly seen or heard about the violence and wanted no part of it.

"How long is your shift?" Tim asked her as sympathetically as he could.

"Another hour, then we close," she replied.

"Are you here alone?"

"Kitchen closed an hour ago, so yeah."

"Would you like us to stay until you close?"

She smiled at him, her eyes tired.

"Yeah that would be nice. Thanks."

"No problem."

She moved off behind the counter, busying herself with cleaning up.

"If I was her I'd lock up early and go home," Melissa said.

"If she did that she'd probably get fired. No shortage of people waiting to take her job."

"Ain't that the truth? You have any idea who we're meeting?"

Tim glanced at the entrance again. "No idea."

At that moment the door opened and in walked a small, white woman in a leather jacket, silk scarf and thigh high boots, carrying a briefcase. She made a beeline for Tim and Melissa, holding a hand out as she approached. She was in her late thirties, early forties and had a face that smiled easily.

"Senator Barns, Miss Jones, so good to meet you."

Tim stood and shook her hand. Melissa did likewise.

"Please, sit down," Tim said. "And you are?"

The woman slid into the bench opposite them and gave that cheery smile again, her blue eyes sparkling behind brown framed glasses.

"My name is Kirsty Frank. I write for darkmice.com, have you heard of it?" Tim and Melissa shook their heads. "Well that's not surprising," she continued. "We're not exactly mainstream. In fact, we have proof that the government is deliberately throttling access to our servers and keeping our hit rates artificially low."

Tim blinked at her. A horrible feeling was forming in the pit of his stomach. The waitress came over and took her coffee order, while suspicions crowded into Tim's head.

"What sort of things do you write about?" he asked Kirsty, dreading her answer.

"Oh you know, we take a deep dive into issues the regular media likes to pretend aren't real."

"You mean conspiracies." Tim wasn't asking a question.

"Sometimes, yes, I suppose you could call them that."

"Oh shit," Melissa said. "Not all that 9/11-was-an-inside-job stuff?"

Kirsty smiled again and shook her head. "Oh no, we would never say anything like that. Although there are some questions about that day that have yet to receive satisfactory answers."

Tim stood up. "I think we've heard enough," he said.

"Wait wait!" she implored them, raising her hands to motion them to sit. "Don't you want to hear how I was able to tip you off about Melissa being tied up in your basement?"

Reluctantly, Tim sat down. Melissa followed suit, though she looked just as uncomfortable as he felt.

"We're listening," said Tim.

"We've been tracking Mr. Granger for quite some time," she explained. "I know you met with him recently and I also know he tried to get you to shelve most of the platform that got you elected."

"How do you know that?" Tim asked.

"Who is Granger?" Melissa interjected.

Tim turned to her. "Lionel Granger. Successful business leader in Virginia who financed my campaign and then tried to control what I did after my election. I was in the process of severing ties with him when you ended up in my basement."

"So you know who kidnapped me?" Melissa appeared outraged. Tim held up a hand.

"I suspected. I don't have any evidence and even if I did, what could I do with it?"

Kirsty nodded. "Granger has people everywhere. It's almost impossible to investigate him without someone noticing and tipping him off. Then his lawyers get involved. He certainly keeps them busy. Sometimes, as in your case, it's not a legal issue, so he uses other means to get his way."

"Like kidnapping?"

Kirsty opened her briefcase and pulled out two

documents. Both were missing person reports.

"These two women had affairs with Granger in the 90s. We know that because they both filed police reports saying he forced himself on them."

"What happened to them?" Melissa asked, gazing at the faces of the women on the reports.

"Both of them disappeared soon after the reports were filed. They were never found."

"And Granger was never linked to the disappearances?" Tim asked.

"They were never investigated. You're looking at the only evidence in police records that these women ever went missing. There was no follow-up, no notes added to the case, nothing. It's like the police weren't interested in trying to find them."

Tim frowned. "Where did you get these?"

"We have a friend at the local precinct. He pulled these out for us a decade ago. This is literally all he could find about these women on file."

"Okay," said Tim. "This looks really bad, but it's not evidence against Granger."

"No it's not, and that's why we've still got it after all these years and Granger is still a free man."

Melissa shook her head. "He should be in jail."

"I agree," Kirsty said. "But no judge will convict him. No prosecutor would dare bring his case before one."

It was Melissa's turn to frown. "Why not? Because he's rich?"

"Even rich people go to jail sometimes."

Tim laughed at this. "Not in my experience."

"It happens, sometimes, usually when the Feds get involved. But there are some people who are untouchable. Kidnapping and blackmail are nothing to these people. They'll do anything to retain power and use every opportunity to wield it."

Tim laughed. "Who? The Illuminati?" He said the word in a mocking tone, like he was talking about the bogeyman. When Kirsty didn't reply, just gazed at him, Tim snorted. "You're not serious."

Melissa looked confused. "I'm sorry, what's the Illuminarty?"

"The Illuminati," Tim corrected her. "They're a sort of shadowy organization dating back centuries. They're supposed to be the ones with the real power, unelected, unknown, unaccountable, pulling the strings from behind the scenes and steering humanity towards a New World Order."

"I've heard of New Order," Melissa said. "My dad was a fan."

Tim laughed. "Not quite. The New World Order is the concept of one world government. No individual nations, just one organization ruling the entire world."

"Sounds creepy," Melissa said.

"It is," Tim agreed. "It's also a myth."

"Really?" asked Kirsty, raising an eyebrow.

"Of course it is. There's no such thing as the Illuminati. They're the stuff of Hollywood B-movies and pulp novels."

Kirsty paused for a moment, taking a couple of sips of her coffee.

"Look, I don't expect you to buy into the truth–" Tim snorted again at the use of the word "–but honestly it doesn't matter whether you believe me or not. We call them 'They', and Granger is a powerful member with deep connections. You will never bring him down."

"I don't want to bring him down," Tim replied. "I want him to leave me alone. I want him off my back so I can pursue the agenda I ran for election on. I want to be rid of his money and his influence. I want the freedom to do my job without being beholden to corporate interests."

"You would never have been elected without him," Kirsty said.

"Well that's... true," Tim admitted. It made him uncomfortable to say it but she was right. Before Granger injected his cash into Tim's campaign, nobody knew who the hell he was and he would likely have sunk in a sea of candidates vying for his seat. "But he broke his side of the deal. He said he wouldn't have demands. He said he liked my policies and wanted to see me go far."

"Sure he did. He said exactly what he wanted you to hear. Just like the TV executive who told Miss Jones she could have her own reality show and might one day rival Oprah."

Melissa sat bolt upright and stared at Kirsty, her mouth hanging open.

"How did you know I was told that?"

Kirsty turned her attention to the young woman.

"Because, Melissa, Harold J. Finch is one of *They*. He says the same things to countless young starlets who come his way. He promises them the world. I guessed the Oprah part, but these bastards tend to profile, you know?"

"So, the contract I signed is useless?" Melissa looked devastated.

"Oh no, it's valid. You really will be starring in your own show. But his motivations for hiring you are not just because of your talent, or your looks, or even the ratings he hopes to achieve. He wants your influence. He sees the vast numbers of millennials who subscribe to your channel, who watch all your videos and hang on to your every word. He, like Granger, knows full well that young adults don't give a shit what people like him say. So he wants you to say it for him."

Melissa was defiant. "Bullshit! I'm not saying words he tells me to say. That's not in the contract and I won't put up with it."

"Oh for sure, you'll start out that way, but eventually you'll take a dip in the ratings, or you'll be offered some lucrative new opportunity, or you'll end up part of some fabricated scandal, and the lifestyle you've become accustomed to will be too risky to lose, and you'll start taking on jobs designed to get his message out there. He'll find subtle ways to do it from the very start and you won't even know it's happening."

"And if I refuse?"

"Those who refuse, or get too close to the truth… well, *They* have ways of dealing with them. Look at what happened with Prince and Michael Jackson. You think their meds were switched out accidentally?"

"This is ridiculous," Tim said. His anger was growing. Any moment now, this woman would be telling them all about chemtrails. "Granger's attempt to control me has nothing to do with the guy who signed Melissa's TV deal. It's just greed, that's all. Granger's protecting his business interests and needs me to pass legislation that will help him do just that. There's no grand conspiracy here; he's just an old white man who wants to make his personal fortune even bigger before he dies with nobody to leave it to. There are a thousand men just like him."

"And most of them belong to the Illuminati," Kirsty said.

Tim stood up again.

"I don't need to hear this crap. Come on, Melissa, let's go."

But Melissa didn't move.

"You said you'd stay until the waitress closes the café, remember?"

Tim stood still. He had made that promise. He glanced at the clock. The café closed in another thirty-five minutes. The waitress looked up from unloading the dishwasher and smiled at him.

"Damn you," Tim hissed at Melissa. He sat down. She'd trapped him. He had no choice but to sit here and listen to these crazy theories with no hard evidence to support them. It bothered him that Melissa was taken in by her words.

"Look," said Kirsty, raising both hands like a preacher imploring her congregation to confess their sins, "you don't have to believe me about what Granger really is. We both know he's bad news, and we both want his fingers out of Virginia politics, right?"

Tim felt like sulking but he knew it was childish to do so. "Yes," he admitted.

"So look, Granger and his… people, they know who I am. I can't get near them, and nobody in his circle will talk to me. I'm looking for the smoking gun I can use to bring him down. I know it's like a drop in the ocean when it comes to the group he's a part of, but it's a start. I love Virginia, and I love Richmond. I hate that he controls everything with zero accountability. I detest that the poor stay poor and stay angry at the wrong things, while the police oppress them and turn a blind eye to the terrible crimes perpetrated by the rich. Our justice system is broken, our prisons are full of our youth who shouldn't be there, our schools and our bridges are crumbling while the money to fix them is syphoned into the pockets of the wealthy. You and I, we share a lot in common, Senator Barns. Unless we deal with Lionel Granger, nothing's going to change in this city or this state."

Kirsty sat back and picked up her coffee mug, watching Tim expectantly.

Tim sighed. "It's a nice speech, but I can't help you. If I'm linked to your Dark Mice site in any way, I'll be a laughing stock. Nobody will ever take me seriously again."

"I'm looking for sensationalist headlines," Kirsty assured him. "I want to do damage to Granger."

"Well on that we can agree," Tim said.

Melissa stared at them both. "This means I don't get to go home, doesn't it?"

"I'm afraid so," Kirsty replied.

"Do you know who hired those men at the protest, the ones who attacked the police and started the violence earlier this evening?"

"I don't know for sure, but I do know the police chief was told to order his officers to block the march. I would guess he also had the agitators hired to provide an excuse for them to attack."

"Why would he do that?"

"I don't know. To perpetuate anti-Black Lives Matter sentiment? To get back at you personally? To give Tim's opponents extra ammunition against the policies he's trying to enact? Who can say for sure? He was undoubtedly behind it though."

"And what about Howie?" Melissa asked, her voice shaking. "Was that part of Granger's big plan? Did he have the police shoot my boyfriend?"

Kirsty put down her coffee cup. "There are plenty of police in Granger's pocket, yes, mostly senior officers like Richmond's chief. The cops who stopped your car weren't acting on any direct orders, as far as I've been able to make out. There's a culture in the States of targeting black people for traffic stops. It's not new, but more people know about it now that everyone has a camera on their phone. The cops had no idea who they were stopping, not until after Howie was dead. I think you were kidnapped as a warning not to go after the cop who shot poor Howie. It was convenient for Granger to kill two birds with one stone, by using you to try to destroy Senator Barns's credibility at the same time. Do I think Granger ordered a hit on your boyfriend? No. I think it was just an unfortunate result of you folks being in the wrong place at the wrong time, and decades of institutionalized racism in our police force."

Tim couldn't tell if Melissa was sad about the state of

American race relations, or if she was disappointed she couldn't direct her rage about Howie's death at a single individual. Either way, it was obvious to Tim that Granger had taken advantage of her and used her as a pawn in his game. Even if she couldn't blame him for Howie's death, he certainly exploited it.

Melissa seemed to come to the same conclusion.

"How do we get him?" she asked.

Kirsty handed over her card. "For now, you two need to keep working on finding out what you can about the kidnapping. Don't trust the police, don't tell anyone what you're doing because you never know if they're Granger's eyes and ears. Look into it as quietly as you can, and look after each other. It could get dangerous. I'll be in touch, and I'll help you whenever I can. You have a good night now."

Kirsty stood up, placed a five dollar bill under her empty coffee cup, and left the café.

Tim and Melissa sat in silence for at least five minutes before either of them spoke.

Eventually Tim said, "9-11 was not an inside job."

Melissa put her hands up in surrender. "I never said it was!"

chapter eleven

THEY: WANT YOU DEAD

Melissa awoke in Tim's spare room to the sound of a door slamming from downstairs. She sat up, listening intently. Was that Tim?

She slipped out of bed and moved to the window. She could see the street and sure enough there was Tim, running off along the sidewalk, out of sight. She relaxed. He wasn't running away from anything, just going for a jog.

She sat back on the bed and checked her phone.

There was a crash from downstairs.

She froze. Tim had left the house. Who the hell else was here? Had someone waited for him to go before breaking in? Her mind filled with images of police raiding the house, or men with guns coming to kidnap her again. Her heart hammered and she fought the urge to hide in the closet. She wished to God she had a gun, or at least Tim's baseball bat. If she was going to stay any longer in this country she would have to arm herself.

Could it just be a friend of Tim's? Maybe Kirsty had stopped by, or someone he worked with? But surely Tim wouldn't leave Melissa alone with a stranger in the house. Not after what she'd been through.

She eased out of bed, trying not to make any noise.

Because she didn't want to face the enemy in her underwear, she slipped on her jeans. As she started doing up her belt, she felt the weight of her Wonder Woman buckle. She wasn't a big superhero fan, but the belt had been a gift from her little sister. Right now though, it wasn't just a symbol of how Tracey viewed her older sibling; it was a potential weapon. She slid the belt out from the hooks of her jeans. The buckle had weight to it, and the belt would act as a good whip. As a weapon it was lacking, and she wasn't exactly trained to use it, but it was better than nothing. It gave her a little confidence to hold something in her hands that could take out an eye.

She crept over to the door, being careful to avoid creaky floorboards. Opening it a crack, she saw that the door to Tim's bedroom was open, but there was no sign of anyone up here.

She was being silly. It was probably just Tim moving about downstairs. She crossed the landing to the top of the stairs and tried to see movement at the bottom. There was definitely someone moving about down there, and they weren't trying to be quiet. It sounded like they were tearing the kitchen apart.

Melissa stepped downwards cautiously, belt buckle held ready to swing, alert for any sign of the intruder approaching the stairs. The front door was closed and locked, so the mystery man hadn't gotten in that way.

She was now below the level of the upper floor and could see the hallway and living room through the railings. She couldn't see the kitchen though. She had to descend to ground level and turn the corner to see into the kitchen at the back of the house. Someone was in there, crouched low, pulling stuff out of a cupboard beneath the sink and making a mess all over the floor. The intruder was obscured by the island in the middle of the kitchen.

Gripped by indecision, Melissa couldn't decide whether to challenge the stranger or retreat to the front door. She wasn't sure how the lock worked, it might be simple or it might make noise and alert the intruder to her presence. Stupidly she'd left her phone upstairs. Should she creep back up and call the police?

The intruder had opened another cupboard and was busily making a mess there too. Melissa wielded the belt and stepped forward.

"Oh for fuck's sake, where is it?" the intruder said in a familiar voice.

Melissa's heart soared and a huge breath of relief released from her lungs.

"Shan?"

The woman with her head in the cupboard withdrew it and turned.

"You're awake!"

Shania Martin leapt to her feet and flung herself at Melissa. The pair hugged like they'd not seen each other in years.

"Oh my God, you scared the shit out of me!" Melissa said after they were done squealing. "I thought you were going to kidnap me."

"Oh, yeah, sorry. Tim let me in this morning but we decided not to wake you. I wanted to make you my special pancakes, so he went to the store to get some stuff. I was looking for a skillet."

"And making a shit-ton of noise!"

"Yeah, sorry about that. Kind of forgot you were sleeping."

Melissa smiled. "So, are you?"

"Am I what?"

"Here to kidnap me?"

"Ha! Sure. Where would you like to be tied up?"

"Ooh, kinky!"

Melissa put her belt back on, which made Shania laugh.

"*That* was you your weapon of choice? You were going to knock me out with a belt buckle?"

"A Wonder Woman belt buckle," Melissa clarified.

"Oh right, sorry. If you hit me with it do I start telling the truth?"

"There's always a first time."

Shania mock-slapped Melissa's arm. "Oh bitch!"

"It's why you love me."

Melissa reached out and took Shania's hand.

"I'm so glad you're here," she said. "It's been… hell."

Shania gave a sympathetic smile. "I can't imagine what you've been through. Do you want to talk about it?"

Melissa shook her head. "Not yet. I'm just enjoying a little normality, you know?"

"I get it? What's more normal than two friends making pancakes in the house of a US senator?"

"*State* senator," Melissa corrected automatically.

"*Dishy* state senator," Shania added with a laugh. "Is he single?"

"He's recently separated."

"Awesome! I've always wanted to be the wife of a senator."

"State senator."

"Close enough. He's pretty hot, eh?"

Melissa turned towards the door feeling a little awkward.

"I suppose so," she said.

"Tell me you've not thought about it!"

Shania was right, Tim was very good looking and she'd be lying if she said she hadn't noticed that he kept himself in shape. He was smart and funny too. A pang of guilt stabbed her heart. How could she think this way? They hadn't even buried Howie yet and she was looking for a replacement. When she turned back to Shania there were tears in her eyes.

Shania realized she'd said the wrong thing and her face collapsed in distress.

"Oh hon, I'm sorry." They hugged, then Shania led Melissa to the living room where they sat down on the sofa. "That was really crappy of me. You must be devastated."

Melissa didn't say anything. She just sat and let the tears roll down her face. Shania grabbed a nearby box of tissues and handed her one. As Melissa wiped her eyes with one hand, Shania held the other in her own.

"Listen, I know I never got to meet Howie –" The mention of his name triggered more tears for Melissa. "–But he seemed like a great guy and I know how much he meant to you. I'm not gonna lie, it's going to take you a while to recover from this. But you *will* recover. You always bounce back, baby girl. You're the strongest person I know and no amount of shootings, kidnappings or riots are gonna keep you down."

Melissa smiled weakly and they embraced.

Shania grinned. "So that means I can make a play for Tim, right?"

Melissa laughed through her tears. She shoved Shania away in mock disgust and they both laughed.

"Make fun of my pain, why don't you?" Melissa complained with a smile, sniffing from the sobs and giggling along with her friend.

The front door opened, closed again, and Tim appeared in the hallway at the entrance to the living room.

"I see you two have caught up," he said as he put down a bag of groceries.

Melissa dried her eyes with her tissue and smiled at Tim. "Good morning," she said.

"She thought I was an intruder!" Shania said and she laughed.

Tim looked shocked. "Oh, yeah, I should have woken you,

sorry Melissa."

Melissa shook her head. "It's okay. I nearly beat her with my Wonder Woman belt buckle but I'm sure she would have been fine."

"Senator Barns here thought I was the enemy," Shania said.

It was Melissa's turn to be shocked. "What?"

Tim held up his hands. "In my defense, I had no idea who she was and I'm not just going to trust random strangers right now. I didn't know if she was with Granger, or a journalist, or really your friend."

"I've mentioned Shania, surely!"

"Nope."

Shania pretend-slapped Melissa's shoulder with the back of her hand.

"You didn't tell him about me?"

Melissa didn't know what to say. After a pause she settled on, "I've been kind of busy."

All three of them laughed.

"You just wanted him all to yourself!" Shania said in mock-accusing tones.

Melissa fell silent at that, feeling awkward.

"Seriously though," Tim said, not looking at Melissa. "You shouldn't be telling anyone you're staying with me. Not after all that's happened."

"Afraid she'll damage your reputation, Senator?" Shania teased.

"Call me Tim. And no, my reputation is already in tatters. I just mean anyone could be snooping, you know?"

"Did he just say, 'snooping'?" Shania said.

"I think he did," said Melissa.

"Who says *snooping*?"

"Snoop Dogg?" suggested Melissa.

Shania laughed. "1950s detectives?"

Tim reached down and picked up the groceries. "Yeah yeah, hilarious. I can tell you two are going to be trouble. Get in the kitchen, woman, and make us breakfast."

Shania's mouth made an 'O' of outrage as she stood up.

"He *is* from the 1950's!" She grabbed the bag from him and headed to the kitchen. "Keep your hair on, daddy-o!"

Tim approached Melissa and sat down beside her.

"I really am sorry for leaving you alone with someone else in the house."

"It's okay, really. I understand."

"I should have woken you."

"Tim, really, don't beat yourself up. Thank you for trusting her and letting her in."

"There's a change in you," Tim said, staring into her eyes. "The difference in you, just half an hour with Shania and I feel I'm looking at the real Melissa for the first time."

Melissa looked away, a little embarrassed.

"Sorry, I didn't mean for that to sound so weird. Anyway, I'm glad she's here. You clearly needed a friend."

Melissa nodded. She *did* feel energized, a little closer to her normal self. Shania had a way of lifting any situation and she was damn glad her friend had taken the initiative to fly out to see her.

Shania wasn't lying about her pancakes. They were good.

Tim helped himself to another couple from the huge stack in the center of the table and then poured on the maple syrup. Nobody said a word since Shania delivered breakfast to the table. But now Melissa took a pause while Tim continued to stuff his face.

"You like the maple?" Melissa asked.

Tim had never tried the famous Canadian export on anything before, but it was great.

"So much better than the usual syrup," Tim agreed through a mouthful. He hadn't realized how hungry he was. It took him a long time to find the maple at the store, and all the while he wondered why Shania had insisted on it. Now he understood and didn't begrudge the extra searching time.

"That's because the usual crap you guys eat is just high fructose corn syrup," Shania explained. Tim was beginning to realize that Melissa's friend was something of a natural food nut.

"Well I'll get this stuff from now on," Tim said. He would have to ask her to write down the recipe too, but he was too busy eating.

"How long are you staying, Shan?" Melissa asked between forkfuls.

"As long as you need me, hon. I have a one-way ticket here and I ain't leaving without you."

Melissa smiled. "I'm not going home just yet."

"Didn't you tell me the police told you to leave? Didn't you get kidnapped because you spoke to Howie's brother?"

"Yeah, but that stuff just makes me more determined to stay. I could run back to Canada but that wouldn't be fair on Howie and it wouldn't be fair on Tim."

His fork paused on its journey to his mouth and he raised an eyebrow.

"If you need to go home, I understand. It's not fair of me to ask you to stay."

Melissa shook her head. "When I was marching with all those people, at the front, leading them…I felt like I never felt before. I felt like I could get shit done, you know? I love doing my channel, and I love connecting with millions of girls and young women and having them hear me and comment and stuff, but this was something different, more real, you know? More direct."

"I know what you mean," Tim said. He rarely felt more

alive than when he was addressing a crowd at a campaign rally or a town hall meeting.

"I guess that was before the violence."

"Yeah. That was horrible."

"It's been all over the news in Toronto," Shania said. "National, even."

"There were a couple of press guys outside the house when I went out," Tim said. "I ignored their questions. I was expecting more after the kidnapping."

Tim had finished his third plate of pancakes and was feeling stuffed. He thanked Shania for the tasty breakfast and then turned on the TV and changed to the news channel. At that moment they were covering some international conference.

"In Canada it's all about Melissa. If nothing else it's doing wonders for your subscriber numbers. I think you're up about a million."

Tim glanced at Melissa. She didn't seem pleased to hear that. He guessed that her priorities may have changed in the last few days.

Shania noticed it too. "Isn't that great?" she asked, trying to get affirmation.

Melissa nodded. She was watching the TV but gave no other reaction to the news.

"Does the press know Melissa is here?" Tim asked Shania.

"I don't think so, at least not when I last checked."

"Good. Probably best we keep a low profile."

The conference item on the news ended and the anchor switched to domestic news. This item was about the last night's violence, but it didn't even mention Richmond. Apparently, other cities in the US had seen clashes between demonstrators and police that had been much worse, with many more injuries and arrests.

The three of them watched with rapt attention. Tim said,

"No wonder the press isn't bothering us much. Looks like Richmond's protest wasn't the only one with agitators."

There were images of violence in Chicago on the screen. Tim saw men with masks actively attacking police lines, while panicked and confused regular protestors tried to avoid the violence. Clouds of gas fired by the police began to fill in the picture, making it hard to see what was going on. Tim watched a massive armored personnel carrier rumbling into view, obscuring the remainder of the scene.

It was happening everywhere, not just Richmond. The President came on, appealing for calm across the nation. Was this really all about him and Granger? Was there more going on here? Or was there just a general movement towards violence and it was a coincidence that he and Melissa had gotten caught up in it last night? Tim didn't voice his unanswered questions. Just a glance at Melissa told him she was having trouble coping with the images on screen. Clearly she was reliving the events of last night. Shania held her hand and Tim was very glad Melissa's friend was here to support her.

Melissa had tears in her eyes now, and Shania put an arm around her. Tim turned back to the TV to see the image of Officer Jason Hagley. The anchor was explaining that the officer had been suspended with full pay while Virginia's Attorney General looked into whether to bring him to trial. Even if Tim had not seen the tape of Howie's death, a trial was obviously the right call. He should call the AG and implore him to press charges.

"Is he going to get off?" Melissa asked.

Tim turned to her, his heart breaking. Putting Hagley away wasn't going to bring Howie back, but it might stop him shooting another innocent man in the future. She understood that, and Tim wished he had a more positive message to give her. Tim didn't know how the justice system worked when cops went on trial in Canada, if indeed they ever made it to trial, but he guessed there was a more balanced outcome than here in the States.

"I'm sorry, Melissa. Given what's happened in the majority of cases where a cop has shot a black man, the case doesn't even come to trial, never mind a conviction."

She didn't cry out. She didn't slam a fist on the table. She held his gaze. Was she thinking revenge? A vendetta? That certainly wasn't wise. No, she was angry, but her poise was impressive.

"We have to keep the pressure on, make sure he goes to trial. Is there anything you can do, Tim?"

"I was thinking of calling Virginia's AG…"

"But?"

"But I doubt it will do any good. He's probably already in Granger's pocket. If Granger wants Hagley let off without charges, then it will happen. The only way to counteract it is via the federal AG They might take my call, but I would guess Williams – that's Virginia's Attorney General, has requested they stay out of this for now."

"So it's a matter of waiting?"

Tim's mind was working fast. He knew that it would be a mistake to reach out to Williams if the AG was in Granger's pocket – and it stood to reason that he was. However, if he could prove that Williams was taking his lead from Granger, he could kill several birds with one stone. It would destroy Williams, and force him to stand down. It would benefit Melissa, because in the absence of a State AG, the Feds would have to step in. It would hurt Granger because he would lose his influence over one of the top people in the State. It would expose some of the corruption in state government, and might even discredit and expose Granger himself. But how could he do it?

"Shania, you're Melissa's tech guru, right?" Tim asked.

"Yeah."

"Can you hack an email account?"

Shania paused for a moment.

"Sure I could," she replied. "If I had the password. Or if I had some heavy-lifting computer equipment that could break passwords with brute force."

"So you're saying you can't do it?"

Shania stood up.

"Are you challenging me?"

"Just spit balling. There's no backdoor into the email system or anything?"

"Someone's been watching too much *CSI*," Shania said. Melissa laughed.

"So how do we get someone's password?"

Shania stared at him for a moment. "I'm not sure I want to reveal all my secrets," she said.

Melissa put a hand on her arm.

"Please Shania. Whatever Tim has in mind, we should do whatever we can to help."

"Okay, if it'll get justice for Howie, then I'll do whatever it takes."

"So?" prompted Tim.

"Okay well you know how sites like Yahoo and Ashley Madison and other had their data hacked?"

"Yeah."

"Well, if we go looking for your account owner on those leaked lists of passwords, we might find a match. Most people use the same password across multiple sites. Oh shit, don't tell me you do that?"

Tim's face must have betrayed his own guilt. "No!" he lied, hoping he sounded convincing.

"Uh huh. Anyway, if you find his password for some site that's already been hacked, you can then use it to try to get into other accounts he uses."

"Like his email?"

"Like his email."

"So I just have to give you a name and you can start looking?"

"Sure thing. I even brought my laptop."

"Great. So the name is Theodore Williams, and he's Virginia's Attorney General."

Shania didn't react for a moment. When she spoke it was in a stage whisper.

"Are we about to do something illegal, Senator Barns?"

"Not illegal, exactly. Okay probably a little bit illegal."

"That's okay, if I get caught I'll just say you tied me up in your basement and threatened me until I hacked the AG for you."

"Shania!" Melissa said.

"I'm not serious!" she protested. She turned back to the Tim. "I'm going to need your Wi-Fi password. And if it's the same as all your other passwords, like your email, your Twitter or your bank account, you might want to change them."

Tim shifted uncomfortably.

"Um, there's no… no need."

"Very glad to hear it. There's one more thing."

Shania excelled at making Tim feel out of his depth.

"What's that?"

"Well I might be able to get one of his passwords from the hacked lists, but I can't use it from here."

"You can't?"

"No. I'd need to be physically onsite at the AG's office, or I'd need to connect via VPN and then login."

"VPN?"

"Virtual Private Network. It allows my laptop at my home to become part of the office's network. It's for security, so not just anyone can attempt to gain access to their servers."

"And I'm guessing your machine has to be registered on the AG's servers in order for you to connect with this VPN?"

"Your IP address would need to have access, and possibly your machine would need a widget, or a rotating authentication ID."

"A what now?"

Shania sighed. "You have a little key with a display on it, and at regular intervals it gets a new code sent to it, which it displays for you. You have to login with that code. Because it keeps changing you have to have the key with you when you connect. How did you get elected again?"

"So what are you telling me?"

"I'm telling you that connecting to the AG's email account would be a lot tougher from remote than it would be if we strolled into the building, sat down and logged in from there."

"Okay then, let's do that."

Shania blinked at him. "Do what?"

"Stroll into the building."

She turned to Melissa, who shrugged.

"Don't look at me!" she said.

Tim grinned at the two ladies. "Who's up for a little role play?"

chapter twelve

THEY WANT YOU DEAD

Shopping for formal clothes with Shania had been fun. For an hour, two best friends went to the outlets and forgot about their troubles for just a little while. They had met Tim back at his place – Tim had given Melissa a spare key to his apartment – and took the opportunity to change their clothes. Now it was time for business. Tim was in one of his own suits, Melissa and Shania wore business skirts and jackets. They stood at the corner of 9th and East Grace Street, facing the statue of George Washington on horseback in Capitol Square. Behind them was the Ninth Street Office Building, which Tim told them was usually known as the Hotel Richmond. These days it was a government office. Melissa would have loved to take a walk in the very pretty park and see all the statues, but she knew they had work to do. The chances of them pulling this off were remote, but as long as they weren't caught they could regroup to fight another day.

"Everyone ready?" Tim asked, adjusting his red tie.

"Ready," Shania confirmed.

"Ready," Melissa said, feeling anything but. On her webcasts she was all about being herself. People watched her for her honesty and genuine approach. She wasn't used to playing a role. She hoped she wouldn't let the side down.

They entered the offices and went through security screening. Tim introduced himself, and told the guards that Shania was his social media advisor and Melissa was his personal assistant. They looked at Tim a little suspiciously, and regarded Melissa with slightly tilted heads and a look of recognition on their faces.

"Aren't you the girl who was tied up in his basement?" one of the guards asked Melissa after she passed through the metal detectors.

"Yes. He rescued me, I convinced him to hire me. Is that okay?"

"Quite okay, ma'am," the guard replied with a slight smile on this face.

They passed security without further questioning and headed to the elevator. They received a few odd looks from suits hurrying by, but nobody challenged them. They ascended in silence. They had already been over the plan; there was no need to rehash it. Melissa tried to concentrate on not looking like she was concentrating. She glanced over at Tim and Shania, both of whom appeared totally relaxed. Did they feel what she felt but were better at hiding it? Or was she the only one of the trio quietly freaking out over here?

The doors opened and they stepped out into a bustling office floor. Nobody paid them much attention as they approached the desk. Tim did the talking.

"Tim Barns. I have an appointment with Mr. Williams."

"Oh yes, Senator Barns. Thanks so much. Please have a seat."

"Thanks. Oh, my assistants want to make a call. Is there somewhere private they could go?"

"Of course. They're welcome to use the empty office over on the right."

"Thank you so much."

Tim nodded to Melissa and Shania, and the two of them hurried over to the indicated office, Melissa trying not to appear to be in a rush. They entered and closed the door. While Melissa pretended to talk on the phone, Shania went straight to the computer on the desk and switched it on. It took a few moments to boot up, then she began typing.

"How many passwords did you find?"

"Half a dozen. Our Mr. Williams has a lot of shady accounts on servers that are always getting hacked. He should learn to cover his tracks better."

"What do you mean shady?"

"Porn sites mostly. Nothing illegal, just stuff that might raise a few eyebrows. Okay, as I suspected, none of them worked. Mr. Williams isn't a complete novice at password security."

"Plan B?" Melissa asked.

"Plan B."

Melissa typed a message on her phone and sent it to Tim.

Plan B.

"Let's hope he's paying attention."

The AG's secretary said, "You can go in now."

Tim thanked her and opened the door to Williams's office.

"Theo! How are you?"

Theodore Williams, a middle-aged, portly fellow with two chins and red cheeks, hurried around his desk and shook Tim's hand enthusiastically.

"Tim! Congratulations on your big win. I had my eye on you, knew you were going places. How's the state senate?"

"Oh, you know, frustrating and slow."

Williams laughed.

"Sounds familiar," he said.

"Thanks for clearing your schedule for me, Theo. I really appreciate it."

"No problem, no problem. Always happy to receive a visit from the legislative branch. Can I get you something to drink? Do sit down."

"I'm fine thanks," said Tim as he took a seat at the desk. Williams' laptop sat just a couple of feet away from him, the lid closed.

Williams shuffled back behind his desk and sat down.

"Now, what can I do for you? Come to thank me for my support during your campaign?" He laughed, suggesting that he didn't really expect thanks.

"Not specifically, no. But while I'm here I did want to say _"

"No need, no need." Williams was all blustering enthusiasm. "Happy to do my part. Like your stuff on the criminal justice reform. Very *progressive*." Williams said that word like it was computer jargon, or some other phrase of which he wasn't entirely sure of its meaning.

"Yes, thank you. So, anyway, I wanted to talk to you about the man who was shot by police the other day, a rapper who called himself Howie Do?"

"Oh yes, terrible tragedy. Such a sad thing to happen. Not that I was into his music of course, absolutely dreadful din, but still."

Tim wasn't quite sure how to respond to that. He soldiered on regardless.

"Right, well, specifically I wanted to talk to you about Officer Hagley, the policeman who shot Howie."

"Yes, my people are looking into whether to lay charges or not."

"Right, well, that's why I'm here. I think you should definitely put him on trial."

Williams frowned. "Bit outside your jurisdiction, isn't it?

You guys make the rules, we enforce them, right?"

"Right, of course. I just… Well, you heard about his girlfriend who I found in my basement?"

"Yes I did hear something about that. Ghastly business. What was that all about?"

"Still no idea, Theo. Wondered if you'd heard anything about it actually. I think someone's trying to frame me and I'm not sure who or why. Anyway, that's not why I'm here. The young lady who was in my basement, her name is Melissa Jones and I think she deserves justice."

"Fond of her, are you?" Williams said.

"Well, I wouldn't say *fond*," Tim blustered awkwardly. "But I do care about her wellbeing, and I do want her to go back to Canada without carrying the message that the US criminal justice system is broken."

"Why on Earth should we care what Canadians think?" Williams said.

"Melissa has a web channel with four million followers, probably a lot more by now. She has a huge international following. Do you really want her telling the world that cops in the US can shoot unarmed black men and not even go on trial?"

"He had a gun, Tim!"

Tim took a breath. He was determined not to get angry. "Officer Hagley was in possession of Howie's firearm when Howie was shot, Theo."

"Are you sure?"

Tim wanted to scream at him. Was he being deliberately ignorant of the facts? How could Howie hope to get a fair trial if the State's Attorney General had wrong information?

"Yes, I'm sure. Check Melissa's statement."

"I will, I will."

Williams reached forward and opened his laptop. Now was Tim's chance.

"Before you do, perhaps I will have that drink."

Williams beamed at him. "Bit early for me, but oh what the hell, why not?"

The big man stood up and walked over to a drinks cabinet on the far side of the room. Tim stood up and walked around the desk to Williams's side. He sat on the desk beside the laptop and, his eyes never leaving Williams, reached down and plugged a small device into the USB port.

Williams returned with two glasses, one of which he handed to Tim, who thanked him and took a quick swig to calm his nerves. He'd never done anything like this before and he was aware his hands were shaking.

"Right then," said Williams. He placed his drink beside the laptop and typed in his password. Tim made a show of not looking while he typed. "Now, let me see. Ah yes, here's the file on Howard Douglas. Got the sworn statements here." He double clicked to open Officer Hagley's statement, then scrolled to the relevant part. "Here we go."

Tim leaned in to read what was on the screen. As he did so he pulled the device from the laptop and slipped it into his pocket. He was interested in reading the officer's testimony, and to his shock it stated that Hagley did not find or take Howie's gun while searching him. He suspected Howie was going for his gun, shot him dead, and then discovered the gun on Howie's person. Not only did the statement not make much sense – how did Hagley miss the gun while searching Howie? – but it also directly contradicted the video evidence and Melissa's account of what happened.

"Theo, you must see this isn't what happens on the video. Hagley took Howard's gun before shooting him. He was unarmed when he died."

"The video is shaky at that moment, Tim. It's hard to be sure."

"What about Melissa's testimony?"

"She was under extreme stress when her statement was taken. She had just seen her boyfriend die. She was in no state of mind to give an accurate account."

Tim was having a hard time concealing his rage. *This*, right here, was why so many cases never even went to trial. Questions about video evidence, contradictory witness accounts, biased readings of the key documents. It was all here in front of him. Tim wanted to scream at Williams, to punch him in his fat face for perpetuating the endless lack of police accountability. The monumental battle he had on his hands to try to change the direction of Virginia on crime and police reform crashed over Tim like a tidal wave of depression. All his usual enthusiasm and positivity seemed to die in that one moment. Was his cause hopeless? Was the system so *automatically* corrupt as to be impossible to fix.

One thing was for sure, Theodore Williams was part of the problem, and Tim hoped to God Shania's little device had done its work. Busting this fat fuck was now Tim's top priority. Nothing would ever change with him in charge of prosecuting police for fatal shootings of unarmed people of color.

"There it is!" said Shania. She waved her phone at Melissa, who smiled in return. Shania had installed an app linked to the device she'd given to Tim, something she'd picked up at the shady looking electronics store they had passed by on their way to buy clothes. Shania was reading the data transmitted from the device to her phone. "User ID, password, perfect!"

She started typing and moments later declared, "I'm in!"

She connected a USB drive to the computer and started downloading Williams' email archive.

Shania had explained to Melissa that the device was small

enough to fit into a USB drive and stay almost invisible – it didn't stick out like a usual USB drive. Inside the device was a tiny wireless transmitter, and the device was designed to captured keystrokes and transmit them to the app on Shania's phone. She could see everything Williams typed while the device was connected, and Williams had typed in his username and password to unlock his laptop.

"Okay, we're copying all his emails off the server. You can tell Tim we're in and he should aim to leave in, er, five minutes or thereabouts."

Melissa texted the message to Tim. Was this really going to work?

Surely someone would walk in on them. Surely someone was monitoring the network looking for unauthorized logins. Surely at some point, Melissa was going to make a huge mistake and give them all away. She resisted the urge to run screaming from the building and instead settled in to wait for the copy to complete.

"So do you see what I'm saying, Theo?" Tim asked, fighting hard to stay calm.

"Oh yes, yes of course. I just… it's just that, normally we don't take these things to trial, you know? Especially if there's sufficient doubt it was an unlawful killing. Trials tend to drag on and they undermine law and order. You think the riots we had last night were bad? Imagine if Hagley went to trial and was found innocent?"

"That's no reason not to try him though. If he's innocent, then he'll be set free. If not, he goes to jail. Either way, we have the perception that justice has been carried out. Right now, there's no justice and people are angry. They're going to stay angry unless we do something."

Tim's phone buzzed, reminding him that this conversation

was just a front for their real purpose in coming here. Tim clung on to the notion that he might be about to bring down this ignorant fuck, this do-nothing yes-man.

"Listen, I have an emergency, but think it over, okay?"

"Of course," Williams said. "Thanks for stopping by. Don't be a stranger."

Tim drained his drink, thanked him for his time and left the office, his head aching with contained fury. He forced a smile at the secretary and headed for the office where Melissa and Shania were working.

He opened the door, making Melissa jump.

"You ladies done?" he asked.

Shania stood up, snatching the USB drive from the computer and slipping it into her pocket.

"Yup. Let's go."

The three of them left the office and Tim called the elevator. It arrived after what felt like an age, and they stepped in, trying to look cool. Melissa was clearly as jumpy as she had been all along, but was holding it together okay. Shania was a picture of serenity – she was a natural spy. Tim hoped he was projecting confidence and calm, but his insides churned with anger. How could Williams not see it? How could he be so cheerfully complicit in the status quo? How was he okay with young men being shot or wrongly imprisoned or beaten and humiliated by cops who could act with impunity? Williams was everything Tim had run for office to oppose. They had spoken before, and Williams had always been supportive of his policies, but now Tim knew that was all just a front. In public Williams was all smiles and support for police and prison reform. Behind that smile, though, was a desire to keep things exactly as they were, not rock the boat or make anything other than cosmetic changes for fear of upsetting his lords and masters. With luck, they were leaving the building with hard evidence that Williams was not his own man, that he answered to someone else, and should step down immediately.

The elevator doors opened at last. The three of them had not spoken a word to each other, and maintained their silence as they crossed the lobby and passed by security on their way out.

Once outside, Shania spoke first.

"I suggest we find an internet café to take a look at what we got. I wouldn't want this bad boy anywhere near our own computers."

"Lead the way," Tim said.

"I'm Canadian," Shania said, "and I'm nineteen years old. I've never even been in an internet café."

Tim sighed. "I think there's one further along East Grace," he said. "Follow me."

chapter thirteen

THEY: WANT YOU DEAD

Melissa sipped her coffee and kept a watch on the door while Tim and Shania scrolled through pages of emails. The café was surprisingly busy. She had expected desolation and despair. It had taken her a while to get coffee for the three of them, and when she returned they were still raking through the coals.

"Here's another one," Tim said, pointing at the screen.

Shania clicked on an email and it popped up in a new window. Tim scanned it but shook his head.

"Nope, keep going."

"Can't you just search for Granger's name?" Melissa asked.

"He's not going to use his own account to tell Theo what to do," Tim explained. "We've tagged a few examples of what looks like Theo receiving instructions or asking questions, but nothing that links them together."

"What are you going to do if you find any?"

"Leak them," Shania answered.

Tim nodded. "Can't take them to the police, so press it is. Whoah whoah! Go back!"

Shania scrolled back up a page. Tim's finger shot out at a particular line, and Shania brought up the email.

Tim seemed excited about something. "This email is about the AG stepping in to prevent a takeover of Villi-Mart."

"So?" Shania asked.

"So, Villi-Mart was eventually taken over by Amberly's, that's Granger's company. Tim turned to the computer in front of him and did a search. Up came a news article about the takeover of Villi-Mart as Tim had said.

"There you go, three years ago almost exactly. They line up. Granger wanted to buy this company but someone else put a bid in first. Granger had the AG block the sale and then swooped in to buy Villi-Mart when the share price dropped."

"So Granger did it to get a better deal?" Melissa said.

"Yeah looks that way. Mighty suspicious."

"It's not enough," Shania said. "We can't link it to Granger's office."

"No," said Tim, "but it's pretty obvious someone is telling Theo what to do, and that's embarrassing for him at the very least. Tag that one, let's keep looking."

"None of these are going to implicate Granger," Melissa said. "This was a waste of time."

"It will still hurt Granger if Theo has to resign. He'll have to groom a whole new AG Plus it will mean the Feds have to step in on Hagley."

Hearing that name caused Melissa to have to close her eyes and calm herself down. Everything came flooding back, a tidal wave she was powerless to prevent. She struggled to fight back tears and the hopelessness overflowing her soul. No, she would not drown. She owed Howie justice. After a moment she opened her eyes again. Her vision was blurred, but no tears had escaped her eyelids.

She kept her voice even as she said, "We need something on Granger. This isn't going to stop until he's dealt with."

Tim shushed her, glancing nervously at the other café

patrons. In hushed tones he said, "Melissa we talked about this when we were planning this stunt. I warned you it would be tough to find anything on Granger directly, and even if we did – he has friends in very high places and if Kirsty Frank is to be believed, he's part of an ancient organization that will pull him out of any fire we can drop him into."

"But if you just bring down Williams and leave Granger untouched, he's going to want revenge."

"Granger is a smart businessman. He won't do anything to connect himself with this scandal."

"He kidnapped me!"

"That was before we proved we can hurt him."

Melissa wasn't convinced. When Tim had explained the plan to her, she had somehow hoped they'd find the mystical smoking gun, the one message that would destroy Granger and his entire hold on Virginia forever. She had not taken the time to consider what it would mean if they fell short of their goal. To say it was disappointing was putting it mildly. Frustration and helplessness clawed at her, threatening to unravel all that she had struggled so hard to keep together. Perhaps the universe would let her have a go at being someone else, just for a little while, until she was ready to be herself again. She liked being herself, generally, but there was rather too much more going on that she could handle right now, and a short time away would be very welcomed.

Two men entered the café. The sight of them froze the air in Melissa's lungs. She did not recognize their faces, but she knew without a shadow of doubt that these were the same men who kidnapped her. One of them was the same guy Tim faced off against in his basement before setting her free. Panic tugged at the edges of her mind, trying to pull everything into a heap of utter insanity.

"They've found us!" she hissed.

Instantly Shania pulled the USB drive from the computer

and closed the files they'd been examining. Tim stood up.

"Out the back," he said to Melissa and Shania. "Don't look back. Go!"

Shania was already moving. As she passed she grabbed Melissa's arm and half dragged her towards the kitchen. Melissa didn't resist, but she looked on helplessly as one of the men dragged Tim from the café. The other kidnapper came after them. Melissa gave a yelp and overtook Shania.

They rushed into the kitchen and crossed the small space quickly, bursting out through the back doors into an alley behind the street.

They didn't wait to see if anyone was following. Shania had always been faster than Melissa, ever since they were teenagers running the 100 meter dash. She made it to the street far faster than Melissa, who was aware of movement in the alleyway behind her. She didn't pause to look around. It was clearly one of the men who had entered the café looking for them. Luckily, Shania had the USB drive, so Melissa wasn't the target. She didn't know if her pursuer knew that, but when she reached the street she saw Shania had run off to the right. Melissa went left.

This time she risked a glance behind her, and was gratified to see the burly man at the exit from the alleyway, staring back and forth between the women running in opposite directions. This was the same guy who Tim had rescued her from in his basement, she was sure of it. His height and build were a match, and the way he moved, agile despite his size, it was a dead giveaway.

The man made a decision and took off after Shania. Melissa felt a little hurt. She was the famous one! Shania had been the one at the computer when they entered the café, so it stood to reason that she had the stolen emails.

Melissa halted, breathing hard. Now what? She couldn't leave Shania. She had a good lead on this guy but he was fast. He'd nearly caught her, Melissa, despite the head start she had.

She hadn't run in so long and already she was feeling a stitch forming. But she couldn't abandon Shania, so she ran back towards the alley and followed her kidnapper, who had just disappeared around the corner of a building.

Melissa crossed the street to follow him, incurring the wrath of a couple of drivers who had to slam on their brakes for her. She ignored them, reached the other side and tore around the corner, only to connect with over two-hundred pounds of muscle.

She bounced off her kidnapper's chest and sprawled backwards into the street. The man had fooled her and she'd run straight into his trap.

"Help!" Melissa cried out to people on the street. Folks glanced at her then continued on their way.

"Shut up," said her kidnapper, stepping forward to grab her. Melissa rolled and scrambled to her feet, escaping from his clutches by mere inches as she backed away. She turned and ran. He was so close she heard his breathing.

"This man is trying to rape me!" she called out as she passed people. "Help me, someone please!"

Still nobody would help. What was wrong with them all? Did the black people think her kidnapper was a police officer and they'd get into shit if they helped her? Did the white people assume she was guilty?

She wasn't sure she could run much longer. Her heart was pounding and her lungs ached. The stitch in her side was like a lance stabbing her with every step. She was vaguely aware that her pursuer was yelling something.

"Richmond PD, stop that woman!"

Maybe that was why nobody was helping her.

She crashed into a big black guy, nearly knocking them both to the ground and costing her precious seconds. Her kidnapper had a hand on her jacket but Melissa let her arms go loose behind her and the jacket slipped off. It was her favorite, the blue brushed leather one, but it was a worthy sacrifice. Melissa ducked around the other side of the man she'd crashed into.

"Please help me! This man kidnapped me but I got away." That much was the truth. "Now he wants to rape me. Please help."

Melissa realized she was outside a diner, and the man was standing in front of a table filled with other guys, all equally big, and a couple of women around the same size. They were all dressed in construction worker uniforms, HiVis jackets and carrying hardhats. The one she'd crashed into was shielding her from her kidnapper.

"Richmond PD," her kidnapper said. "She's a wanted fugitive. Please hand her over."

The construction worker's friends stood up and moved to flank their fellow. They formed a protective shield around Melissa. She couldn't believe what she was seeing.

"Show my your badge," the black man said.

"Get out of the way, Sir!" her kidnapper insisted.

"Not until I see your badge."

This guy was Melissa's hero.

The other workers nodded. Her kidnapper flashed something at them but it clearly wasn't a police badge, even a Canadian could see that.

"I suggest you run away before we take you over to our site and bury you under twenty tons of cement."

Her kidnapper glared at the construction workers for what must have been a full minute. Then he turned and stalked away.

"Oh my God, thank you so much," Melissa said.

"No problem," said her savior. The others nodded their agreement. "I knew he ain't no cop. I'm Amos." He held out his hand.

Melissa shook it. His hand was huge but his grip was surprisingly gentle. "I'm Melissa. And no, he wasn't a cop. He's a bad man who really did kidnap me."

"Hey, I seen you on the news, right?"

Melissa smiled and gave an awkward little wave. "Yeah, hi, that was me. I was the girl in Senator Tim Barns's basement."

"Yeah that's right. You're Howie Do's lady. Shit, you weren't kidding. I thought you was yelling a line to get people's attention."

"Well, to be fair I don't think he planned to rape me. But he did kidnap me."

"Shit, if I'd known that we'd have pummeled the guy."

Melissa wasn't usually happy to hear talk of violence, but in this case she'd make an exception.

One of the other workers said, "Didn't you just sign a TV deal?"

Melissa turned to him. "Yeah, but since Howie died I've no idea if it's happening or not. But if it does, I'd love to have you guys on to say thank you for what you did for me today. Let me give you my number."

Melissa took a scrap of paper and pen from one of the workers and wrote down her number.

Amos smiled. "We were at the demonstration the other night, when the police charged."

"Oh you were? Thank you." It sounded lame to say, but she really was grateful for their support.

"Yeah I'm glad you are all right. You were at the front, yeah?"

"Yeah. It was terrifying. Look, I have to go make sure my friend is all right. Thanks again guys, you saved my life."

She shook Amos's hand again, waved to the others and headed off in the direction Shania had gone. This time she didn't rush around that same corner. She peered around it carefully. There was no sign of her kidnapper.

There was no sign of Shania either.

chapter fourteen

THEY WANT YOU DEAD

Tim didn't have to wait long for company. The location was so close they didn't have drive him there, they simply walked him to a nearby building on a side street and took him inside. This room was windowless and kept deliberately gloomy. There was a distant dripping noise coming from somewhere. He wasn't cuffed, but the door was locked and there was no other way out of there.

Eventually the door opened and in walked the two FBI agents who had interviewed Tim at his house the day before: Agents Clark and Ortega.

Tim smiled at them as they entered. "Ah, familiar faces. How nice. Can I get a coffee?"

"Senator Barns, we… have a few questions for you." Again with the drawl, Clark's voice grated on Tim's nerves. But he simply smiled again and held his arms wide.

"Of course, fire away. If I may, I'd like to ask you a question first."

Clark seemed about to refuse him but Ortega got there first.

"Go ahead," she prompted. She sat down opposite Tim. Clark stayed standing and clicked his tongue in irritation.

"Why are two FBI agents interviewing a state senator in a

meeting room in an almost empty office building in downtown Richmond, instead of at a police station or federal building, especially when said senator has been captured and brought here by independent operatives who don't work for the police or the FBI?"

"We're asking the questions," Clark said coldly, contradicting his fellow agent.

"Okay, well that's fine. I would make one request then. I have to open a school on Monday so if you're going to start hitting me, do you mind avoiding the face?"

Clark did not look amused at this. Ortega gave a wry smile.

"We're not going to hit you," she assured him.

Tim sat back. "So again, why am I here? You didn't even put me in cuffs. Am I under arrest for something?"

"You and your associates stole confidential data from the offices of Virginia's attorney general."

"If that's the case, why is this a federal issue? Surely this is a state matter."

"This is part of a wider investigation into the kidnapping of a foreign national. Since we were already running an investigation that involves you, we were asked to talk to you about this."

"Asked by whom?"

Clark stepped forward. "That's… none of your concern. Do you recognize this?"

He placed a small device on the table with a USB connector. It was the wireless keystroke transmitter Tim had planted in Williams's office. He picked it up and made a show of examining it, acting as if he had never seen it before.

"It's a USB drive, but I'm guessing it's more than that. Some sort of espionage device?"

"It… records keystrokes and transmits them over Wi-Fi to

a… synched device. You used it to… capture the Attorney General's password so you could… login to his account and steal his email archive."

"Did I?"

Clark leaned in, still standing, his face inches from Tim's.

"Yes. You did."

"And the evidence you have for this theft, is this device?"

"We have more."

"Oh good. Because you didn't even hand it to me in a bag. My prints, your prints are all over it. It's contaminated. You can't use this as evidence to link me to any crime you think happened."

"Were you at his office today?"

"Yes."

"Why?"

"I wanted to talk to him about the police officer who shot Howard Douglas. I urged him to seek criminal charges against that officer."

"Was anyone with you?"

"Yes. Melissa Jones and Shania Martin."

Ortega asked, "The same Melissa Jones who you found tied up in your basement."

"Yes," said Tim. "I hired her to be my PR rep."

"You… hired her?" Clark didn't sound convinced.

"That's right. Nothing official yet. She said she was interested in the role and so I agreed to take her on for a few days to see how she does. If it goes well, I'll hire her full time."

"You see how this looks, right?" Ortega said.

"How what looks?"

"You and… Miss Jones hatched a plan to steal emails from Williams, you dragged Miss Jones's Canadian… friend along for her tech skills, and now these two… ladies are on the run with the stolen data in their possession."

"Well, that's quite the story. It doesn't sound like the sort of thing I'd do. So am I free to go?"

"Why… would we let you go?" Clark asked.

"Because I'm not under arrest, I'm not even in a federal, state or town police station. There are no cuffs on me, and you don't have any evidence directly linking me to any crime, and if a USB with stolen data on it exists, you don't have that either."

"You can't leave yet," said Ortega.

Tim studied their faces for a few moments. They weren't giving much away, but he could see just a tiny slice of humiliation in her expression.

"Oh," Tim said, "now I get it. You have to wait for your real master to come talk to me. He just wants a quick chat, right? You guys aren't in charge here, he is."

"We'll be back later, Senator Barns," Ortega said. She stood up, joined Clark and together they left the room.

"So no coffee then?" Tim called out just before the door slammed.

"Come down, bitch!"

"No way. I'm not coming with you."

Melissa hugged the wall out of sight and listened to the exchange between Granger's thug and Shania. Peering around the corner, she could see Shania on a roof top. Melissa's kidnapper was on the ground, calling up to her. There was a metal ladder running up to the roof on the side of the building, which was clearly how Shania had gotten up there. Now she had nowhere to go. She couldn't jump from rooftop to rooftop like Spiderman. The flat roof of the next nearest building was at least ten feet away and it was slightly higher. Shania had been better at school track and field than her, but Melissa doubted Shania could make that distance without falling.

The thug, for his part, seemed reluctant to climb up after her. Melissa had not arrived early enough to hear the full exchange, but when she saw Shania wielding a plank of wood, it became a little clearer.

Shania was taunting him. "Please, come on up. I would love to smash your ugly fucking face in."

Melissa's kidnapper was pacing back and forth, clearly at a disadvantage. He must've realized that if he climbed up after her, he would be vulnerable at the top before he could step out onto the roof. Shania could knock his head off with the plank before he climbed high enough to block her or try to grab the makeshift weapon.

Melissa considered going back to get Amos and his friends. She didn't want to leave in case this guy decided to go for broke. He probably had a fifty-fifty chance that Shania would fumble or be too slow, and he could gain access to the roof before she took a swing at him. Shania was tough but she was hardly a combat veteran. Melissa knew she couldn't take him down, unless she could find a weapon too.

Then she remembered that she'd taken Amos's number. She pulled out her phone and sent a text, praying he would hear it and not be operating a jackhammer or something.

Urgent! Need your help. Can you come?

To her delight, the reply came back almost immediately.

Where are you?

Melissa thought about how to answer. She had no idea what alley she'd followed that had led to this parking lot. This is where employees parked, not customers. Melissa was looking at the backs of various commercial buildings in all directions. There were no titles or logos visible, just nondescript delivery entrances and back doors, extractor fans and windows.

There was one obvious landmark in sight. A crane stood some distance away, possibly more than a whole block. Using the compass feature on her phone Melissa could tell it stood to the south west of her current position. She texted this information to Amos. He responded:

I see the crane. We'll find you.

Melissa felt a surge of relief and gratitude. She peeked around the wall again. Mr. Thug had stopped moving. He was texting someone too.

Shania peered over the ledge at him.

"Calling for backup? Are you scared of a little woman?" She cackled in delight, swinging the makeshift bat a few times to punctuate her laughter.

Mr. Thug seemed unhappy with the response from his phone because he made to hurl it at the wall. In the end he put it back in his pocket. Either his backup was too far away to help, or had refused his request.

He seemed to come to a decision. He started climbing.

Shania stopped taunting him and hurried over to the top of the ladder, waiting with her plank of wood held ready.

Indecision gripped Melissa. She looked back along the alleyway hoping she would see a group of burly construction workers coming to her aid. Nobody was there. She looked back, now standing in the open, heart hammering, hand to her mouth as she anticipated the inevitable clash.

Mr. Thug was almost at the top. Any moment now his head would poke over the top of the ledge and Shania would strike. Melissa could hardly stand to watch. Without thinking she ran forward.

"Hey!" She reached into her pocket and drew out the first thing she grabbed, a lipstick. It was small, black and rectangular, and Melissa was banking on Thugman not being able to see exactly what she was holding. "Looking for this?"

He paused, just four rungs from the top, and turned to look at her.

"Come get it!" Melissa cried, waving the lipstick at him

while being careful to conceal most of the object with her hand. "Leave her alone and you can have it!"

Now it was Mr. Thug's turn to be indecisive. He descended a couple of rungs, then paused again. He was just a couple of feet from Shania, who stood with the plank raised over her head. She was staring at Melissa as well, a look of astonishment on her face.

"Come on!" Melissa yelled again. She hoped her voice would carry so her knights in shining armor could locate her faster. "I'm waiting!"

Melissa's kidnapper started moving downwards. He was part climbing down, part sliding, making rapid progress. Shocked into action, Melissa turned and ran.

She could go back to the main street, where all the people were, but they might just ignore her again. She could head back in the direction of Amos, but he might be coming at them from a different direction. Either way she had to move. Glancing back, she saw her kidnapper on the ground, turning from the ladder to pursue her. She already knew he could outrun her. This may have been a mistake.

"Hey, moron!"

Shania was calling from up on the roof. Melissa slowed and looked back, and so did her kidnapper. Shania was waving the zip drive in her hand, or at least Melissa assumed that's what it was.

Melissa hurled the lipstick at the ground by Mr. Thug's feet and ran. Glancing back, she saw him stop to pick it up, curse and then hurl it away. She had managed to put some distance between them now, she was at the entrance to the alleyway. She was among people again, though she knew she could not count on them to help. Her kidnapper seemed torn once again. Melissa didn't have the drive, Shania did, but he was clearly considering using her to bring Shania down from the roof.

Melissa stole a look down the street. Amos and his friends were coming! They were still some distance away though. Melissa made a decision and ran towards them. She left Shania behind, not knowing if her kidnapper would follow her or return to the ladder.

Amos spotted her through the throng of shoppers, and quickened his pace. Melissa ran towards him, dodging and weaving between people, nearly colliding with a woman carrying multiple shopping bags, and leaping over a small dog dragged precariously by its leash by another woman. Melissa didn't dare look back. Her right shoulder crashed into the arm of a man but she barely noticed and refused to slow down to say sorry. She heard him yell an expletive at her, and to her horror a cry cut him off as someone else crashed into him.

Mr. Thug.

Melissa didn't dare look back. She increased her stride, her lungs bursting. She couldn't call out for help because she was breathing so hard. Panic welled in her chest and drove her onwards. Amos was perhaps a hundred meters away, crossing a side street and narrowly avoiding a car hitting him as it turned the corner. She could feel his breathing on the back of her neck now. Fingers brushed her back, grabbed at her shirt. She had no jacket to shrug off this time. People were staring, jumping out of her way, realizing something was wrong. He was so close. She was sure his hand would close around her shoulder any moment.

And then Amos was there, right in front of her. She dived to the ground, sprawling awkwardly and painfully onto the sidewalk. Above her she heard the collision between Amos and her kidnapper, who had been unable to stop. Amos crashed to the ground beside her, but so did Mr. Thug.

All three of them lay there on the hard cement, staring at each other and breathing so hard they couldn't speak. Then suddenly Mr. Thug made a grab for Melissa. Amos threw himself in between them, knocking her kidnapper away. Amos's friends arrived. They surrounded her kidnapper while Amos and Melissa helped each other to their feet.

"Did you not understand what I said?" Amos spat at Mr. Thug.

"This is police business," he said, dabbing a finger at a cut on his forehead.

Amos shook his head. "I know police," he said. "At my school, cops were everywhere. Police stop me nearly every day because I'm a big black guy. I've spent time in police cells for nothing more than walking down the street. I know cops, and you ain't one. What's your name?"

"Bruce," said the man. It suited him.

Melissa was still breathing hard but she'd recovered enough to get out her phone. She texted Shania and told her she could come down now. A moment later, her friend responded that she would.

"What do you want us to do with him, Melissa?" Amos asked. His friends closed in on Bruce, whose expression had turned from defiance to concern.

"You work for Granger?" Melissa asked Bruce.

He nodded. Clearly he had no need to lie at this point.

"You have family, Bruce?"

He nodded again. "Wife. Two boys."

"So why are you doing this? Why are you trying to hunt down two teenage girls on the streets of Richmond?"

"Mr. Granger pays me pretty well for the work I do."

"Which is what? Intimidating people?"

"I do what I'm told."

"You kidnapped me."

"It was a warning. Mr. Granger wanted you to get out of the country and not cause trouble. We used you to get Barns in trouble too. That was my idea."

"Oh very good," said Melissa. She gave him a little clap. "Before you kidnapped me I was heading to the airport. I was leaving for Canada. If you hadn't grabbed me off the street I'd be gone by now. Not such a clever idea after all."

Bruce shrugged.

"You want us to pour some fresh cement?" Amos asked with a meaningful nod towards Bruce.

Melissa shook her head. "I want you to hold him here until I get Shania. Please."

"Sure, we'll do that."

It took Melissa a good ten minutes to find her friend. Shania was hiding behind a group of dumpsters, and wouldn't come out even when Melissa called her name.

Eventually Melissa stumbled across her.

"Why didn't you answer me?" she asked.

Shania looked suspicious, glancing around as if expecting someone to leap out at her.

"I thought that guy had you. I wasn't going to step out if he was forcing you to call for me."

"Well that's smart I guess. Anyway, come on. Some friends of mine are holding him."

By the time Melissa and Shania returned to the workers, Bruce had gone.

"I'm sorry. He got away from us just a few minutes ago." Amos glared at one of his coworkers, a younger man who looked suitably abashed. "You girls had best be careful in case he comes back for you."

"We should wait for Tim," Melissa said.

"It isn't safe," Shania said. "If that guy, what's his name, Bruce? If he comes back…" she trailed off.

"You could stay with us," Amos offered, except we're just about done for the day. I'll stay with you if you like."

Melissa smiled at him. "That's very kind, but we should be getting back. Shania's right, we shouldn't be on the streets while Bruce is looking for us."

"Okay, well at least let me get you a cab."

Melissa nodded. She and Shania stayed with the other workers while Amos went to the street. It took him a minute or two but he hailed them a taxi.

Melissa was texting Tim to let him know they were heading back to his place. She was glad he'd given her a key. She had no idea where he was and hoped he was okay. She and Shania thanked Amos for his help and climbed into the cab.

As the driver sped away, Melissa checked her phone. No response from Tim. Where the hell was he? Was he in trouble? Should they go looking for him? Indecision ate at her. Maybe he'd already gone home, though that was unlikely.

For now all they could do was ensure they kept themselves, and the zip drive, safe. Tim's house probably wasn't the safest place they could go, but at least it got them off the streets where they were vulnerable, and there was a lock on the front door.

She hoped to God Tim wasn't already lying in a ditch somewhere. She also hoped Bruce and his fellow goons weren't waiting for her at Tim's house.

When Lionel Granger entered, Tim was feeling more relaxed than he expected to. He wouldn't let this old bastard humiliate him. Granger wore a quiet smile and seemed subdued. Tired even. He sat down at the desk opposite Tim, took off his glasses and peered at the senator, without saying a word.

"You know," he began, punctuating his words with a wave of his glasses, "you and I could really achieve something in this state. We could make Virginia the greatest state in the nation. But we can't do that if we're heading in different directions."

"Sure we can," Tim replied. "Because I'm the elected official, and you're a concerned citizen."

Granger smiled. "I am far more than just a concerned citizen."

"Well the Constitution might disagree with you there."

"You are a public servant. You should be serving me."

"I do serve you, Mr. Granger. I also serve all the people of Richmond who elected me to the state senate, and all those who didn't, and everyone else in this great state."

Granger sighed. He put his glasses back on, sat back and folded his arms, his eyes never leaving Tim.

Tim, for his part, sat still and calm, and stared straight back. A door banged somewhere outside the room, but neither of them broke their gaze.

"Come on, Lionel," Tim said. "Kidnapping the girlfriend of a rapper shot to death by the police and tying her up in my basement. What the hell were you thinking? That's how you control people? It's 2017, you don't have to resort to nineteenth-century tactics."

Granger smiled in a smug, knowing way that angered Tim, though he tried not to show it. "I'm just getting started."

"Do you have anything else to take from me? My wife is gone, and I'm starting to suspect you had a hand in that. Any progress I made since taking office has been negated by all the rumors flying around since the kidnapping, so I have to start again anyway. I'll quit before I become your puppet. So really, what do I have left that you can take?"

"Melissa."

Tim stared at him. "She's not mine to take."

"But you care about her. Oh I'm sure you don't have romantic feelings for her, at least I assume not." Granger paused and stared deeply into Tim's eyes. Tim held his gaze.

"Hmm, perhaps you do. Regardless, you care about her. You feel partially responsible for some of what's happened to her since her boyfriend died, and you've taken her under your wing. You feel responsible for her well-being, and you would probably die for her."

"Everything that's happened to her since she came to Richmond is your fault."

"Nonsense." Granger interlocked his fingers behind his head and tipped his chair back. "I had nothing to do with the police shooting."

"And Officer Hagley? Why isn't Williams prosecuting? Why isn't the Federal AG getting involved?"

"It's important that we don't undermine law and order. Hagley will be dealt with, but not by… official channels. We want the police on our side when the time comes."

"If Hagley isn't brought to justice, there'll be more protests, maybe riots."

"Officer Hagley's conduct is the unfortunate result of decades of failed policies regarding law and order, policing and the war on drugs."

"If you think those policies have failed, why are you trying to stop me changing them?"

"Some of what you propose is of use to us. A society at war with itself is not what we want. Some other aspects of the status quo we wish to maintain."

"You're a barrel of contradictions, you know that?"

"Not contradictions. You lack the full context of our aims. I'm not going to explain it all to you now, but if you knew the full plan then you'd understand why we act as we do."

"Who is *we*?"

Granger gave him that knowing smile again. "Surely I don't have to spell it out for you. I'm sure Ms. Frank has been filling your head with conspiracy theories, and you're welcome to draw your own conclusions."

"So, you're too ashamed to admit what you're part of. Interesting."

Granger laughed. "A secret organization has certain rules and policies, you know? It's not smart for its members to go around advertising. We get more done from the sidelines, by influencing and guiding. We have no desire to be in control until…" Granger trailed off.

"Until what?"

Granger didn't answer. Instead he said, "This past election was more polarizing than ever. Frankly it was exhausting, and it completely ran away from us. There is a large part of this country that is not interested in enlightenment, nor in discovering a better way. Instead they care only about themselves, about racial purity, and about ephemera such as flags and pledges. There is so little common ground these days."

"If your people have been influencing us for decades, maybe longer I don't know, aren't you to blame for these divisions?"

"Only partially. Not everyone subscribes to our way of thinking. Sometimes we have to take a more direct approach."

"Like with me?"

"Yes, your policies are progressive but they don't fully align with our wishes, and you would certainly end up causing more divisions, not bringing the country together."

Tim's head was spinning. Trying to pin down exactly what Granger and his ilk were trying to achieve was like trying to catch clouds in a net.

"To me," he said after a moment, "it seems like you want to keep people as slaves, regardless of their race. You want to remove democracy from those you feel are unfit to decide."

"Democracy is an illusion."

"You say that, but the last general election didn't go the

way the majority of voters wanted, yet westill abided by the result."

"Of course, but look at what folks had to decide between. In the end, it doesn't make much of a difference. We made sure of that." Tim understood that there was no possible way to verify Granger's claim, so he let it slide. He continued, "Elections are decided by money, fear and bigotry, and sometimes by the Russians. They are not changed by any grand hope that things are really going to get better. That's just the way we like it. Change too quickly is rejected, but as long as the country is on the right path we are content to influence, to guide, but not to meddle directly."

"You're meddling with me."

"The country is not on the right path."

Tim paused, trying to read Granger's inscrutable expression. How much of this was truth, and how much propaganda? Was he being allowed just a glimpse at the surface of some global conspiracy, and further demonstrations of loyalty would reveal more and more layers? Or was Granger delusional, convinced he was part of a worldwide movement to achieve something great. Great for them, anyway, perhaps not for everyone else.

"Why is Melissa involved in all of this?"

"She was already on our radar, and yes we influenced the deal she signed in Hollywood. Reaching Millennials is exhausting frankly. The ways they communicate change so fast, it's hard to keep up. We need to recruit people like Melissa, even if they don't know they've been recruited, to help us influence and guide the next generation. Fail to do that and one day we become irrelevant, and everything we've worked for is for nothing."

"So why threaten her?"

"To keep you both in line. You are too noble to care what happens to you, but you care about what happens to her.

Melissa is too young to care about much beyond the wellbeing of herself and her friends. You are still useful to us. It's not too late. You can choose to be a part of something greater, to work with me, with us. You can make a real difference. Perhaps not the exact impact you hoped to have when you took office, but careful, constructive change."

"Even if it means that divisions get worse and people I don't like end up in power, I will defend the right of the people to choose their leaders. I can't sign up to some mysterious, aloof organization with nebulous goals calling the shots and telling people what to think."

Granger shook his head. "You've gotten it all wrong," he said. "But it's your choice." He leaned forwards across the desk, coming closer to Tim. "I warn you though, don't try and reveal what I've told you here. Don't tell everyone that Virginia's Attorney General is in league with a shadowy organization involved in a giant conspiracy. We have worked hard to appear to be nothing more than the deranged fantasy of discredited conspiracy theorists. If you start to sound like one, your career will not be a long one. If you try to damage my position in any way, the consequences for you and your young friend will not be pleasant. Am I making myself clear?"

Tim stared back defiantly, refusing to blink.

"Perfectly," he replied, trying to inject just the right level of flippancy into his tone. Too little and Granger might think he was fully capitulating. Too much and he might make good on his threat right away. Granger eyed him suspiciously but sat back in his chair again.

"Your two friends have given my people quite the runaround," he said, suddenly conversational again. "I'm impressed, and a little annoyed."

"So can I go?" Tim asked, standing up.

Granger made no move to stop him.

"Of course. You were never a prisoner here."

"Been nice talking to you," Tim said. He headed for the door.

"Just one more thing," Granger said. Tim stopped. "The zip drive. Bring it to Rocketts Landing Marina tomorrow morning at 10am. Don't copy it. Don't distribute it. Do that and I'll let your friends return to Canada. Do we have a deal?"

Tim didn't say a word. He opened the door and stepped from the room.

Ortega and Clark waited in the corridor, but they didn't say anything as Tim passed by. He retraced his steps to the building's entrance and stepped outside. It was already growing dark. He took out his phone and saw texts from Melissa saying they had gone back to his apartment and hoping he was okay.

He could already hear the unmistakable sounds of gathering protestors nearby, but for now he had more pressing issues. He had to make sure the girls were okay.

chapter fifteen

THEY: WANT YOU DEAD

Melissa jumped up when Tim came through the door and rushed to give him a hug.

"Oh my God!" she said. "We were so worried about you."

"I was worried about you too," Tim said, hugging her right back. They separated awkwardly, avoiding each other's gaze.

Melissa waved Wilson over to meet Tim. They shook hands.

"Wilson Douglas," said Wilson, shaking Tim's hand.

"Oh right, Howie's brother. Nice to meet you. I'm Tim Barns. You were arrested at the protest, right?"

"Yeah that's me. Sorry to come to your house. Wanted to check on Melissa."

"That's fine, no problem. You're more than welcome." He paused, trying to read the situation. "Er, do you two want to be left alone?"

Melissa and Wilson made noises to the contrary, both feeling awkward.

Melissa broke the moment. "Do you want something to eat?" she asked Tim. "We grabbed Thai. That okay?"

Tim nodded. "First thing's first though, do you still have the zip drive?" Shania took it from her pocket and handed it to him. “Damn you girls are good,” Tim said, examining it in his hand.

Shania went to get Tim some food from the kitchen while Melissa led him into his living room to sit down with her and Wilson.

“We thought we’d lost you, in the café,” said Melissa, so relieved that he was in one piece and back at home. She picked up the wine bottle and poured some into a glass. It occurred to her that she had just thought of this place as “home”. That was weird.

“Yeah, I figured I would be locked up,” Tim said.

“That’s where I just came from,” said Wilson. “Released late this afternoon.”

Tim seemed surprised. “You’ve been locked up since the protest?”

“Yeah.”

Tim accepted the glass of wine Melissa handed him. “Did they charge you with anything?”

Wilson shook his head. “Nah, man. I was in with twenty people, I know most of them. None of us was charged with anything.”

“I’m glad you were all let go.”

“So?” Melissa prompted Tim. “What happened to you?”

“I was taken to some building Granger owns. It’s an office building but there doesn’t seem to be any tenants. Granger himself paid me a visit. That was after his two goons from the FBI asked me some questions.”

“The same pair who came here after the kidnapping?”

“Yep, Ortega and Clark. I suspected they might be in with Granger but now I know for sure. Their ‘interview’ with me after the kidnapping was probably just a way for Granger to find out what my state of mind was.”

Melissa poured Wilson and herself some more wine. “So, what did he say?”

At that moment Shania appeared with a plate of food, steaming invitingly. Melissa caught the aroma and wondered if she had room for another helping. Tim gratefully received the plate and a fork.

"Well, on the one hand, he says he had nothing to do with Howie's death."

Melissa frowned. "And you believed him?"

"He was being pretty open the whole time actually. I don't think he was lying. Everything from the kidnapping onwards was all him." Tim took a mouthful and was unable to talk for a moment. Shania poured wine for herself while Melissa and Wilson drank their own. "He told me about the organization he is a part of –"

"You mean the Illuminati?" Melissa interrupted.

Wilson laughed. "Shit no! That's some bullshit right there."

"It's true!" said Melissa.

"We don't know if it's really the Illuminati," Tim said. "Honestly I'm still wrestling with a lot of what he said. It didn't make a lot of sense to me, and I deal with Republicans." The joke raised a smile with Wilson. Melissa knew enough about American politics to know who Republicans were, but felt like an outsider at that moment – which of course she was. She might think of Tim's house as home, but her real home was to the north, in a different country, and she missed it.

"He confirmed a lot of what Kirsty said, about the kidnapping and the Attorney General."

"What about the Attorney General?" Wilson asked.

"He's in Granger's pocket," Melissa explained. "We stole his emails so we'd have evidence."

Tim swallowed his mouthful of food. "Yeah, about that."

"What? The zip drive?"

"Yeah. I have to give it to Granger."

Melissa and Shania both reacted angrily.

"What?" Shania said. "Are you nuts?"

Melissa couldn't believe what she'd just heard. "Do you have any idea what we went through to keep that drive from Granger's thug?"

"He was going to kill us!" Shania agreed.

"Don't you dare hand it over!"

Tim held up his hands in surrender, still holding his fork in one of them.

"Relax, I'll take a copy. I think it's just part of the evidence we need anyway. It's not enough on its own. Anyway, tomorrow morning I'm going to give the drive to Granger and then he'll let you two return to Canada."

"We don't want to go back to Canada," said Shania. "We need to take this guy down."

"That's impossible," Tim told her. "He's too well connected. We could hurt him, but then he'll strike back in ways we can't imagine."

Shania was having none of it. "That's bullshit. You're already assuming we've lost."

They continued to argue, but Melissa's mind was wandering. She missed her mom and dad. Mom wasn't getting any less sick, and every day Melissa was here was another day that might be her mom's last. She was terrified of being arrested at the border, or of something horrific happening to her or Shania if they stayed here and continued to meddle in Granger's affairs. Bottom line, maybe Tim was right and it was time for them to go home.

Tim and Shania were still arguing. Melissa cut through them both.

"Tim's right. We should go, Shan."

Shania rounded on her with her mouth open.

"I'm sorry, what?"

"We should go," Melissa repeated. "If we don't take the

opportunity to get out now, we might not be allowed to later. We might even be arrested. I don't want to go to jail."

Tim put down his fork. "I led you both into committing a felony. For what we did today, all three of us could go to prison. I don't want that for you two. Today was a mistake."

"We have to fight!" Shania said.

"*I* have to fight," Tim replied. "This is my country and I'm an elected public servant. It's my duty to root out corruption. You are Canadians. You're young. You shouldn't have to carry this burden.

Shania got to her feet. "That's a bunch of crap. We're in this together. I came here to help Melissa but now I want to help both of you."

Melissa reached out and took Shania's hand, trying to calm her.

"I want to help too, but I'm scared we might not be allowed to go home."

Wilson put down his wine glass. "If it comes to that, I'll drive you both over the border. Ain't no way you girls aren't going home. Granger can't keep you here."

"I'm concerned that he can," said Tim. "If *They*, whoever *They* are, have enough influence, they could ensure that Melissa and Shania can't leave via the airport or across a bridge into Canada."

Melissa had tears in her eyes now as she implored Shania.

"It's time to go," she said. "I need to be with my mom. She was stable when I left, and dad says she still okay but he might be saying that so I don't worry. I should have been back yesterday."

"You owe this to Howie!"

Melissa's cheeks were wet now. "Shan, please. Don't do that. Don't tell me that. I can't bring him back, I can't do anything to have him back…" she trailed off.

Shania knew immediately she'd gone too far. She pulled

Melissa into a hug and stroked her hair, while Melissa sobbed into her shoulder.

"I'm sorry, hon. I'm so sorry. That was really shitty of me. I know you need to be with your mom."

Tim said, "This isn't over. I'm not done. Once you two are safely out of the country I can fight back without worrying what happens to you. Granger threatened your lives, you know? He said if I didn't play ball he would hurt you two. While you're here, I can't do what I need to do."

Melissa prised herself from Shania's embrace. She sat down and rubbed her eyes. Images flashed through her mind. Thoughts of her TV career going down in flames – althought that seemed gloriously irrelevant right now. Horror stories of people of colour getting stopped at the border, detained, questioned, never allowed back into the country. Nightmares crowded her mind's eye, of her and Shania wearing prison clothes and being beaten in America's toughest prisons. Next, pictures flooded into her head of what condition her mom was in – Melissa didn't know for sure but her imagination was going all out, feeding her images of a frail lady in a hospital bed, knocking on death's door. Then of course Howie, poor Howie. It burned her, a white-hot searing pain in the middle of her chest, to even contemplate for the merest second never being with him again. Then came Hagley, laughing at her, standing with Granger. Both of them telling her she was out of her depth, to run along home and never bother them again. She desperately wanted Howie's killer to be arrested, tried and put away for a long time. But she knew fighting Granger on this was an uphill struggle. Today's "hack" had been daring, fun even – a brief distraction from the pain of what she had lost – but ultimately it was a criminal act, and she did not want to risk finding out for real what life was like for two black girls in an American jail. Aside from the hardships, she would never see her mom again.

"Give him the drive," Melissa said to Tim. Shania didn't protest. She was clearly upset about handing over the fruits of their efforts, just like that, but she was a good enough friend not to challenge Melissa's decision. "I'll ask Jasmine to book us a flight. She must be sick of booking tickets for me by now. Anyway, Shan, let's go home. If Tim runs into trouble and needs our help, we can always come back. If we don't play ball, we might not be allowed home and even if we are, they probably won't let us ever come back to the States."

Shania looked crestfallen. It must be hard for her, to have walked into this exciting situation and then to have it pulled away from her. Shania had always been the daring one, always willing to push it just that little bit farther.

"You're abandoning my brother." This came from Wilson in an accusatory tone. Once again, just like in the café, he was placing obligations on her shoulders, responsibilities she was ill-equipped to deal with. Did he not see what had just happened when Shania pushed this line of reasoning? Was he so blind to her feelings?Melissa took a breath. He was hurting too. He'd lost his brother. He'd known Howie all his life. She was just some fly-by-night who'd known Howie for just a short time. She was abandoning Wilson too, fleeing the country and leaving him to pick up the pieces of a shattered life without his beloved brother. She felt a wave of sympathy for him.

She stepped forward and gave him a hug. After a moment, he accepted it. His closeness reminded Melissa of Howie, and she released him awkwardly. "Of course I do. I just don't think we stand much chance of making it happen. Tim has a shot, if we're not around for Granger to threaten."

"Honestly, you guys are all I have to lose," Tim said.

Melissa found this touching. Shania found it infuriating.

Shania had backed off arguing with Melissa, but felt no such restrictions with Tim. “So you want us gone?” she snapped at him. “Well I’m sorry we’re causing you so much trouble.”

“It’s not like that,” said Tim. “I’m going to make Hagley’s prosecution and jail time a condition of my capitulation. I’ll hand over the drive, tell Granger I’ll play ball, and I’ll quietly look for other ways to oppose him.”

“It sounds like giving up,” Shania said.

“It sounds sensible,” Melissa said.

Shania regarded Melissa curiously. “I get your reasoning for leaving, Mel, and I sympathize, but this isn’t you. You don’t let shit get on top of you. What happened to the girl who rallied her subscribers and got asylum for the Kahn family? Where’s the Melissa who helped prevent St Harriets closing in Thunder Bay? You did those things on your YouTube channel. You had no army, no resources, no help – other than me – and you still did it. That’s why people love your channel and that’s why people love you. This is what got you your TV deal, regardless of what Granger says.”

Melissa had a hard time looking Shania in the eye. “This is bigger than both of us, Shan. Let Tim do what he needs to do, we’ll let all this die down and then we’ll find a different way to fight that doesn’t involve breaking the law or kidnapping or thugs chasing us through the streets.”

Shania did not look convinced. "Fine, I’ll go get my case." She left the room, clearly dissatisfied with this turn of events.

“She’ll come around,” Melissa promised Tim. “I’m going to book our flights.”

“You’re doing the right thing, Melissa,” said Tim. He picked up his fork and went back to eating.

Was she? It felt like running away. Was she abandoning Tim and Wilson? Should she stay and help or was she really a hindrance? She hated to think she was in the way, but she,

Shania and Tim *had* succeeded in stealing Williams's emails. They made a pretty good team. Were they capable of bringing down Granger and his shadowy organization that may or may not be the infamous Illuminati? Probably not. What did they want to achieve? Justice for Howie, certainly, but Tim was hoping to secure that in return for his surrender. The rest of it wasn't her fight, not really. This wasn't her country after all.

Wilson checked his phone and stood up. "I'm gonna join my brothers and sisters on the front lines. Thanks for dinner and good to meet you, Senator Barns." He held out his hand, more out of politeness than any kind of warmth.

Tim stood also and shook Wilson's hand. "Likewise. Stay in touch, okay? I want to help Black Lives Matter any way I can."

"I appreciate that."

Melissa walked Wilson to the door. He called goodbye to Shania and she yelled in response.

"Tim's a good guy," Melissa said to Wilson when they were alone.

"Sure he is, I just don't trust politicians. And his encouraging you to leave, I don't like that. I need your help. Your voice carries weight. I know I'm being selfish but we need all the help we can get."

"I understand. I'm not sure I could do another protest right now even if I wanted to."

"I get it," Wilson said with genuine sympathy. "I'm really sorry about the other night going south. They gassed me and hauled me into the back of a van. I couldn't come looking for you. I know it must have been rough if you weren't expecting it."

Melissa shook her head. "It's okay. I figured you had your hands full. Tim pulled me out and helped me recover." The protest seemed like a lifetime ago. "I'm sorry you had to spend the night in jail."

"Yeah, not my first time."

"You've been locked up before?"

"Five years," Wilson replied.

Melissa was shocked. "What for?"

"I got in trouble at school, sprayed some graffiti, did some weed."

"That's it? Five years for that?"

"Well, more than that. The police at high school, they knew me because I was a bad kid and got into trouble. So when I left school I already had a record. I got stopped on the street with some more weed in my pocket and it's three strikes, bye bye baby."

"Five years for some pot?" Melissa couldn't believe it.

"Uh huh. That's the way it works here. They rack up the charges while you're at school, then once you're old enough they hit you with the final bust, any way they can. If they don't find nothing on you, they plant it. I've seen that happen. Got to the big house and it's like a big reunion. All my brothers from high school in there with me."

"That's awful. God, I'm so sorry."

"Don't be. Like I said, that's the way it works here."

Melissa shook her head. "Not where I come from. I mean, sure, black kids tend to get busted more often than anyone else, but nobody gets five years for a minor possession charge. That's insane."

"It is what it is," Wilson said. "Listen, I gotta go before the protest ends. I'll give your apologies, right?"

Melissa shifted uncomfortably. "Er, yeah. Thanks. Maybe in a week or two, when this blows over."

"It's okay, I get it. I'll come see you in the morning, maybe take you to the airport or whatever. Text me, okay?"

"I will. Listen, Tim's going down to Rocketts Landing Marina in the morning to hand over the zip drive. Can you come with us? Safety in numbers and all that."

"Sure, I'll be there."

"Thanks. I'll let you know what time."

They hugged briefly and Wilson left the house.

Tim had just finished eating as Melissa returned to the living room. As she sat down he thanked for the food. She told him it was nothing and then there was an awkward silence.

"I'm sorry," Melissa said eventually.

"What for?"

"For leaving."

"There's no need for you to be sorry," Tim assured her. "I'm the one who should be sorry. I encouraged you to break the law. It could have ruined your career, ruined your life. I should never have made you go through with it."

Melissa shook her head. "It was just as much my decision as yours. I could have said no. I could have said you were crazy."

"I think you did, at one point."

Melissa laughed. "I appreciate it though, everything you've done for me and Howie," she said, turning serious. "And I'm sorry Shan had a go at you."

"Oh that? Jeez that was nothing. I deal with far far worse in the senate. Honestly, I barely noticed."

Melissa tried to smile but something prevented her. She was crying again. Fuck! This was embarrassing. She was a fighter, like Shania said. She championed causes when she felt invested in them. She rallied people to help the downtrodden. Was she incapable of fighting for herself?

Tim noticed her sudden turn and came over to her. Melissa allowed him to put his arms around her. She felt secure and cared for in that moment, something she craved given the turbulence in her life these past few days. The hug went on for a while, and it reminded her of the way she used to hold on to Howie for as long as she could whenever they were alone. She had missed the warmth of Howie's body pressed against hers. She allowed herself to sink into his arms, to let him consume her world.

But this wasn't Howie. Suddenly the hug felt too much like something else.

The pair broke apart.

"Tim, I…" she faltered.

"I know," he replied, sensing her disquiet. "It's just a hug. I'm not expecting more, I promise. You looked like you needed one, that's all. I'm sorry if you…"

"No, I did need it. Thank you."

She really did mean that. A sympathetic hug with no expectation of more was exactly what she needed, in theory. In reality, it had felt good to be in the arms of a trustworthy man. Oh God, she was terrible. Her boyfriend wasn't even buried yet. What was she thinking? How could she even consider that anyone else could replace him, even for a few seconds.

The pair sat down and didn't say anything for a few moments. Then Shania returned. Melissa was glad she had missed the hug, which she might have misconstrued.

"I had my tantrum, now I'm back. What did I miss?"

Melissa and Tim shared a look and a small smile.

"Oh hell, did I miss something important? Dammit!"

chapter sixteen

THEY: WANT YOU DEAD

Melissa awoke feeling bleary-eyed and unrested. She hadn't slept well last night, reliving Howie's murder, the gassing at the hands of the police, and Bruce chasing her up and down the streets of Richmond. She wasn't used to having such literal dreams: usually they were abstract and weird, if she remembered any details at all. Last night had been draining though, with multiple interruptions to her sleep cycle as her brain tugged her awake, convinced another adrenalin-fueled emergency was happening.

When she went downstairs she was extremely grateful that Tim had coffee ready. She sat on a kitchen stool and drank slowly, blowing on her drink at times to help cool it.

"How does it feel to be going home at last?" Tim asked as he cracked eggs into a frying pan.

"It's a relief, but I feel guilty."

"I get that." The eggs sizzled. Tim added diced ham and cheese, followed by green peppers and mushrooms. "But you shouldn't feel that way." He smiled at his choice of words. "Sorry, I shouldn't be telling you how to feel. But none of this is your fault and you've been through more in a few days than most people experience in a lifetime. There's no shame in going back to your own country to take time to mourn, to be with the people who love you. To be with your mom when she needs you. Live to fight another day."

"I guess." Melissa didn't feel convinced.

Shania joined them then.

"What time are we off to the docks?" she asked.

"I'm meeting Granger at 10am," said Tim, loading a plate with a steaming omelet. "It's out in the open so there should be lots of witnesses. There's really no need for you guys to come." He handed the plate and a fork to Melissa and then started on the next batch.

"Screw that!" Shania said. "We're coming."

Tim shook his head. "Nope, you're not." He put down the egg he was about to crack into the pan. He reached into his pocket and pulled out a USB drive, which he handed to Shania. "I need you to take this to the airport and wait for Melissa there."

"Um," said Shania. "What's this?"

He picked up the egg again and this time opened it into the pan. "A copy of what we took from Williams. I want you to take it to Canada. Keep it there until I tell you. No safer place than out of the country."

Melissa stood up in alarm. "He said he'd know if you took a copy," she warned.

"How could he know? I didn't upload it anywhere. I just copied it on my laptop."

"You're playing with fire, Tim," Shania said. "He might have spyware on your machine."

"Whatever, it'll be fine. Wilson will be here soon. He's going to take you both to the airport and I'll be in touch once you're safely home."

The plan made Melissa feel very uncomfortable. She didn't argue though. She already knew what she was going to do. She finished her omelet and then told Tim she was going to pack. Shania stayed to eat her breakfast and after she was done, followed Melissa upstairs.

"So what's the real plan?" her friend asked as she entered the spare room where Melissa had been sleeping.

"You take an Uber to the airport with the copy. I've asked Wilson to bring his bike. We're going down to the docks to make sure Tim's okay. Once we know he's safe, Wilson will bring me to the airport too. We should still have plenty of time to catch our flight this afternoon."

"Tim's not going to like you guys being there."

"Nope, but he doesn't get a choice. I'm not going to abandon him to Granger. If he gets kidnapped, someone should be looking out for him."

"Fair enough. Just be careful, okay? Stay at a safe distance and watch out for his goons."

Melissa laughed. "Did you just use the word, 'goons'?"

Shania mock slapped her arm. "Shut up! I'm serious. I don't want you ending up in someone else's basement who isn't as nice as Tim."

"So you like him too?"

Shania looked affronted. "Fuck off!" she said, but then she smiled. "He's nice for an older guy. For a white guy. For a politician! Hey, what do you mean, 'too'?" Shania's eyes widened.

Mercifully, Melissa's phone buzzed. It was a text from Wilson.

I'm down the street.

"Okay," she said. "Time to go."

The two women descended the stairs with their luggage.

"Wilson's waiting. Good luck!" Melissa gave Tim a hug. "Thanks for everything."

"Least I could do." Tim hugged Shania too. "Stay in touch, please!"

"You ain't getting rid of us!" Shania said.

Tim glanced through the window at the street outside.

"Where's Wilson?"

"Oh he's waiting around the corner. He thought there might be press."

"Thankfully they've lost interest in me for now. Still it's smart. Granger's people might be watching the house."

They said their final goodbyes, and then Melissa and Shania left Tim's house. It was a short walk down the street to where Wilson was waiting. He brought his bike as requested. A driver waited nearby, ready to take Shania to the airport with Melissa's luggage.

The two women embraced.

"Be careful, okay?" Shania said.

"Always," Melissa replied. Then she climbed on the back of Wilson's bike, put on the spare helmet he handed her, and they tore off down the street, away from Tim's house.

Melissa tried to control her nerves. She wasn't going to get involved, she was just there to observe. Why then was the omelet she'd eaten threatening to make a return appearance?

Tim passed through the police roadblock with a rising sense of trepidation. The police had closed Old Main Street at the entrance to the marina, and the officer he asked the reason for the roadblock didn't answer, he simply waved Tim through. Was this for him?

Tim drove the short distance past the Boathouse restaurant with its distinctive brick chimney. To his right, the James River curved around westwards towards downtown Richmond. There were no cars parked along the street, but when he got to the turn onto Orleans Street, he realized that there was another roadblock up at the top of that street too. He stopped the car on the corner, between two restaurants, both deserted at this time of the morning. Was that normal? He wasn't sure. There was a featureless impressionist sculpture of a squat man standing in the middle of a grass area. Tim got out of the car and walked towards it. He couldn't hear anyone, just the distant roar of traffic and the lapping of the river against its banks.

Here in between the two buildings, he couldn't be seen from the hotel or apartment building to the south. Across the road was a warehouse with no windows, and on the other side of the river he could see only trees and shrubs. Nobody could see him from this angle.

Granger and his men emerged from the restaurant. They were laughing and joking with one another. Tim noted there were a few women with them too, dressed in suits just like the men. At least Granger was an equal opportunities despot.

"Do you have it?" Granger asked?

A seagull passed by, squawking at them with indignation.

Tim reached into his pocket. Every one of Granger's people reached for weapons as he moved. He froze, one hand inside his jacket pocket. The other he raised in the air. With finger and thumb, he pulled out the flash drive, and then held it above his head for them to see.

Granger's people relaxed.

"Did you make a copy?" Granger asked.

"Yeah, I'm an idiot," Tim replied, laying the sarcasm on thick to prevent misunderstandings. It occurred to him that now wasn't the time to be snarky, but he couldn't help himself. "Honestly this is a lot of fuss for nothing. We found plenty to incriminate Williams but nothing that linked him back to you."

"Well that's good to hear," said Granger. He nodded to one of his men. Tim recognized him as one of the guys who had come after him at the internet café – the one who had run after Melissa and Shania. What did they say his name was? Bruce? It hardly mattered. Tim flashed him a genial smile as he reached up and grabbed the drive from his upraised hand. As Bruce stalked back to his master, Tim dropped his arms to his sides. He wasn't going to be intimidated by this man and his paid army. It bothered Tim more that Richmond PD cops were in Granger's pocket too, manning the roadblocks that kept this area free of unwanted traffic.

Bruce handed the drive to a woman carrying a laptop. She sat down on one of the benches by the sculpture, opened the laptop and plugged in the drive.

"This is it," she said after a moment. "It's all here."

Granger turned to Tim with a smile. "Excellent. Thank you so much. I'm sorry for all the firepower and the John le Carré bullshit. Can't be too careful can we?"

"No, no I totally understand," Tim replied. And he did. This wasn't about ensuring Granger's safety. This was about intimidation. The whole display of police obedience, and hired guns, was to demonstrate to Tim in no uncertain terms that Granger owned this town, and he didn't appreciate Tim running around trying to spoil it for him. "Know this though. All this won't last. Eventually of these people here today will retire or go work for someone else. One day you'll be a has-been, a nothing. Your influence will be gone and your reputation will be in tatters. Nobody will listen to you any more, and you won't have any money to pay them to listen to you. Your time is ending, just like all those like you. Your hold on this town will be dead one day soon, that is if you don't keel over and die first."

Granger cocked his head at Tim. "Are you threatening me? Are you still thinking that you can possibly bring me down? Did you learn nothing here today?"

"Oh no, not me. At least, not just me. This whole city will turn against you eventually, and then you'll have nowhere to run."

"That is fascinating," Granger said, walking much closer

to Tim. His hired guns looked wary, reaching for their weapons again. “Can you see the future then, Tim? Did you read your tealeaves this morning?”

“I don’t need ESP to see where you’re headed. Corruption will out eventually.”

Granger gave a short, bark-like laugh. “You think I’m corrupt? Seriously? You really haven’t understood me at all, Tim! I’m not corrupt. I belong to an ancient organization that stands for enlightenment and reason. We are the force holding this country and this planet together. Without us, *everything* would be corrupt.” Granger was just two feet away from Tim now, their faces close enough that Tim could see every line, every deep crease in Granger’s craggy face. “Now I’m going to ask you one more time, and this time I want you to tell me the truth. Did you make a copy of the contents of this drive?”

Wilson and Melissa sped under the Williamsburg Avenue Bridge over Orleans Street and screeched to a halt on the motorbike. Wilson flipped up his visor. Melissa got off the back of the bike, taking the opportunity to stretch her legs. She took off her helmet.

The police roadblock stretched across the road just beyond the intersection with VA-5. Its mere presence made Melissa nervous. It might be a coincidence, or it might have been set up for a very specific reason. Either way, she and Wilson had to get past it. Wilson indicated she should get back on the bike, and once she was on they turned left and headed along the Old Osborne Turnpike, turning right at the old Cedar Works, into the village of Rocketts Landing, according to the sign on the iron bridge they passed under. To their left, Melissa saw a water tower high above them. They turned right at a roundabout and the sign said they were on Old

Main Street. The end of the road, where it met Orleans Street, was also blocked by a single police car. Wilson took the bike up to a parking space next to an apartment building and the two of them got off and removed their helmets.

"This way," said Wilson. He led her along a path beside the apartment building. Ahead of them was the river, and to their right stood two buildings, both restaurants according to Wilson. The one furthest north sported a tall brick chimney on the far side. Wilson led Melissa past the restaurant to a slope leading down to a wharf where a number of pleasure boats were moored. Instead of continuing to the river, he led her over a fence onto a patio running the entire length of the glass-walled restaurant in parallel with the river. Melissa thought it would have been a lovely place to sit and have lunch or a drink and watch the boats go by, but right now she had other concerns.

They heard voices ahead and crouched down between chairs and tables. They were nearing the north side of the restaurant now, and could see a patch of grass in between this building and the restaurant with the brick chimney. In the center was a weird statue of a squat figure and a couple of benches, and then next to these was a steep slope down to the river wharf. Wilson motioned to Melissa and they stopped moving closer, now as near as they dared to the people talking. If she raised her head slightly over the table, Melissa could see. There was Tim, surrounded by people, talking with an older man who must be the infamous Lionel Granger. Beside him stood Bruce. From here, Melissa could not make out what Granger and Tim were saying. She took out her phone and launched the broadcast app, but then noticed she didn't have any signal. That was odd. Nowhere else in Richmond had she experienced this problem. In fact, signal loss in the States was no problem for her at all. After all, she was signed up with a Canadian provider, which meant in the US she was roaming. That meant she could make use of multiple carriers depending on who had the best signal strength in her current location. She couldn't remember ever being without a signal while in this country, regardless of where Howie had taken her.

For now then, she had to settle for recording video of what was going on.

A woman on a bench closed her laptop and stood up. She handed something that could only be the flash drive over to Granger, who slipped it into his pocket. As far as Melissa could tell, Tim seemed relaxed and confident. She didn't share his blasé attitude. She knew if Granger's men discovered her and Wilson, Tim would be in huge trouble. She couldn't have let him go through with this alone though. Granger had proven himself capable of kidnap and worse, and Melissa would never forgive herself if Tim disappeared and nobody knew he'd gone.

"I didn't copy it." Tim was shouting now so every word carried to Melissa's position. He was starting to look agitated. "You have the drive, now let me go."

"You know what," said Granger, loud enough for Melissa to hear. "I don't care."

Granger pulled a gun, took aim at Tim's head and fired.

chapter seventeen

THEY WANT YOU DEAD

Tim died instantly, his forehead exploding, his body crumpling to the ground before tumbling down the slope towards the river.

Melissa stood. "No!" she cried, hands flying to her mouth, unable to process what she'd just seen.

Wilson launched himself at her, knocking her to the ground as the first bullets ricocheted from table legs and chairs around them. One of the large restaurant windows exploded, showering them in what was thankfully safety glass. Melissa was aware of Wilson grabbing hold of the neck of her jacket and yanking her away.

"Move!" he yelled.

Melissa came to her senses and ducked down beside him, still weaving in and out of the patio furniture as quickly as they could. Another window exploded causing Melissa to let out a shriek, but as far as she knew the shower of glass again caused no harm to them.

Glancing back, Melissa saw Bruce and a couple of other men clambering over the fence between the grassy area and the restaurant patio. More gunfire rattled after them, impossibly loud, the shots reverberating over the river and echoing back to them. They reached the south end of the restaurant and both Wilson and Melissa threw themselves over the fence. Bullets punched small holes in the wood as they struggled to get to their feet and keep moving. Wilson led the way, heading back to the parking lot on the east side of the restaurant, intending to go back along the side of the apartment building to the south and return to his bike.

They reached the south-east corner of the restaurant but Wilson put up a hand. He stuck out his head and immediately pulled it back as a burst of gunfire came in response. Behind them, Melissa saw Bruce clamber over the fence. They were about to be pinned down.

Melissa grabbed Wilson's arm and together they ran directly away from the restaurant, towards the apartment block. It meant taking a slightly longer route than cutting diagonally across the parking lot, but it meant that the building shielded them from Granger's men coming around the front of the restaurant. It did nothing to block Bruce's line of fire, but to her surprise he motioned to his two fellow thugs to stop firing. They still ran in pursuit, but at least the bullets had stopped firing. Melissa guessed Bruce was either under orders to bring her to Granger unharmed, or else he had taken the executive decision himself. Either way, she was grateful for the respite.

Melissa and Wilson reached the apartment building and, keeping as low as possible, ran along the path beside the building. For now, Granger's thugs were not shooting at them, but they were still exposed here. Only a couple of men were chasing them. The others, including Bruce, had doubled back, presumably to fetch their vehicles.

She could hear the pounding footfalls of their pursuers. They were so close to Wilson's bike now. Melissa could see flashing lights moving along the road to the east. The police roadblock was on the move, heading this way.

Finally they reached the bike just as their pursuers caught

up with them. One of them grabbed Melissa's shoulder. Wilson leapt onto the bike and handed her the spare helmet. Without pausing to think, she twisted round and slammed the helmet into side of her assailant's head. He let go and dropped to the ground like someone had chain-sawed his legs from under him.

The other guy was trying to pull Wilson off the bike. Wilson slammed his helmet into the man's face causing him to spin around. He stared at Melissa, dazed. She brought her helmet up hard under the guy's chin, causing his head to snap backwards. He too went down.

Wilson gunned the engine as Melissa jumped on behind him. She was still putting on her helmet as the bike roared into motion, tires screeching on the asphalt. Melissa could hear the dirge of multiple sirens drawing closer, but now they were moving the noise of the bike and the muffling effect of her helmet reduced the intensity of the police's cacophony.

The bike tore along East Main Street, Wilson not daring to look back. The water tower and the roundabout were ahead, but Melissa saw police cars streaming towards them from the left. In the middle of the roundabout was a kind of black obelisk. Wilson was heading straight for it, but at the last moment as the bike drove across the center mini-island, he swerved around the tall object and they were off, continuing south parallel to the river. They turned left at the end of the street, the bike leaning precariously as Wilson took the corner at speed. As they cornered, Melissa looked to her right and saw another of the slender, towering, red-brick chimneys. She didn't have time to muse on what this area might once have been. They were now bombing eastwards, away from the river before meeting a major road, where Wilson turned right without slowing.

Now they were hurtling along a street Melissa didn't know the name of, and they were racing a freight train on their left.

Daring to glance behind her, she saw a phalanx of police cars with their lights blaring, struggling to keep up. Wilson terrified Melissa by taking the bike off the road, closer to the tracks where the train was still thundering past. There was a rough track here, running between the main road and the rails, and Wilson used it to double back the way they had come. Trees sprang up to shield them from the road as they passed the police cars, and the noise of the train masked – or hopefully masked – the roar of the bike's engine. Melissa realized that Wilson might just be a genius.

They were running out of track as it narrowed, coming closer to the rail tracks. Wilson turned sharply and they bumped over grass and down an embankment, skidding back onto the road again. Now they were heading back towards Richmond. They had entirely evaded the police.

Unfortunately, Granger's people hadn't been in such a hurry to follow them. Bruce and the other thugs in Granger's employ had presumably waited on the corner in case she and Wilson had doubled back. Wilson didn't slow down, instead he swerved around the makeshift roadblock before any of them could react. Melissa's scream would likely have deafened Wilson if he'd not been wearing his helmet. Melissa forced herself to be quiet but in truth she was barely hanging on. Tim's death had not registered yet, and she found herself questioning the finality of what she'd witnessed.

The road curved back towards the river and they passed the other end of the street with the restaurant and its brick chimney. The remains of a police roadblock were still here, and the remaining pair of officers jumped into their cars when they saw Wilson's bike zip by. They had to wait before they could pull out because three cars and one motorbike came zooming past in pursuit, blocking the officers' exit.

Melissa risked a glance back as they sped along beside the river. There were trees and buildings in between at intervals, but most of the time she could still keep the river in view. The bike's acceleration and ability to take the corners without slowing left the cars pursuing them way behind. The guy on the bike, however, was keeping pace, matching them and even gaining a little.

Wilson was weaving in and out of traffic, which wasn't too heavy as it was late morning and rush was well over. Melissa tapped him on the shoulder, hoping not to distract him and cause them to crash. Wilson looked back and saw the bike pursuing them. Its rider was dressed in black leathers with a neon green helmet. Not exactly inconspicuous. He was drawing closer. He was close enough that Melissa could see a gun strapped to his belt. She had to do something. She had no weapons, no way of throwing the rider off or getting him to stop. She had literally nothing.

She glanced at his bright green helmet again and an idea occurred to her. With one hand still holding Wilson around the waist, she used the other to take her own helmet from her head. The wind whipped at her hair and made her eyes water, but she held on tight and twisted round to see where the other rider was. Trying to time it exactly right, she tossed the helmet at him.

The rider braked and swerved as Melissa's helmet bounced off the roadway and came hurtling towards him. In a moment he was back on track. He'd lost a little ground but kept on coming.

Melissa cursed loudly. Wilson had seen what she'd done and took off his own helmet. He handed it to her quickly then put his hand back on the handlebars just before having to move out around a slower car in his lane.

Their pursuer was gaining on them again, and this time he was riding with one hand. The other was reaching for his gun. It was now or never. He was so close now. Melissa waited for the last possible second, as the rider drew his gun and aimed it at them, he was just meters away.

She let go of the helmet.

The heavy object didn't have time to bounce off the road, and the rider didn't have even a second to react. The helmet slammed into his shoulder, twisting his body with the impact. The bike tipped beyond the point at which he could rescue it. Melissa watched in horror as rider and bike went sideways, skidding across the roadway in a shower of sparks and the sound of tortured metal.

Melissa turned away, burying her face into Wilson's back, trying not to throw up. She didn't look back to see if the other rider had survived. She heard the screech of brakes coming from other vehicles as they swerved to avoid colliding with the fallen rider. Then came the sound of impact as they no doubt collided with each other or with the man they were trying to avoid. Melissa couldn't look. As the sound of chaos died away beneath the rush of the wind in her ears and the roar of Wilson's bike, she told herself she had done only what she must do. Those bastards had killed Tim. She had not asked to be a part of this. He had reached for a gun, clearly trying to kill or maim her and Wilson.

It didn't matter how she tried to justify it: she had probably just killed someone.

Sirens.

Wilson shouted something she couldn't hear over the deafening noise of their flight.

But she could hear the sirens.

All other sounds drifted away. The sirens sounded and Howie stopped the car. She saw Officer Hagley telling Howie to get out of the car, but couldn't hear the words he spoke over the deafening noise of the police sirens. She saw Howie with his hands on the car, saw the papers drop to the ground and Howie instinctively reaching out to grab them.

The shot. That first shot, then more. Howie slipping out

of sight.

Another shot, Tim pitching to the ground, blood erupting from his forehead.

The crash and scrape of the rider's bike skidding across the asphalt.

Bruce tying her up in Tim's basement. Chasing her down the high street.

Arriving home from school at the age of seven and her father telling her that her older sister, Sabrina, was dead.

Standing in her beautiful dress at prom watching her handsome date kissing the most popular girl in their year.

Holding her dog, Chaser, at the vets as they put him to sleep.

Posting the wrong selfie to her Instagram and deactivating her account for a week after the disgusting and dehumanizing avalanche of hate-filled comments.

Finding out about her mom's cancer.

Her mom. She had to see her mom again.

Melissa opened her eyes. She gasped for breath, realizing she'd been holding it for some time. She felt dizzy, and clutched tighter to Wilson's back to prevent herself falling off. She felt exposed without her helmet, but at least the wind in her hair helped to revive her. Wilson was pulling into a side street now and slowing the bike as they passed a row of parked cars.

A few moments later, he stopped, turned off the engine and disengaged the key.

"Off, quick!" he said.

Melissa dismounted, still in a daze but fighting to hold it together. Wilson pushed out the kickstand and got off the bike. He pulled another key from his pocket and pressed a button on the fob. The gleaming new BMW to Melissa's right bleeped and she heard the doors unlock.

"This is yours?"

"A gift from Howie," Wilson said.

"Isn't the bike faster?"

"Yeah but two black people without helmets riding a motorbike through downtown Richmond are a bit conspicuous. Get in."

He had a point. She got into the passenger seat and felt dazzled by the array of tech on display. She felt like she'd just gotten into the car from that TV show her dad used to watch when he was young. What was it called? *Knight Rider*, was that it? Anyway, this was like that. The memory of her dad showing her clips of a cheesy talking car and David Hasselhoff's hair made her feel better. She was back in the present again and ready to keep fighting.

Wilson started the engine and carefully edged the car out of its parking spot.

"We need to go to the airport," Melissa said.

"You crazy? That's the last place we should be!" Wilson protested. "Nah I'm not going there."

"Please, Wilson, we have to. Shania is there. She's waiting for me. She probably has no idea what happened to Tim and to us. They might try to take her."

"Fuck!" Wilson slammed a hand on the steering wheel in frustration. "We need to lie low, not go strutting around a heavily guarded, very public place with 24-hour video surveillance!"

"I know. But I can't leave her."

For a moment, Melissa believed that Wilson might tell her to get out and leave her to make her own way to the airport. Instead he cursed again and pulled away.

It was getting close to the lunch hour and traffic had built up significantly. Melissa wished they were still on the bike as they'd have made much faster progress. However, when a cop car drove slowly past in a line of traffic, the officers didn't even glance in their direction. They had traded speed for anonymity, at least for the time being. If and when the police found the bike, they would surely be able to find out what car Wilson had switched to driving instead.

It seemed to take an age to get to the onramp of the Highway 95, but once they did the going became much faster. A police car waited at the side of the ramp, checking for speeders. Wilson cruised past him at the speed limit. No siren or flashing lights indicated they'd been rumbled. If they had stayed on the bike they'd have half the Richmond P.D. on their tail by now.

"Did you message her?" Wilson asked.

"My phone has no reception."

"Shit. Take mine." Wilson reached awkwardly into his pocket with one hand while keeping the other on the wheel. Eventually he managed to extract his phone and he handed it to her.

"Yours has no reception either."

"What? That's not true."

"It's true. No signal."

"My phone ain't never out of coverage, least not in Richmond. What the fuck?"

"Do you think there's an outage?"

"Dunno."

Melissa suspected that this was no city-wide issue. Wilson was locked into one provider but she was not. The fact that neither of them had coverage proved it wasn't a problem with her phone. The fact that she couldn't roam onto any network, either suggested that all providers in the city had gone down, or else she and Wilson were being targeted. She suspected she knew which of those was the right reason.

"Granger," she said.

"What? No. That's not possible."

"Is it so far-fetched?" Melissa handed Wilson back his phone. "Granger has a high up friend in the phone company.

They owe him a favor so they put a block on our phones. I bet Shania's phone is blocked too."

"Do you think they're trying to stop you sharing the emails you took?"

"Williams' emails? Yeah maybe."

"Well that sucks. Richmond airport is fucking huge. How are we going to find Shania?"

Melissa smiled. "She's probably at the bar getting hammered."

Wilson steered the car onto an exit ramp to join another highway, 64.

"We check there first then."

chapter eighteen

THEY: WANT YOU DEAD

Wilson drove the car into the short stay parking lot, dutifully taking a ticket and parking as close to the terminal as he could. It wasn't exactly the best place to keep the car for a fast getaway, but they couldn't risk parking at the terminal and having the car towed. Melissa wasn't worried about their location. There were two ways this would end. One involved walking out with Shania and driving away as if nothing had happened. The other involved police, handcuffs and more flashing lights.

Wilson looked more nervous than she was, and she was crapping herself. Armed police were everywhere. But, she realized, they weren't Richmond P.D. They were Federal officers. Melissa knew that Tim had encountered a pair of FBI agents who were in league with Granger, but that couldn't be true of the majority of Federal officers, could it? Granger had warned her she wouldn't be allowed to leave the country, and it was likely she was on a watch list. Still, if she didn't actually head through security, would they be looking for her? Was Shania already in custody somewhere in the terminal?

Again, it didn't matter what happened to Melissa. She needed to know Shania was safe and there was only one way to do that.

Once inside the doors they headed to the second level for departures. Melissa hoped Shania hadn't passed through security yet. Wilson tapped her on her arm and waved his phone at her. At first she didn't realize what he meant, but then she glanced at her own phone to see a welcome screen and an acceptance of terms and conditions button.

"Wi-Fi!" she said.

Wilson put his finger to his lips and the two of them sat down on a bench opposite the ticket counters.

Melissa's phone came to life as soon as she pressed the accept button. She couldn't send or receive texts or make calls, but she could get email and her IM was buzzing with notifications. She scrolled through the messages from Jasmine, from her dad, from random men sending her pictures of their junk. There was Shania. An hour ago she had sent a simple message.

Where are you?

She messaged back.

We're at the airport. Where are you?

She waited for the response, tapping her finger against the side of her phone. Wilson was scrolling through his own phone, clearly with a lot to catch up on also.

Finally the little bouncy symbol appeared to show that Shania was typing.

At the bar. Where have you been?

Melissa tapped Wilson on the shoulder and they stood up. She followed the signs that showed an image of a knife and fork, past the ticket counters and through a wide corridor leading to the security checkpoints and terminals. The deeper they moved into the terminal, the more apprehension she felt. She was sweating slightly despite the reasonable temperature in the building. Her eyes darted this way and that, searching out cops as she tried to assess their likelihood of advancing on her and Wilson. Her stomach was churning and she realized she was in urgent need of the washroom.

What could be more normal and nonchalant than using the washroom?

She steered Wilson towards the ladies.

"Washroom," she said.

"Washroom? What the hell's a washroom? Oh, the restroom. Really?"

"Yes, really. Don't worry, it adds to our cover."

"Sure."

Wilson didn't look happy to wait outside for her, but as she entered the *restroom* she noticed with amusement that he was heading into the men's. It had been a long time since they left Tim's house.

Tim.

She made it into a stall before the tears started falling. She sat down to pee, but she was now sobbing so hard she couldn't go. She didn't care who could hear her. She cried for Howie. She cried for Tim. She cried at the injustice of her and Wilson and Shania being the hunted ones while the real criminal was a free man. Untouchable. She cried for the anonymous bike rider she was convinced she'd killed.

Her phone bleeped.

Where are you now?

Shania.

Melissa relieved herself while she dried her eyes. When she left the cubicle she got a few odd looks from other women but she ignored them. She glanced in the mirror. She was quite a sight. She forced herself to slow down, take a deep breath and clean herself up a bit. She would draw attention if she went out there with streaky makeup and puffy red eyes.

When she finally emerged from the washroom, Wilson looked stressed.

"Shit, I thought you'd gotten arrested or something. I was seconds away from coming in!"

"I just needed a minute or two to process."

"Is it the bike rider? You did the right thing. It was a good idea."

Melissa didn't answer. She smiled her thanks for his support, but she couldn't take a lot of comfort from his words.

"Come on, let's get Shania and get out of here."

Melissa knew she wouldn't be leaving for Canada today. She might have to take Wilson up on his offer to drive her over the border on his bike. She'd have to buy him new helmets first.

As they entered the dining and shopping area, Melissa checked her phone.

"Shit. The Wi-Fi ran out."

Wilson confirmed on his own device. "There's a time limit?"

"I guess so."

"Now what? Did she say what bar she's in?"

"No."

"Shh, police."

Two armed officers were heading their way. There were so many people walking by it was impossible to tell if they were coming for Melissa and Wilson. For a moment, Melissa considered grabbing Wilson's jacket and pulling him in for a kiss. The prospect wasn't an unpleasant one, but she was relieved from the embarrassment when one of the cops got a call on his radio. They stopped while he listened, acknowledged and then led his partner in a different direction.

Melissa let go of the breath she'd been holding.

"Shall we split up?" Wilson asked.

"God no. I'll lose you too. She must be here somewhere.

How many bars can there be?"

It turned out there were quite a few. Shania of course, was in the last one they checked.

She leapt from her bar stool and hugged Melissa tightly.

"Oh shit, bitch, I thought you'd been arrested."

"Nearly was," Melissa replied.

Shania hugged Wilson and then started talking.

"I couldn't check your luggage because some of its yours and I'd be over my allowance so I put all the luggage in a locker so we should go and get it quick because our flight leaves in less than an hour and we still have to get through security and why are you looking at me like that?"

Melissa realized she was grimacing.

"I'm afraid we're not going home, Shania. Not yet."

"Oh God, why? I want to go home."

"I know. I'm sorry. Listen, I have to tell you something but you've got to promise not to yell or make a scene, okay?"

"Okay."

"Tim's dead."

To Shania's credit, her face did all the talking and she managed to keep silent.

Melissa continued, "Granger shot him in the head. We only just got away. They blocked our phones so we had to come here to find you. Now we have to leave before Granger has the airport police looking for us."

"He doesn't know you're here, right?"

"It won't take him long to work it out. Does your phone have reception?"

"Only Wi-Fi. I paid a fee with my credit card to get longer than half an hour. No idea why roaming's not working."

Melissa gave a knowing glance to Wilson.

"Shan, they're blocking our phones. I have video of Tim's shooting which I'm only now realizing I should have uploaded to the net while I had Wi-Fi."

"Pay for it, that's what I did. It's five bucks for two hours."

Melissa looked around. Had those cops just outside the bar been there for long? Were they checking on the patrons?

"I don't think we have time," she said. "We have to go."

Wilson had reached the same conclusion.

Shania dropped a ten dollar bill onto the bar and they headed for the exit. Unfortunately the only way out was directly past the two officers. The three friends kept their heads turned away as they left the bar.

"Excuse me!"

Melissa froze. Her companions did likewise. With mounting terror, fighting every instinct to run, Melissa turned around.

One of the officers was holding out a couple of pieces of paper to Shania.

"I think you dropped your tickets."

"Oh. Oh God." Shania didn't seem able to function.

Melissa smiled and took the tickets and smiled.

"Thanks so much, officer. That's very kind of you."

"No problem, ma'am. Is your friend okay?"

Shania still didn't seem able to speak.

"She's fine," Melissa said. "We were just arguing over which of the two of you is the hottest. She's crap around nice looking boys."

The cop flushed and stammered. Wilson rolled his eyes. Shania gave a weak smile.

"Well please tell your friend," the cop said, his eyes on Shania, "that she too is very, um, hot."

"I will. Thanks again, officer."

"No problem, you have a good day now."

Melissa steered Shania away while Wilson chuckled to himself.

"That was quick thinking," he said.

"I do live comments on my channel sometimes. I have to

be quick."

Shania still hadn't said anything, but Melissa didn't need her to speak. She needed her friend to move. Glancing back, Melissa saw the cop she had spoken to was talking into his radio. Convinced this was it and the game was up, she quickened her pace and dragged Shania along with her. A wall mounted television displaying local news showed Tim's face on the main part of the screen, with a ticker at the bottom and weather on the right. Shania paused to look but Melissa pushed her forwards. There would be time for watching the news later.

They moved as quickly as they dared without drawing attention to themselves. They saw plenty of people running in the opposite direction, towards the terminals, but nobody was running away from them. An emergency exit to their left looked inviting, but Melissa steered them away from it. If they went through it would trigger an alarm.

They were back at the check in desks now. Police seemed to be moving with purpose in all directions. She was painfully aware that cameras were everywhere, so if the cops were looking for her and Wilson, it wouldn't take them long.

They hovered around a long line up of people at one of the check in desks, looking for an opportunity to leave. The exit to the parking garage wasn't far away, but officers were gathering around in that area.

"We're not going to get out of here," said Wilson unhelpfully.

"Come on," said Melissa. She grabbed Shania's arm and led her and Wilson past the check in desks, in between the coiled line up of waiting passengers and the folks checking their luggage in. Several passengers flashed them dirty looks, believing they were trying to skip the line. Melissa ignored them. With so many people waiting, and the mass of people crowded in front of the desks with kids and strollers and luggage, the police patrols could not see them.

They reached the end of the row of desks and had to open a temporary barrier. Melissa was careful not to let go of the stretchy band until they were all through, and then she slotted the end back into the post. The escalators down to the arrivals area were located here. Melissa took them, making sure the other two were following. They walked down the moving stairs, squeezing around groups of people who weren't keeping entirely to one side.

On the lower concourse the trio headed straight for the exits, but once again they found police everywhere. Convinced they were about to be spotted, Melissa hurried over to the nearest carousel and stood as if waiting for her luggage. The others joined her.

"The longer we stay here, the harder it's going to be to get away," Wilson said.

Melissa pointed to a rack of carts standing to one side of the carousel. "Get me two of those," she said. Wilson and Shania dutifully complied, returning moments later with two carts. Melissa started grabbing bags from the carousel at random, waiting for a moment or two between bags to avoid looking like she was stealing. Wilson followed her lead, loading his own cart.

Melissa prayed the real owners of these bags weren't nearby, or this was going to get ugly. She now had a stack of bags high enough that if she crouched down a bit to push them, her face wasn't visible. Wilson did the same. Shania, who the police were least likely to be looking for, led the way, helping to guide them towards the exit to the parking garage. They rolled straight past a couple of police officers who didn't even glance in their direction. Just moments later, they were out of the terminal and on the ramp to the garage.

Wilson was ready to abandon his cart but Melissa told him no.

"Let's keep them until we pay the ticket."

In front of the elevators were a line of automated payment machines. One was free so Melissa took Wilson's ticket and fed it into a machine, using cash to pay. Long, agonizing seconds later, the machine spat out an exit ticket.

"Let's go," Melissa said. She continued to push the carts to the elevator, placing hers off to one side of the doors. Other people were waiting here but they weren't looking at the trio. Wilson pushed his cart to stand beside Melissa's. When the elevator doors opened and they followed the group of people inside, they quietly left the carts outside. Since they weren't visible from inside the elevator, nobody paid it any mind.

Going up one floor, they exited the elevator and Wilson led the way to their car. There were no police patrolling the garage, which was a relief, but they weren't in the clear yet. They reached and entered the car, and Wilson drove them to the exit. They joined the lineup of cars waiting to get out of the garage through the automatic barriers.

Melissa's nerves were at breaking point. When she saw a cop car pass by on the road beyond the exit ramp, she had to grip her seatbelt to avoid throwing open the car door and making a run for it.

The cop passed by without stopping, and a long, agonizing couple of minutes later, Wilson wound down his window, inserted his ticket and drove through when the barrier lifted. A minute after that and they were on the ramp leading away from the airport towards the highway.

"Are we clear?" Shania asked after they'd been on the highway for a few minutes.

"I think so," Melissa replied. "We were lucky as hell. If they'd gone for us at the airport, they could have locked the whole place down and there'd be no way of getting out."

"We need to lie low for a bit," Wilson said. "Unless you have any other friends wandering around very public spaces, like the train station?"

"Ha ha," Melissa said without humor. She was too distracted watching for anyone following them to find Wilson's comment funny.

"So where are we going?" Shania asked from the back seat. "I'm guessing we can't go to Tim's house."

"Cops will be all over it," Wilson said. "I know a place though. We can stay there a little while until I find somewhere better."

"So what the fuck happened to Tim?" Shania asked.

Melissa fought back tears as she explained what had happened. "He met with Granger to give him the flash drive. There were a bunch of Granger's people there, all armed, but Granger didn't believe Tim hadn't taken a copy of the emails, so he shot him."

"Just like that?"

"Yeah, just like that. Straight in the head. So fucking cold. I still can't believe he's gone."

"You didn't see him die though?"

Wilson scoffed. "Ain't no way anyone can survive a bullet to the head fired at point-blank range. No way. He's dead, Shania, sorry to say it out loud."

All three of them were quiet for a time after that. Melissa leaned her head against the window and thought about the kind, handsome senator who had rescued her from his basement, from the protest and from losing her sanity. She owed him so much yet when he'd needed her most, she could do nothing. A single tear rolled down one cheek, the one facing away from Wilson so he didn't see it. There was no justice here. Howie and Tim were good men and she couldn't stand to lose them both. What if Shania was next? Or Wilson. What if Granger decided to shoot Melissa for what she did to his rider?

Images of Wilson's helmet striking the rider and knocking

him from his bike flashed in her mind. She knew it was a memory that would haunt her for a very long time. Tim's death, the moment his head had exploded from the impact of the bullet, was indelibly marked on her mind's eye also. The cop firing on Howie too. So many horrible images she knew she'd see every night when she closed her eyes. Perhaps a bullet with her name on it, delivered by Granger's gun, would be something of a mercy.

Not for the first time she wished she had stayed in Canada. The temptation of the TV deal, the chance to spend time with Howie and the lure of making new fans in the US, it had all been so appealing. She never imagined for a moment she might be sucked into this nightmare.

They were driving now through a pleasant suburban street. Melissa had no idea where they were, having lost track of their journey in her musings. Parents met their kids from school busses, and Wilson had to keep stopping when the bus lights flashed. Melissa didn't know where they were going, but it was nice to be in the midst of normality for a little while. This neighborhood reminded her very much of her parents' place in Toronto. The houses dated back to before Melissa was born and she wasn't good at pinpointing the exact decade. They were pretty though, and upscale, with relatively new cars in the driveways and mature trees lining the street.

They pulled into the driveway of a small, single-story, well-kept home and parked next to an imported compact car.

"Where are we?" Melissa asked as they got out of Howie's BMW.

"My folks' house."

It took a moment for Melissa to process this. She swayed on her feet, lightheaded and dizzy. This was where Howie intended to take her, before he died. Here. To his mom and dad's house in the suburbs of Richmond. This was where she was supposed to come before everything went to hell.

Wilson was already at the front door, ringing the bell. Shania came over and put an arm around Melissa.

"I'm here, hon. It's all good. You just relax, okay?"

The door opened and Wilson greeted a plump lady with a kindly face, close-cropped hair and piercing brown eyes. She hugged Wilson and then caught sight of Shania and Melissa standing in the driveway by the car, Melissa still frozen.

Howie's death hit her harder in that moment than at any time since the shooting. Howie told her that this house was where he grew up, so the place would be full of memories of him. Was she ready for this?

Wilson's mom – Howie's mom – stepped over the threshold and walked towards Melissa. Her face was full of sympathy and mutual pain. Tears streamed down Melissa's cheeks as she stood there, leaning against Shania for support.

This lady, this stranger, whom she had never met before, reached her and drew her into a tight embrace. Melissa sobbed into her shoulder, wracking sobs that soaked the poor woman's shawl and threatened to bring them both tumbling to the ground. Howie's mom held her strongly, patiently, waiting for the deep mourning to rise out of Melissa from every fiber of her soul.

Melissa lost track of how long they stood like that, just holding each other while she cried. She didn't know what Shania and Wilson were doing; they might not even still be there. In that moment it could have started raining and Melissa wouldn't have noticed.

As it happened, Wilson had brought some tissues from inside, along with a tall, good-looking senior man with a rough beard and shaved head. Melissa blinked at him through her tears, unable to focus on his face beyond the superficial. Melissa finally broke away from Howie's mom and realized that this lady had been crying too. There were tears in the eyes of everyone present, and as Melissa hugged Howie's dad those tears reappeared immediately.

Melissa did not hold the embrace with this man for as long as his wife; emotionally she did not have much more to give. Nevertheless, the instant bond she formed with these two people was palpable. Their acceptance of her was overwhelming. She had no idea what she'd done to deserve it, but it moved her deeply.

Wilson handed her the tissues, and saved some for Shania and his mom, and then they led Melissa inside the house.

Melissa laughed through her tears. "I'm so sorry," she said.

"It's okay, my dear," Howie's mom replied. "I think we all needed that."

Melissa nodded and blew her nose as politely as she could into a tissue.

The house was cozy but didn't feel cramped. Pictures of Howie and Wilson were everywhere, at all stages of their life. Instead of prompting more tears, Melissa found this comforting. The love exuded by this home was obvious, and it did her spirit good to know that Howie had grown up here.

Wilson's parents led them through to a small sitting room with a threadbare sofa and a scratched up coffee table. The furniture was old and the walls could use a coat of paint, but the place was spotlessly clean yet felt homely and lived-in. Melissa loved it.

She and Shania sat down on the sofa while Howie's parents chose chairs across from the coffee table.

Wilson was over by the window, peering out into the street.

"No reporters been round today, Dad?"

"No, Wilson, not today. We had one guy come around yesterday but we said we didn't want to talk any more and he went away. We did our speaking out the day after Howie died. We've said our piece. It's up to the justice system now. Since then it's been much quieter. Nothing like the day after…"

"Are you in trouble?" Wilson's mom asked. There was no hint of accusation or disappointment in her tone. Instead it was filled with concern.

Wilson nodded. "Yeah, we are."

"You can stay here as long as you need to," Wilson's dad said.

"Thanks, Dad."

Howie's mom said, "Now, we know who you are Melissa. Howie showed us photos and we've seen you on the news." She turned to Shania. "But I don't think we've been introduced."

Wilson sprang forward like he'd been launched out of a cannon.

"Oh, yeah, sorry, Mom! This is Shania. She's Melissa's friend from Canada."

Shania shook hands with his parents and they greeted one another.

"I'm Jackie," Howie's mom said, "and this is Trevor."

"Thank you for inviting us into your lovely home," Melissa said through the occasional sniff. She wiped at her face with a clean tissue, finally feeling herself return to some kind of normalcy.

"Oh that's no trouble at all, honey. You've been through a lot, so it's the least we can do."

"You've been through a lot too."

Jackie seemed very wise at that moment, at least to Melissa. She nodded and blew air through pouted lips. "Well, that we have. But when you're the mother of two black children in America, well you always know and fear the day might be coming."

"That's horrible," Melissa said.

"That's life. I've mourned for my sons every time I hear someone else's been shot by police. That goes for any unarmed person, of any color, just minding their own business. I thought what with Howie getting famous… I thought that would protect him. Cops would recognize him and leave him alone. Guess he didn't get quite famous enough."

"It's open season on us right now," Trevor said.

"Ain't that the truth," Wilson agreed.

Melissa gave a wry smile. "You'll get no argument from me. You said you talked to reporters the day after it happened?"

"Oh yeah. I couldn't stop Jackie here. She raged fire and brimstone all over the news networks."

"I wish I'd seen it. I've been… avoiding the TV."

"Don't blame you," Jackie said, taking hold of Trevor's hand. "The things some of them are saying about our boy, it's sickening."

"Like what?"

"Like he's into drugs, he's a criminal so he deserved it. Makes you sick. I screamed at them so called journalists. Gave them plenty of drama for their audiences."

"Since then we've tried to keep a lower profile."

Jackie seemed to snap out of something. She smiled at Melissa.

"I'm sorry. I didn't mean to dredge up bad memories."

"No problem," Melissa replied awkwardly.

"Are you hungry?" Melissa and Shania nodded. It was well after lunch and they'd not eaten since breakfast. "I'll fix you something. Trevor, come help me."

Mr. and Mrs. Douglas left the room. Melissa, Shania and Wilson were alone.

"How likely is Granger to work out where we are?" Shania asked.

Wilson shrugged. "We should be fine for now, but we shouldn't stay anywhere too long."

Melissa took out her phone. "Do your folks have Wi-Fi?" she asked Wilson. He shook his head. "Damn. I wanted to upload the video of Tim…"

It occurred to her that she'd not yet watched it. Making sure Howie's parents weren't coming back, she took out her phone and found the video, noting that the device still had no signal.

She watched it. The first few frames were shaky but clearly showed Lionel Granger, talking to Tim while his men surrounded them. Melissa's phone tracked around the area, taking in the faces of each of the people there. This proved to be a mistake, because when the shot rang out, the camera was not on the shooter or on Tim. Melissa had completely forgotten she had done that. This was followed immediately by furious shaking and more gunfire, the phone failing to capture images of anyone with a gun.

As video evidence, it wasn't that great. It put the right people at the scene of the murder, but it didn't prove that Granger pulled the trigger, and it didn't prove that Tim was shot at that moment. Before the camera had moved, Granger hadn't even been holding his gun, never mind firing it. Melissa recalled how sudden that moment had been. No gun; gun; blam. She shuddered.

Shania watched over her shoulder. "Shit!" she said softly.

"It's not clear enough. It doesn't prove anything."

Shania shook her head. "Coupled with a confession, it will prove enough."

"How the fuck am I going to get…?" Melissa trailed off as Jackie and Trevor returned with two trays piled high with sandwiches and chips and drinks. They arranged them on the small dining table off to one side of the room and invited everyone to come and help themselves.

Melissa realized how hungry she was, and heaped a plate full of food. The five of them sat around eating, laughing and sharing stories for some time, until the light started to fade outside. It was the most normal Melissa had felt since all this started, and she was heartened to find out that Howie's parents were such lovely people. There was a bitterness there, a deep resentment and anger in the face of their pain. But they concealed it for her sake, and they were kind hosts. They didn't have to. They could have refused to shelter her and Shania. It was putting them in danger, and potentially turning the spotlight back on them. She admired their resolve.

With no internet access, Wilson was growing restless. Despite his parents' protests, he switched on the TV and changed the channel to a local news outlet.

Currently the anchor was talking about a murder investigation that had nothing to do with what had happened to them today, so they ignored it and went on talking for a time. Five minutes later, the anchor turned to an item about Tim.

"And more about the murder of Senator Tim Barns now we turn to our correspondent on the scene, Celia Ophernan. Celia what's the latest you have?"

"Jonathan, I'm standing at the place where Senator Tim Barns was shot this morning, down here at the Boathouse restaurant at Rocketts Landing Marina. Police say there are no eye witnesses but they did provide one new piece of information. There are two suspects in this murder, and police are working to identify two people, a male and a female, who were in the area at the time and were seen speeding away on a motorbike. As soon as we have more information, we'll of course keep you updated. We did find something interesting though. The police chief stated to us earlier that the roadblocks in this area intended to prevent the public from accessing the scene of the crime were set up after Senator Barns's murder. However, the timelines don't quite match as we've spoken to a couple of passers by who say that the roadblocks were set up much earlier than when the murder was alleged to have taken place. I'll continue to investigate this discrepancy and I'm also trying to get an interview with the police chief. When I do, I'll let you know, Jonathan."

"Thank you, Celia. We'll come back to this developing story as soon as we have more information for you."

For now that was the end of the segment. Melissa wasn't surprised. She just felt tired and overwhelmed. At the back of her mind she'd expected Granger to make use of the presence of her and Wilson as a way to assign blame for Tim's death. She had handed him a gift there. No need to pay off reporters and police, just tell everyone that the two people who weren't supposed to be there did the crime and let the press do the rest. She knew it was just a matter of time before her picture and Wilson's were splashed over the news. It would be a lot harder to get around town if that happened.

The next item on the news was about protest organizers talking about a big turnout tonight in memory of Senator Barns. "He was an ally," said one of the BLM organizers. This surprised Melissa. The cops didn't shoot Tim. He wasn't black. A murder committed by someone other than the police did not usually trigger protests.

"What's going on?" she asked Wilson.

He shrugged. "I dunno. I've been offline most of the day. I should go find out. I should be there."

"Breaking news just in," said the TV anchor, as the graphics surrounding him turned red and the words, "Breaking News" appeared in every place imaginable on the screen. "We've just learned that Officer Jason Hagley, who shot and killed Howie Douglas, will not be charged by the State of Virginia for murder. We also understand Officer

Hagley has been reinstated effective immediately into the Richmond Police Department. No word yet on whether the Federal Attorney General intends to step in here and press charges, but for now, Officer Jason Hagley is back on the force as of tonight. More on this as we get it."

"Are you kidding me?" Melissa would have cursed but she felt uncomfortable using bad language in front of Howie's mom and dad.

Jackie seemed to deflate, looking crushed by the news. Trevor reached out and took her hand. As angry as Melissa was about the ruling, it was for them she felt most sorry. The officer who had killed their son was still out there, still serving, and could easily kill someone else's son or daughter.

Wilson was putting his jacket on.

"You're going to leave us?" Melissa's voice shook.

He grabbed his car keys from a table by the door. "You'll be safe here. Mom and Dad will look after you."

"Wilson, I don't think you should go," said Jackie.

Shania agreed. "What if they put your pictures up on the news? You'll be a wanted man in the middle of a televised protest."

"I'll be fine," Wilson argued. "I gotta go. If protestors were already gonna be out for Tim, Hagley's acquittal may send people over the edge. You guys stay here and I'll be back after I find out what's going on. I hate not having my phone connected!"

There was no talking Wilson out of it. Jackie and Trevor seemed well used to losing arguments with Wilson about what was best for him.

Wilson addressed Melissa directly. "I'm sorry. I should be with them."

Melissa wanted to be there too, but truth be told she was afraid. She was surprised the TV news hadn't put up their pictures already. When they did, it would not be safe for her in public. Today had been what was probably her last chance to go home. Now she didn't know how she was ever going to see Toronto again. If she was arrested would the Canadian government come to her aid? Or would she spend the next twenty years in an American prison for murder?

"Wilson," she said. "First thing tomorrow morning, will you drive us to Canada?"

"Yeah," he replied. "I'll do that for sure."

"Thanks."

Wilson left then. Melissa watched his car pull away with a sinking feeling. She felt safe, for now, but also helpless. She wished she could do something for Tim. And Granger? Frankly, a man who could brazenly gun down a senator in broad daylight and then try to pin the blame on that senator's friends…

Clearly he was capable of anything, and considered himself untouchable. Melissa would dearly love to take him down, but how could she, a nineteen-year-old Canadian YouTube star, possibly do that?

She wished she'd never started her channel, and never tried to pursue fame. She should have continued her marine biology courses and followed her secondary dream of helping to preserve ocean wildlife and ecosystems. Instead her ambition had gotten her into this mess. She wished she could say she was glad to have known Howie at all, even for just a short time. She wished she could say that the time they spent together was better than no time at all. But quite honestly, the pain of missing him and the terror she had been through since he died – if she had never met Howie she'd have no idea what she was missing. Now she knew *exactly* what she was missing and it was almost more than she could bear.

Jackie brought them all coffee and the four of them continued to talk about Howie for some time. It was comforting but at the same time it stirred the pain and made it feel fresh, like ripping open the stitches of a knife wound and letting it bleed out.

It was dark outside now; Wilson should have reached his friends. Sure enough, when they tuned to the news again, the footage was of protestors marching through downtown Richmond, waving hastily-created signs that bore Tim's name and calls to bring his killers to justice.

"And on the subject of Senator Barns's killers, for those who've just joined us, the police have now named the two suspects they are seeking in connection with the murders. The first is Wilson Douglas, brother of rapper Howard Douglas who was shot and killed by police a few days ago. The second is Melissa Jones, a Canadian YouTube star who was in a relationship with Wilson Douglas's brother when he died. Police sources are telling us that these two fugitives are considered armed and dangerous. They fled the scene of Senator Barns's murder on a motorbike heading west. This security camera footage shows Douglas and Jones at Richmond International Airport this afternoon, where they met another woman who police have not yet identified. You can see close up pictures and descriptions of the fugitives on our website, and if you see them police say do not approach them, instead call 9-11."

"Great," said Shania.

Melissa said nothing.

Jackie and Trevor didn't seem fazed by what the news was saying.

"I take it you didn't kill Senator Barns," Jackie asked Melissa.

"He was my friend. No, I didn't kill him. Wilson and I know who did. That's why we're hiding here for now."

"That's what Wilson said," Jackie continued. "We believe you and you're welcome to stay here as long as you need to."

Melissa smiled. "Thanks, Mrs Douglas."

"Oh please, call me Jackie."

Melissa was grateful, but she couldn't help wishing Wilson had brought them somewhere with Wi-Fi. Perhaps it was smart of him. They could be traced if they attempted to access any of their online accounts, possibly back to this house if they weren't careful. Maybe it was better to be off the grid for a little while.

The landline telephone rang and Jackie answered it.

"Melissa who? Melissa Jones? Why would she be here?"

Melissa and Shania sat upright, listening keenly. There was no way they could make out what the voice on the other end of the line was saying, but Melissa strained to hear it anyway.

"I don't care if you need to speak to her, I can't give her the phone if she's not here to receive it."

Perhaps it was a reporter? Or one of Granger's thugs? Either way, Jackie was doing a great job of covering for them.

"I've never even met the woman. Okay, yes I'm sure you'll call back later. She still won't be here. Goodbye." Jackie hung up the cordless phone with the press of a button.

"Who was that?" Shania asked before Melissa could.

"Someone called Kirsty Frank."

"Oh," said Melissa. "She's actually a friend. I wouldn't mind talking to her."

"I'm sorry!" Jackie said, clearly horrified that she'd treated an ally so curtly.

"No no, if anyone will understand why you were being careful, it's Kirsty."

Shania sat back on the sofa. "Do you trust her?"

Melissa realized that Kirsty and Shania had not actually met. "I don't think we have much choice," she said. "She knows stuff that we can only guess at."

"Yeah but most of it's crap. I did some research on her and Darkmice.com, and they're into some seriously wacky stuff. Chemtrails, faked moon landings, the works."

"I know, but when it comes to Granger she's been on the money. The enemy of my enemy and all that."

Shania nodded. "She's no friend of Granger's, that's for sure. There were several stories about him on the site, with her byline. Nobody takes them seriously though, do they?"

"I don't know. Look, a lot of stuff she believes is, well, out there, but we need all the help we can get. I think we can trust her. Without Tim, honestly I don't know where to turn next. Maybe Kirsty can give us something we can use."

"All right. Assuming she calls back, I guess we can at least hear what she has to say."

The phone rang. Jackie answered it and then put it on speaker phone.

"I'm here," said Melissa.

"Hi, thanks for talking with me. I'm… sorry about Tim."

"Yeah, so are we."

"He was one of the good guys. How are you holding up?"

Melissa glanced at Shania, who gave her a supportive smile. "We're surviving," she said. "How did you find us?"

"I have my ways. Listen, if I worked out where you are then Granger's people and the police won't be far behind. You should keep moving."

"But if we go out, we'll be recognized and arrested, surely?"

"Most of the police force is at the protest. Most black people out on the streets are at the protest. Anybody else isn't going to give you a second glance, especially if you're not with Wilson. He's more at risk because he looks like his famous brother." Jackie and Trevor did not look happy about Kirsty's comment on their son. "Just avoid the protest and you'll be fine."

"Okay, where?"

"Why don't you come to our office? You'll be safe there and nobody will turn you in."

Melissa took down an address from Kirsty.

"See you there in half an hour."

The line went dead.

Shania stared at Melissa. "Um, Wilson's not here. How do we get to her?"

Melissa reached for her phone, then remembered she couldn't use it to go online. "Oh, no Uber."

"Can we take a bus or something?" Shania asked.

Jackie smiled. "Oh you Millennials," she teased gently. "I'll call you a cab."

"Nonsense," said Trevor. "I'm not letting you go into the city in a taxi. I'll drive you."

Melissa and Shania smiled to each other.

chapter nineteen

THEY WANT YOU DEAD

"You don't have to come in with us," Melissa said. "We'll be fine."

"I'm not letting you out of my sight," Trevor replied, pulling into the parking space. "You girls have been through hell and I'm not leaving you out here for the police to find you."

Melissa smiled at him. "Thank you," she said.

"Anything for my Howie's girl."

"And her best friend," Shania added from the back seat.

Trevor laughed. "And her best friend."

They got out of the car. Trevor paid for the parking and displayed the ticket, and they walked to the street nearby. Darkmice was located on the fifth floor of a high rise tower block, and when they asked for Kirsty at the security desk they were allowed up in the elevator in no time.

The three of them rode in silence, unsure what they were about to walk into.

They emerged into an unremarkable corridor. A sign on the wall listed a number of businesses and suite numbers, and Darkmice was number 505 further along the corridor. They passed a chiropractor, two web development companies and a dental office before reaching Darkmice's door. Melissa was going to knock but Shania just opened the door and stepped in.

It seemed like any other office suite, with a reception desk, a large sign with the company name over the top, and beyond the desk a series of cubicles and meeting rooms. The receptionist smiled at them and didn't take their names. She simply waved them to a waiting area. They had barely sat down when Kirsty arrived.

"Thanks for coming, guys." She gave Melissa a hug. "I'm so sorry about Tim." Melissa had no reply to that, but appreciated the second hug Kirsty gave her.

"This is Shania Martin," Melissa said as she and Kirsty parted.

Kirsty shook Shania's hand. "Of course, I've heard all about you." She turned to Trevor. "And you are?"

"Trevor Douglas," Trevor said. "Howie and Wilson's dad."

"Oh right, yes. Welcome." She shook Trevor's hand. "I'm deeply sorry for your loss. Please, come over to my office."

They followed her past a number of empty cubicles and one or two occupied. It was late in the evening so most people had gone home, but Melissa was surprised at the size of the operation. She had expected a pokey office in a seedy area, with a couple of old desks in a dank corner with people huddled in corners whispering to each other. This seemed like a business, and a reasonably successful one at that.

The walls of the office were covered with framed prints of articles, presumably taken from Darkmice.com itself, written by the people in this office. Other prints showed images of various conspiracy theories, some of which Melissa had heard of, others that were new to her. A picture of the moon landing, with the caption, "Real or Faked?", next to an image of a jet plane passing through the air leaving a long trail of vapor in its wake. The caption on that one read,

"What are they spraying?"

Melissa passed a picture of a man photographed in a lab coat. She didn't recognize him, but the caption read, "Cured AIDS?" and at the bottom added, "But They Killed Him in a Plane Crash!"

She wondered who "They" were. The Illuminati? Did that even make sense? Why would they want to kill a man who had cured AIDS? Was the disease part of their plan?

She shook herself mentally. She did not want to get caught up in this stuff. But where did it end? How much of it was true? Was Granger really part of the shadowy, global organization hell bent on reshaping the world to its own vision? And had Prince really been murdered, like Kirsty said?

Tim would have laughed at these thoughts and the pictures on the walls of Darkmice's offices. Perhaps he would have reacted by turning around and storming out of the building, calling it all ridiculous. Melissa sympathized – she did not believe the moon landings were faked – but Lionel Granger was certainly a man of influence and power whether he was Illuminati or not. Melissa had precious few people she could trust, and Kirsty certainly appeared to want to take down Granger in a big way, and she had resources and people, and that made her a useful ally even if some of her beliefs might a somewhat out there.

Kirsty took them to her office. She invited them to sit at her desk but she only had two chairs, so she went to the office next to hers to borrow a chair for Trevor, who insisted on the girls having the two seats available. Her office was simple but neatly organized, with more framed pictures adorning the walls. One of them appeared to be an album cover by an artist Melissa knew of but hadn't heard much of his music: Tupac. The album title, *The Don Killuminati: The 7 Day Theory*, certainly seemed pertinent to their discussion. Another picture, a grainy image of a UFO with the caption, "I want to believe," looked a bit like a movie poster, but perhaps Kirsty and her friends were convinced aliens existed too.

"I don't want to be rude," Kirsty said to Melissa and Shania, "but I assume you are okay with discussing anything in front of Trevor here?"

"Do you want me to wait outside?" Trevor asked, making to stand.

"No," Melissa said, reaching out and putting a hand on his arm to encourage him to sit. "He can definitely stay."

"Thank you," said Trevor. He was looking at the posters too, and had chuckled at the UFO one. Melissa wondered if there was some joke she wasn't getting.

"Do you guys need anything? Coffee?"

"We're good, thanks," said Melissa.

Shania had been watching Kirsty with an odd look on her face. Now, out of nowhere, she said, "You're the one who thinks Granger is Illuminati, right?"

Trevor laughed, then fell into an awkward silence.

Kirsty ignored him. "I know it. But you don't have to believe it. If you believe Granger can do whatever he wants in this town with impunity, he can shoot senators in the head and acquit police officers of murder charges, then you don't have to care what he really is. You know he's dangerous, and you know we have to stop him."

She handed them a battered copy of *The New Yorker*, and pointed out an article. "This man was investigating the effect of the world's second most popular herbicides, and he found out they were impacting multiple species, including frogs. When he published his results, the company that hired him tried to ruin his reputation and his career. That company was Synpertia."

"Why are you telling us this?"

"Because Granger is on the board of directors for

Synpertia. We believe he was instrumental in discrediting this research. The company is enormous and multi-national, and is a major source of funding for Illuminati activities. Granger will stop at nothing to protect his investments and his interests. No Senator or independent website will stop him alone. And that's why I need your help."

"Hey, er, wait," Melissa said. "I think Shania and I are done. Look, we want Hagley charged and we definitely want Granger to face justice for what he did to Tim, but we're just a couple of Canadian teenagers who never asked to be mixed up in this shit? What can we do?"

"Everyone thinking it's too much trouble and it's too dangerous is why Granger stays powerful. If enough people oppose him, his influence crumbles."

"Well that sounds fine and dandy," said Shania, "but speaking for myself, I'd like to go home."

Kirsty eyed her with a note of irritability. "And how exactly are you going to do that?"

"Wilson's going to drive us over the border tomorrow," Melissa said.

Kirsty shook her head. "Uh uh, not going to happen. Border security will be on the lookout, and if both of you are together you'll be easily identifiable."

"I'll take them then," said Trevor defiantly.

Melissa smiled at him with gratitude.

Kirsty shook her head. "Better, but chances are they'll take one look at Melissa's passport and you'll be arrested."

"That's so not fair," said Shania.

"Short of digging a tunnel, you're stuck in the US for now. I want to get you out of Virginia though. It's not safe for you and if you're arrested, I'll have a hard time getting you out of jail."

"Why are you helping us?" Shania asked.

"Because you didn't kill Tim Barns, because Granger is an

asshole, because the organization he's a part of needs to be opposed, and because you can help me too."

"Why are you being blamed for Senator Barns's death?" Trevor asked Melissa, looking surprised.

Kirsty answered. "The press is reporting that Melissa and Wilson killed Barns because they were present when he died. That's true, they did see it happen, but they didn't do it."

"So who did kill him?" Trevor asked.

"Lionel Granger," Melissa replied. "But he's not going to take the hit for it. And since we were there, we get to be the convenient scapegoats."

"Exactly," Kirsty agreed. "And also, he saw you take a video of the shooting. If you're arrested, he can have your phone destroyed and nobody else will get to see it. Which reminds me, can I borrow your phone please?"

Melissa hesitated. "Why?"

"I want to make a copy to use as evidence against Granger. We've got all sorts on him, but until now nothing concrete. This could be the smoking gun we've been looking for, quite literally."

"How did you know about the video?"

"We know Granger blocked your phones but he didn't bother blocking Tim's. We knew something was going down but we didn't know where until after it happened. And then we heard that the police were looking for you in connection with Tim's death after you fled the scene on Wilson's bike. It wasn't too hard to assume you taped the murder and that Granger wanted your phone before you could share that video."

"You make a lot of assumptions."

"It's my job. I'm right though, aren't I?"

"Yeah. To a point."

Kirsty tilted her head a little. "What do you mean?"

Melissa sighed. "I recorded the meeting but neither

Granger nor Tim was on camera when the shooting happened. The video puts them both at the right location at the right time, but it doesn't show the murder."

Kirsty seemed visibly upset by this. "Really? Shit! Goddammit. Damn, I really thought…" She tailed off. She looked about to stand up and storm out of the office but she restrained herself, instead clenching her fists several times over. "Shit! I really thought we had him."

"I'm sorry," Melissa said inadequately.

"The video was meant to be the headline piece in the exposé we're working on. I wanted to get you out of state, then reveal the video and everything else we have on Granger. There's no way he could have survived that. But without a solid video, the whole thing collapses."

Melissa grew defensive. "I did the best I could. They shot my friend in the head right in front of us. I wasn't really thinking about getting the best angle."

"No, it's not your fault," Kirsty conceded, despite her palpable frustration.

"Damn right it's not her fault," said Shania. "How could she know Granger would whip out a gun and plug Barns in the skull in a split second?"

"She couldn't," Kirsty agreed. "It's really not your fault, Melissa. I'm just frustrated, you know? Usually Granger gets someone else to do his dirty work. But I heard in this case Granger did the shooting personally, and that there might be a video of it. Can I see it anyway?"

"Of course," Melissa said. She handed her phone to Kirsty, who took a cable and connected it to her laptop. A few moments later, she unplugged it and handed it back.

"Thank you. I'm uploading it to our servers now. I won't release it to the net yet, but I'm storing it on a special site my coworker built. It copies files to three separate locations, and scrambles the IPs so nobody has any idea where they really are. They can't be deleted, only copied by those who have the right key to access them. Granger won't have any way to get rid of them."

"Sounds thorough," Melissa said. She looked to Shania for confirmation that this was a good plan. Shania nodded, which was something of a relief to Melissa. She'd not yet had a chance to transfer the video from her phone, and now the pressure to guard the video and her phone evaporated thanks to Kirsty's smart thinking.

"Do you have anything else we can use against Granger?" Melissa asked.

"We believe he's ordered over a dozen hits over the past decade on political enemies or those who have opposed or failed him. We have some evidence of payments made, but nothing more concrete. As I said, usually he gets other people to do his dirty work, which is why I was really hoping your video would show him pulling the trigger personally."

Melissa felt a stab of guilt again.

"He has around twenty state senators in his pocket, as well as the attorney general of course. Tim Barns sent us the emails you grabbed from the AG's office before he died, which we're very grateful for."

"So Granger was right," Melissa said. Granger knew what Tim had done and had punished the senator for it. But if Granger knew Tim had sent a copy of the emails, he must know *where* he sent them. And that meant he was fully aware of Kirsty's involvement and that Melissa would likely also send a copy of the video to this office too. And since Melissa didn't have any internet connection on her phone, she would have to deliver it in person. Which meant they knew she'd be…

"We need to get out of here," Melissa said, standing up.

"What? Where are you going?" Kirsty asked.

"What's wrong, Mel?" Shania asked, her face full of

concern.

Trevor stood up too, following Melissa's gaze out of the office door towards the reception desk.

"We shouldn't have come here," Melissa said, stepping towards the office door. "Granger knows we're here."

"That's not possible," Kirsty said. "We took every precaution…"

But something was going on at the reception desk. There was a flash and the loud crack of a gun going off.

Melissa froze but Kirsty was already moving. She barreled into Melissa, shoving her out into the corridor and then grabbing her arm, pulling her in the other direction, away from reception. Shania and Trevor followed, and seeing their panicked faces woke Melissa up. She turned in the direction Kirsty pulled them in, allowing the conspiracy theorist to drag her along.

"Where are we going?" she hissed.

"Back exit," Kirsty said.

Another bang sounded from the front of the suite, but Melissa didn't stop to look. Kirsty slammed into the crash bar of an emergency exit at the back of the suite. The door flew open and they spilled out into a stairwell, starkly illuminated with bright strip lighting, leading up to higher floors and down to ground level. Shania, Melissa and Trevor headed towards the stairs leading down but Kirsty, halted them with a hissed warning.

"They'll be coming up that way. We go up!"

She grabbed the handrail nearest to them and began to climb at a rapid pace. The others followed, confused but assuming she knew what she was doing.

After two or three floors had passed and they had turned on another landing to continue upwards, Trevor held up a hand.

"I ain't as young as I used to be," he complained. "You

guys go on but I need a breather."

"We're not going without you," Shania said.

Melissa peered over the bannister, down the gap between the staircases, which allowed her to see a glimpse of multiple floors below them and, right at the bottom, the ground floor. People were moving upwards, maybe four or five floors below them. Melissa couldn't see faces, but a hand that reached out to steady its owner on a handrail was carrying a gun.

"They're coming!" whispered Melissa urgently. Had their pursuers come from Kirsty's office? She had not heard the crash door open, so it was likely these guys had come up from street level, looking to cut off their escape. What the hell did Kirsty have in mind, leading them upwards?

"Come on!" hissed Kirsty. She had already reached the landing above them.

Shania and Melissa grabbed an arm each and heaved Trevor up the stairs. He puffed and panted but did his best to keep moving, aware that now there was an urgent need to get out of the building.

From below, Melissa heard a crash door exit flung open and a series of footsteps entering the stairwell. She heard shouts and questions as the two groups of armed men converged. The newcomers presumably being told that their prey had gone upwards, instead of the expected downwards. Glancing over the railing again, Melissa saw more of them now, moving quickly up the stairs in pursuit, only about four floors below them. Rallying Shania, the two women heaved Trevor upwards as fast as they could manage. Kirsty was on the landing above them, which appeared to be the top of the stairs. No further flights extended upwards. She stood holding open a door revealing the darkened sky, beckoning to them to hurry.

Finally, with a last burst of effort, Shania and Melissa got

Trevor to the top step and shoved him through the doorway. Kirsty followed them, slammed the door shut and locked it behind them.

Melissa barely had time to take in the roof, to survey Richmond's array of lights and buildings and highways from this vantage point, to catch her breath as the wind whipped across the flat roof of the office block, before they were off again.

Trevor begged for a break but they couldn't give him one. The locked door wouldn't hold Granger's men for long. Melissa had no idea where they were going, but trusted Kirsty knew what she was doing. Everyone she worked with might be dead, so regardless of her trustworthiness, her own sense of self-preservation was strong enough to convince Melissa to blindly follow her.

They reached the far side of the building, and to Melissa's horror, Kirsty jumped over the edge and for a moment, disappeared out of sight. Despite their terror of the threat pursuing them, both Shania and Melissa cried out and halted at the same time.

Kirsty's head re-emerged a second later. Melissa looked over the edge and realized she was standing on a fire escape ladder, which she had ducked down to deploy from its stored flat position. Already she was rushing down the staircase to the next platform. Melissa and Shania helped Trevor to climb over the edge onto the platform. Kirsty was on the next level, again ducking down to release the next stage of steps.

She did this for each floor, and had reached just two stories above the ground before Melissa heard boots landing on the stairs above them. She glanced up, peering through the metal mesh of the emergency stairs above. She couldn't make out faces or any people in their entirety, but it was clear that men were hurrying down the steps from the roof. She heard one talking on a radio or a phone, no doubt signaling to any of their friends still in the building or waiting on the ground that the four fugitives were about to make their escape.

Kirsty waited at the bottom of the final ladder, impatiently waiting for Melissa, Shania and Trevor to reach the ground. As soon as they did, she reached up and pulled a lever and immediately, all the stairs flipped back into their horizontal positions, all the way up to the top. There were cries and shouts of alarm. Melissa saw several of their pursuers falling or grabbing onto handrails to prevent themselves from tumbling over the edge.

"Nice!" Shania said, gazing up at the disarray above them.

"Little adaptation my friend Celine installed. Let's not waste it, come on!"

She hurried away from the stairs, in the opposite direction to the main entrance on the other side of the building. The crack of a gun going off issued from the stairs above their heads, and all four of them ducked down instinctively. One of Granger's men had recovered enough to take pot shots at them from on high, but he was too far away to hit them with a pistol. Still there was real danger of a stray bullet finding its mark, so they moved as quickly as they could, Trevor now breathing very hard, until they had ducked around the corner of another building, shielding them from the gunfire.

Trevor took the opportunity to place his hands on his knees and try to get his breath back. He shrugged off help from Shania and Melissa and headed after Kirsty at an unsteady jog. Shania followed him and Melissa brought up the rear, concerned that Trevor might have a heart attack before they reached safety.

In fact Kirsty took them in a circle and they arrived back in the lot where Trevor had parked his car.

"I saw you arrive," Kirsty explained, pointing at a security camera mounted high over the lot.

"If you saw us, Granger's people saw us too," Shania said.

Melissa turned just in time to avoid the pistol-whipping her face nearly received from one of Granger's heavies. He was the only one, clearly assigned to watch the lot in case the fugitives tried to return to their car. Melissa had not noticed him hiding behind the ticket machine. She backed away from him swiftly, avoiding another two wild swings with the butt of his handgun. Melissa didn't know why he wasn't firing it but she didn't complain, although she doubted she could keep avoiding him forever.

She didn't have to.

Kirsty jumped in between Melissa and her assailant. While Shania and Trevor stood frozen in surprise, unsure of what to do, Kirsty ducked low and kicked out, connecting with the assailant's shin and knocking one foot out from under him. Now in a crouch, Kirsty swept her leg in an arc and took out the man's other leg. He crashed to the floor, letting out a cry of shock, his gun bouncing off the pavement as it slipped from his grip. Kirsty was on him in a moment, punching at his face and then slamming a hand into his neck. The man clawed at his throat with his fingers, gasping for breath, his eyes bugging out.

Kirsty stood up.

"We'll take your car," she told Trevor, quite calmly. He nodded, dumbfounded.

Shania was whooping in appreciation but Kirsty told her to be quiet. "The others aren't far away. Save your applause until we're safely away."

Shania fell silent like a schoolgirl told off for chatting at the back of the class.

The four of them climbed into Trevor's car. The big man, still wheezing, started the engine, slammed the lever into drive and floored the gas. The Toyota screeched with some wheel spin before catapulting them from the parking lot, rattling along the short alleyway that led to the street.

Melissa held on to the handle above her rear door's window. Kirsty yelled directions to Trevor as they sped away on well-lit and crowded roads, avoiding cabs, pedestrians and buses in their rush to get away. Around every corner she expected to see a police roadblock, but for the time being the only slowdowns were other cars and cyclists, or people jumping out in front of moving traffic to cross the road without waiting for the lights to give them safe passage.

When their flight had settled a little and Trevor was able to drive a little more normally, Shania could hold her tongue no longer.

"That was awesome!" she blurted to Kirsty. "Where did you learn to fight like that?"

"I take lessons, twice a week," Kirsty replied. "When you know someone is out to get you, you try to make sure you're ready for them." She had her phone out and fell silent as she texted, presumably asking her colleagues if they were okay or warning them to stay away from the office. She stopped for a moment and went very quiet, her hand wiping at her eye.

"Did you lose someone?" Melissa asked as gently as she could.

"Jeanie, our receptionist," Kirsty replied haltingly. "And Brad, one of our staff writers."

"I'm so sorry," Melissa said, reaching out from the back seat and placing a hand on Kirsty's shoulder.

"I never thought it would come to this," Kirsty said, descending into tears.

Melissa glanced at Shania, who returned her look of empathy. More people dead at the hands of Lionel Granger. It brought to the surface all of the pain and hurt over the loss of Howie and Tim, and Melissa was getting sick of adding names to the list.

"I got a text from Wilson," Kirsty said. "He wants to meet

us at the café where I first met you and Tim, Melissa. Any objections?"

"Is that safe?"

Kirsty shrugged. "Depends if we were followed. I don't think we were, but if we were, it doesn't matter where we go."

"Maybe we should all go back to my house," Trevor suggested.

"If you were spotted with us, which I'm sure you were, then your home isn't safe either. They'll be watching it for your return."

"What about Jackie?" Trevor said in alarm.

"They'll be watching the house, but they're unlikely to move in on it unless we turn up. They should leave her alone. If you want to call to warn her to stay put, that might be an idea."

Trevor nodded and gratefully took Kirsty's phone. With one eye on the road, he dialed the number and spoke urgently to Jackie, telling her to stay put and not to go out for now. Melissa felt for him terribly. Now they had dragged his wife into this mess as well. Howie's loss and the threat to Wilson must already have been weighing heavily on him. Now he had Jackie to worry about too. It wasn't right. These were good people. They had not asked to be dragged into this. Just another couple of victims of Granger's struggle to protect his position.

They would meet with Wilson and talk about their next steps. Melissa wanted to explore options available to them to fight back, but she was realizing she was way out of her depth and her priority now was to keep everyone else she cared about alive. Nobody else would die to keep her and Shania safe. If that meant leaving the state or the country for a time, then so be it. Perhaps that would be best. She would listen to Wilson's opinion, and then likely do as Kirsty had suggested. She dearly wanted to return to Canada, but for now had accepted that wouldn't be possible. She wished her phone was connected so she could tell her mom she was still okay.

"Kirsty," Melissa asked, "can I borrow your phone?"

"Of course," Kirsty replied, handing it back to her.

Melissa thanked her and started writing a text to her dad.

"I'll borrow it after you, if that's okay?" Shania asked.

"Yeah of course," Kirsty said. She fell quiet again, and Melissa could hear the occasional sniff from her direction, and watched her wipe away a tear now and again.

She wished there was a way to fight back.

chapter twenty

THEY WANT YOU DEAD

Unlike the last time Melissa was here, the café was busy. Kirsty, Melissa, Shania and Trevor found a booth in the far corner of the room and sat down. Kirsty was no longer crying, but her eyes were puffy and red, and she sniffed from time to time. They ordered coffee, and as the waitress retreated from their table, Wilson arrived. Trevor stood up and hugged him, clearly relieved to see him still alive, and introduced him to Kirsty.

"Thanks for meeting me here," Wilson said after he had shaken hands with her. "I heard something went down near Ryland and Grace. Anything to do with you guys?"

"That's where my office is," Kirsty explained. "Granger paid us a visit."

"In person?"

"No, just his goons."

"Are you okay?"

"We're fine," Melissa answered as Kirsty fell silent. "But not everyone was so lucky."

"I'm so sorry," Wilson told Kirsty. She gave him a weak smile of thanks and a heavy silence fell over the table. The waitress broke the fog of despair, bringing four coffees and taking Wilson's order.

"Hey," said Wilson to Melissa and Shania, changing the subject. "I've asked one of my friends to pick up your luggage from the airport, is that okay? Since you're not leaving the country any time soon I figured you could use your stuff."

"Thanks," Melissa said. "That's really thoughtful."

"Can you give me the locker number and the code?"

Shania handed him a piece of paper with some hastily scribbled numbers on it. Wilson texted the details to someone he clearly trusted, so Melissa decided she was okay with it too.

"Your phone's connected again?" Melissa asked Wilson.

"Nope, I borrowed a friend's. I called home to check on you and mom gave me Kirsty's number."

Kirsty gave a wry smile. "I don't usually respond to texts from random numbers, but I'm aware of your friend."

Wilson looked coy and Trevor raised an eyebrow.

"Something you want to share with us?" he goaded his son.

Wilson refused to make eye contact. "Her name is Yolisa," he said at last.

Trevor smiled. "And how long have you been seeing her?"

"Oh, we're not together any more. We're just friends now. But we have a one-year old son."

Melissa's jaw dropped open.

"What?" Shania seemed equally astonished.

Trevor was the most surprised of all. "I'm sorry? Did you say Yolisa gave birth to your son?"

"Yeah, sorry I should have told you guys."

"Yes you should! You have a son!"

"Yeah, his name's Curtis."

"And you didn't tell me and your mom?"

"No, Dad. I'm sorry. Yolisa wanted to keep it quiet. She has an ex who might have a claim to the baby, so the less people who know the better. I guess that doesn't extend to our resident conspiracy theorist."

"You're sure it's yours though?"

"Dad, he has my ears. Curtis is the best, man."

"I'm a grandpa! I don't believe it!"

Kirsty put down her coffee cup with a bang, making them all jump.

"Sorry to piss on the bad news, but we need to focus. I don't want to stay out in the open longer than is necessary. Wilson, I'm sorry for outing you. It's not like I'm a top secret spy. All of this information is easily available on social media if you just take the time to look."

"If you're the sort of person who likes to snoop into other people's business, sure," Wilson said.

"My point," Kirsty said, ignoring the jibe, "is that our families and friends are not safe. Two of my co-workers, people I cared about very much, are dead tonight." Tears sprang back into her eyes again. "We should all make it a priority to keep those we love safe."

"Trevor, I suggest you return to Jackie alone. As I said, I don't think Granger will move on either of you as long as none of the rest of us comes with you. No more fiery statements of outrage to the press, okay?"

"Mom's in trouble?" Wilson said, making to stand up.

Trevor put a calming hand on his arm. "She's fine for now. We just have to be careful not to put her in danger."

Wilson sat back down but did not look at all relaxed. He took out his phone and started texting someone. "I'll have your luggage sent to Tim's house. I don't want anyone going to mom's house she doesn't know or spooking anyone who's watching her."

Melissa nodded. It made sense.

Kirsty waved her coffee mug as she spoke. "My job right now is to keep you and Melissa safe and out of prison. So, here's what I'm thinking. Wilson, I'm going to help Melissa and Shania get out of Virginia. You might want to go with them. I don't think Granger will have an easy time convincing police departments in other states that you're guilty of killing Tim, at least not right away. I think we should take you into Maryland for now, just until things die down a bit. I'm working to get the truth out about what happened to Tim, but it will take a while. Once the public knows you weren't responsible, the arrest warrant for you two should go away."

"Okay so once my parents are safely home and Melissa, Shania and I are out of Virginia, then what? What about you?"

"Granger will come after me. He'll know I have the video. Given he attacked my office I doubt he knows that the video doesn't show the killing. In fact, I would expect by now..." Kirsty trailed off as she pulled her phone out of her pocket. She woke it up and cursed. "Yup, no surprise there." She showed them the screen. *No Carrier* appeared at the top. "Granger cut off my phone access. It won't be long before he cuts off Yolisa's phone too."

Wilson, who had not looked at his phone for a few moments, now checked it automatically. "Still connected, for now," he said.

"Okay, I suggest we head out of here and go south a block. I have a lockbox there with a couple of burner phones in it. If we can grab those then we can head to the state line. I've already contacted a friend of mine in Maryland who is willing to take you guys in, but I need to contact him when we're close. I need one of those phones to do it. You guys can keep the other one so I can stay in touch with you."

"Sounds like a plan," said Wilson. "But I'm not going."

"What?" Melissa said.

"Take Melissa and Shania over the border, but I'm staying

here in Richmond."

"That really isn't wise," Kirsty said.

"Son, you should go until it's safe."

"Nuh uh," Wilson said, shaking his head. "I ain't leaving the movement. Every night we get more people coming out, membership is through the roof, people are pissed, and they need leaders. They look to me, not just me but they are looking. I need to stay. I can't abandon them. We're out there every night making noise and making our voices heard. I ain't gonna abandon them just because of some trumped up charges against me. They have no evidence. They can lock me up but they can't keep me down. I need to take a stand and I need to be here. I can't do nothing from Maryland."

"Wilson, you need to stay free," Kirsty said. "You can come back and fight another day."

"Please, Wilson," Trevor implored him.

"My mind is made up. This is my home, and I will defend it from trigger-happy police and shitstains like Lionel Granger. No way am I letting any one of those motherfuckers so much as bruise another one of my brothers and sisters."

Trevor stood up, as if about to grab his son and wrestle him back to the car. Melissa put a hand on his arm.

"I think you need to let him stay," she said.

"Like hell," Trevor said, the volume of his voice rising. "I already lost one son. I ain't losing another because he's too pig headed to listen to reason. Think of your son, Wilson. He needs his daddy alive."

"I am thinking of my son," Wilson said, rising to his feet with a scrape of his chair. Other people in the café were staring at them now. "I don't want him to say his daddy was a coward, that he ran away when things got tough. I want him to know I took a stand and I defended his town."

"But that's no use if you're dead."

"Shut the fuck up, both of you!" Kirsty was on her feet now. The two men glared at her, but backed down after a moment. All three of them sat together. "Jesus, you want every cop in the city to hear you?"

Wilson and Trevor said nothing. Melissa smiled at some of the other patrons who were still staring. Eventually they all went returned to their own business.

"I'll take you to the border," Wilson said to Melissa and Shania, "but then I come back here."

"No need," said Kirsty. "I've got a car. It's not in my name so the police shouldn't be aware of it. I'll take them. Your car is probably marked now anyway."

"I can take them," Trevor said.

"You need to stay with Jackie," Kirsty said. "I can't guarantee Granger won't make a move on her. In fact, as soon as we leave here, you should go straight home. We'll call you when we're safe."

"Okay," said Trevor. He was clearly making a point of following Kirsty's advice, in stark contrast to his stubborn son. Wilson said nothing.

Melissa feared for his safety, but there was no dissuading him. He had made up his mind. She admired him for that, although it probably wasn't smart. She wished she could stay and make a stand too. One of them had to stay safe. They were both witnesses to Tim's murder, and eventually one or both of them might have to testify, if Granger ever faced charges for the terrible things he'd done.

"If we're done arguing," Kirsty said, "I suggest we get going."

She had not even stood up before the squealing noise of a bullhorn came from outside the café. All the patrons stopped talking and twisted around in their seats to see what was going on. To Melissa's horror, the sidewalk outside was full of police officers.

"Melissa Jones. Wilson Douglas. Step out of the café with your hands up."

All eyes within the eatery were on Melissa and Wilson. Melissa froze, her gaze darting urgently between each of her friends. Perhaps it had not been a good idea to meet Wilson here. She returned some of the stares of accusing strangers, wondering which of them had sold them out. She knew she couldn't blame them, given that their pictures were on the news with big wanted labels all over them. Still it felt like a betrayal. Wilson, at least, was one of their own.

"Melissa Jones and Wilson Douglas," the officer with the bullhorn repeated. "Put down your weapons and step out into the street with your hands raised."

The impact of this announcement was immediate. Every person in the café scraped their chairs back and got to their feet. Every person except Kirsty, Shania, Wilson, Trevor and Melissa scrambled for the exit with terror in their eyes. Desperate to leave, they squeezed and shoved to get through the door. They spilled out onto the sidewalk screaming and crying. Melissa couldn't see the police for a minute or two while the other patrons cleared out. Terror gripped her. She didn't want to go to jail. She didn't want the world to think she had murdered Tim. She'd heard all the stories about American prisons and she never imagined she'd come anywhere near one, never mind be locked up in one. It was suddenly hard to breathe. She leaned on Shania for support, and once again her best friend was there to hold on to her. She had pulled Shania into this mess, if she went to jail too it would be Melissa's fault. This made her feel sicker than her own prospects. How could she live with herself?

The five of them were now alone in the café. Even the waitress had disappeared. Shania still wanted to leave but Melissa held her arm.

"It's too late," she said.

"She's right," Wilson said. "Don't move." He was still on his phone and texting furiously. Who was he talking to?

"Is there a back way?" Trevor asked.

Kirsty said, "Police will be at every exit. If you try and run they will have an excuse to shoot."

"So we're fucked?" Shania said. Melissa could tell Shania was as close to panic as she was.

"Not yet," said Wilson.

He turned his phone around. It was showing a video on a loop. Protestors breaking away from the main march and starting to run.

"Is this tonight's protest?" Kirsty asked.

"Yep. They're on their way."

"How is that going to help?" said Shania.

"We're out of time," Melissa added.

"Last warning. Step out now or we will come in."

"We need more time," Wilson said. "Come on, come on!"

Kirsty stepped forward. "We need to start surrendering. I suggest we go one by one to draw this out as much as we… Where the fuck is he going?"

Trevor was striding towards the door.

"Dad, no!"

But Wilson's cry went ignored. Trevor stepped through the doorway, deliberately taking his time. The police called out to him to step forward and then get down on his knees. His response was dangerously slow.

"Do what they tell you, idiot!" Wilson hissed under his breath. "Don't do it slow. Do it fast."

Finally Trevor was on his knees, and to everyone's relief, the police rushed forward and cuffed him. They weren't gentle, but as they dragged him off Melissa was thankful no shots had been fired.

Shania looked at Wilson.

"How much more time?"

"Seconds? Minutes? I don't know!"

Shania strode towards the exit.

Melissa moved to stop her but Kirsty grabbed her arm.

"Shan!" she cried. "No! Jesus no!"

Shania was now at the door. The police also told her to step forward and get on her knees, hands behind her head.

Melissa was in tears. She couldn't fathom what was happening. It felt like they were picking off everyone she cared about one by one. Thankfully they arrested Shania without incident and took her away peacefully.

"I'll go next," said Kirsty. When it's your turn, don't delay like we do. Don't run. Be purposeful and do exactly as they say. Don't reach for anything. Hold your hands over your head."

Melissa tried to reply but her lip was quivering.

"Do you understand?"

"Yes! Yes I understand."

"Okay then. Here I go."

"Wait!" called Wilson. "We can all go."

"Are you sure?" said Kirsty, already stepping forward.

"Yes. Let's go."

"Okay, keep behind me in case they get trigger happy."

Melissa didn't need telling twice. She cowered behind the conspiracy theorist, feeling ashamed for not walking tall as Trevor and Shania had done. Wilson too hung back behind Kirsty. To be fair, if anyone was likely to get shot it was the two of their group with their faces on wanted posters. Still, she wasn't proud of hiding.

All three of them walked from the café and stepped out into the street, their hands held high above their heads. Melissa felt like she was going to wet herself. She had never been more terrified. Not when Howie died, not when they kidnapped her and tied her up in Tim's basement, not when they gassed her at the protest, not when they stole emails from Virginia's Attorney General, not when Granger shot Tim and they fled on a motorbike. Facing at least a dozen officers, standing behind their patrol cars, their guns out pointing straight at them, lights trained on them. It went against everything her instincts told her, to offer herself up to the people who were supposed to protect her, yet would likely gun her down without hesitation if she acted in a threatening manner. Or even, she was uncomfortably aware, if they simply *perceived* her to be a threat. After all, what had Howie done to deserve to be shot, over and over? Now she was a fugitive, wanted for a crime. Did she think for one second they would show restraint?

These moments could be her last.

But to Melissa's surprise, she, Wilson and Kirsty were not alone. A steady stream of people, mostly African-American, came streaming in to fill the gap between the trio of fugitives and the line of police officers. A handful at first, and then many more. Melissa didn't understand what was happening for a moment. Then she realized where these people were coming from. It was Wilson's friends. Most of them from Black Lives Matter. They had broken off from the protest and hurried over here to try to keep them safe. Melissa's mouth dropped open. Despite what the news was telling them, they still felt compelled to put themselves in harm's way to protect their friend. She wasn't sure if they would do the same if Wilson wasn't here and it was just the Canadian girl who needed defending, but she wasn't about to complain.

"All newcomers step aside," said the officer on the bullhorn. "You are shielding fugitives. Stand aside."

"You are on camera!" yelled one of the protestors, his phone in the air, the camera directed at the police.

"Start shooting, we're recording," said another.

"I can't breathe," called one woman.

"Hands up, don't shoot!"

There were at least a hundred of them now, all calling out chants and slogans, waving signs and recording on their phones. Would the police open fire and risk the broadcast of a massacre to the world? Melissa couldn't see much of them through the crowd of protestors closing ranks in front of them. She did catch sight of one officer lowering his gun but could not see any more.

Emboldened, she turned to Wilson.

"What now?" she asked. "Can we escape? Will they move in?"

"They might. A lot of people will get hurt if they do."

"How long do we have?" Kirsty asked, shouting to be heard over the chanting.

"No idea," said Wilson. "But more cavalry is coming."

Before Melissa could ask what he meant by that, a rumbling noise shook the ground beneath their feet. Looking to their left, along the line of protestors towards the far end of the street, a line of police reinforcements had arrived, marching in riot gear and carrying batons. It was a terrifying sight, but not as frightening as the armored tank rumbling along behind the police line. It wasn't technically a tank, Melissa knew that, but it was huge, desert-colored and heavily armored. It was clearly a military vehicle, but it appeared to be police owned. It was certainly intimidating and completely over the top.

Wilson tugged at Melissa's shoulder and she turned to her right, looking along the line of protestors in the other direction towards the other end of the street. Just coming into view were more protestors, but this wasn't just a handful of people. This was the entire movement. That became obvious as soon as the first few lines of marchers emerged.

The police reinforcements would reach them first, and when they did the officers with their guns pointed at the hundred or so people blocking them from her and Wilson, would be emboldened and would likely make a charge. If they did that, Melissa and Wilson had nowhere to run. Wilson had clearly seen the same thing. He was shouting instructions to their defenders, trying to herd them away from the café, towards the slowly advancing bulk of the protest.

Melissa joined in, grabbing shoulders and arms to try to pull people away. She lost sight of Wilson and Kirsty for a moment, but the group was starting to move at last. Gradually, Melissa helped build a wall of people between herself and the police that backed her onto the street rather than the café, so that behind her now she could see over her shoulder the marching masses as they drew steadily nearer.

The dozen officers shifted their position. They glanced over their shoulders, looking to see when their reinforcements would arrive. Unless they started firing their guns, they weren't going to break through the line of people protecting Melissa. When the riot police arrived, they would have other tools like gas and shields much better suited to breaking the wall. Then it would be over. The line would collapse, and Melissa and Wilson would be arrested or shot.

The relatively small group of protestors linked arms and stood in lines across the street, around to one side of the ring of patrol cars outside the café. The officers couldn't shield themselves behind their vehicles any more. They were forced to emerge and follow, moving away from their reinforcements, advancing with their bodies held in a firing stance and their guns pointed at the wall of people. Protestors taunted them, inviting them to go ahead and shoot, all the while filming every move they made on their phones. The officers hesitated, aware that protestors were broadcasting them. Melissa sent a silent prayer of thanks to the inventors of the internet, the smart phone and the live video broadcast app.

"Step aside! You are shielding known fugitives. Step aside."

But the wall held strong. Nobody broke away. Nobody ran.

Melissa was in awe.

Behind the wall, she reunited with Wilson and Kirsty. She was surprised the conspiracy theorist was still there. She could have run away at any time, or even stayed in the café. They probably would have assumed the white woman wasn't with the rest of them and left her alone. She could have ditched them when everyone else fled the café. But she was still here, backing up slowly as the wall retreated along the street. Why was she still with them? Did Melissa represent Kirsty's best chance of bringing down Granger? Could she really trust this woman? Was giving her a copy of the video the right move?

Never mind, she was here and in danger just like they were. She needed all the allies she could get, so for now she would have to trust this woman.

The main body of protestors was perhaps five minutes away. At the other end of the street, the riot police were closing in on the dozen officers quickly. Had they increased their pace? They knew that if Melissa and Wilson and their small band of defenders mixed with the larger protest crowd, the fugitives would be a lot harder to find.

Some of the officers with their guns drawn attempted to move around the sides of the protest wall shielding Melissa and Wilson. The marchers responded by curving the wall around, so it became a semi-circle of bodies around the fugitive's position. Wilson was directing them like a general on the battlefield. He was shouting loud enough for those nearest him to hear and pass on his instructions, but not so loud that the police could hear him over the relentless chanting.

Through the occasional gap in the wall of defenders,

Melissa saw that one of the officers had stopped moving. He was looking up and down the street, seeming to reassess the situation. Melissa guessed he was in charge of the team, and now he appeared to make a judgement call. The smaller group of protestors was accelerating, which meant that Melissa was now walking backwards quickly. They were on course to join the main throng before the riot police arrived. This was a critical moment. Was he about to call on the other officers to fire?

She grabbed Wilson's arm.

"I think they're going to fire on us," she yelled. She pointed at the man in charge, who had started moving again and was calling to his fellow officers to draw closer together. "Should we run?"

"No," said Wilson. "If we break away now they'll intercept us."

"But if they start firing, these people are going to die."

"They know what they're getting in to. All of us are prepared to die for the others."

"That's not right," Melissa insisted. "I won't have these people lay down their lives for me."

"It's not just about you," Wilson said coldly. "It's about taking a stand. It's about telling the police they can't bully us any more. It's about making a statement and broadcasting to the world what's really going on."

Melissa stared at him open-mouthed. "You want them to shoot!"

"Of course not," he replied, looking irritated. "But if they do, we can turn that to our advantage too."

Melissa tried to peer through the wall to see the police. All at the same time, it seemed, they dropped to one knee and assumed a firing position.

She could not let this happen. She tried to reverse course, break through the wall so that she would emerge in front of the police and make herself a target. Wilson grabbed her shoulder and pulled her back.

"No!" he commanded.

Melissa tried to duck away from his grip but at that moment, he broke out into a run. He dragged Melissa along behind him, and Kirsty followed suit. They ran towards the much larger protest, now just a short distance away. Melissa allowed herself to be pulled along, her eyes locked desperately on the wall that had previously protected them. The rumble of the military vehicle was much more intense now, and she could hear the sound of batons striking shields in a coordinated rhythm. The police backup had arrived.

But the defensive wall held. The line did not break. And then, without warning, at some prearranged signal that Melissa didn't see or hear, the wall exploded in all directions. Protestors ran in all directions, deliberately making it hard on the police to pick out a target or to aim their advance at some single point.

And then Melissa lost sight of them as she was plunged into a sea of people, some white, some black, some young, some old, even some kids. She, Wilson and Kirsty had reached the main protest and had been absorbed into it. A dense pack of hundreds, likely thousands of people surrounded them, many with placards and homemade signs, waving and chanting. Some protested Tim's death, others Hagley's acquittal, a few still held signs for Howie or his album covers. These were not organized activists. These were regular folks who had come out to have their voices heard and to shout out against injustice. Plenty of people among whom she and Wilson could hide, but not fighters, not people they could count on to defend them.

In fact, a new threat was raising its head: recognition.

Several folks in the crowd pointed to Melissa and Wilson and managed to place them.

Someone yelled, "Those guys killed Tim!"

Others joined in, and jostled Melissa and Wilson. With rising panic, Melissa wondered if some of these people might physically attack them, or turn them over to the police.

Kirsty stood before them, telling the people the police lied to them. She explained that Melissa and Wilson were innocent, but she wasn't having much luck. Nobody knew who Kirsty was, so her words had little effect on them.

But something else was occupying the attention of the protestors. The march had stopped, and the cessation was rippling back through the crowd. Melissa realized the people convinced she was a killer were not moving, and as she looked back towards the front of the protest she knew why, even though she could not see anything at any distance in the throng. She heard them though. The rumbling of the tank-like military vehicle, the rhythmic slamming of batons against riot shields, the marching of the police to meet the protestors. The sounds and presumably the images sent shockwaves through the protestors.

Some people tried to grab at Melissa and Wilson, perhaps thinking if they gave up the fugitives, everyone else would be spared. Melissa doubted that would be the case, but she had no way to make them listen to her. Most people seemed distracted, concerned. It wouldn't take many running away to break up the whole protest. If that happened, they were all vulnerable. People would get hurt.

But Wilson's friends were making their presence felt. They'd managed to merge themselves into the main group and were now calmly taking charge, steering the protest in another direction. With agitation and confusion still prevalent, the marchers slowly started moving again. Melissa didn't know where they were going, but as long as it was away from the riot police lines she wasn't going to argue. At any moment she expected them to come charging in, to stop the protest and to use tear gas and other methods to break up this gathering. Perhaps they knew that if they charged in, people would scatter in every direction and they could very easily lose their targets, i.e. Wilson and Melissa.

One of Wilson's friends handed him a couple of bandanas, and he passed one on to Melissa before putting the other on himself. It wasn't exactly master-of-disguise standard, but it would help them avoid being picked out from the larger crowd. As she, Wilson and Kirsty allowed themselves to drift back deeper into the marching throng, those who had previously recognized them drifted away as the march progressed. With the bandanas on, they attracted some suspicious stares but no positive identifications. This came as a relief. It was scary enough to be a part of a big protest march after what happened last time out, but to have the people *within* the protest threatening to beat you up or identify you to the police added an extra dimension of terror Melissa could do without. Was this her life now? Always on the run? Hiding among people who might sell her out to the authorities at every turn? Wondering who she could trust?

She glanced again at Kirsty, who had foregone a bandana given that she was not a specific target and her face had not been all over the news. The conspiracy theorist seemed concerned for Melissa's safety, but had relaxed since the bandana had provided some anonymity. Their position was close to one edge of the protest march now, and Kirsty moved herself in between Melissa and the police officers who had taken up positions along the edges of the street. This was a new tactic from last time, and Melissa's theory about the police being reluctant to try to break up the protest seemed to be holding water. They were being patient this time, watchful. At some point they would spot Melissa or Wilson, and then they'd make their move. Or they were waiting until the protest naturally dispersed, whereupon they would move in and arrest the fugitives.

Wilson was texting on his phone, and upon receiving a particular message he moved forward, pushing through the throng towards the front of the march. Determined not to be separated from him, Melissa grabbed Kirsty's hand and followed him. Lunging forward, she grabbed his hand. He turned, looking surprised, but clung on to her. The three of them slipped through the mass of protestors like a snake through thick grass, heading towards the front. Melissa had no idea why they were heading this way, but she allowed Wilson to lead her.

When they reached a point near the front of the protest, Wilson could talk with his fellow leaders in person. Melissa caught small snatches of the conversation, something about deciding where to lead the march where minimum harm would come to the people assembled. There was much debate as to whether they should continue on to East Main Street because the police might be waiting for them there in force. Kirsty interjected herself into the conversation. She was saying something about a Federal building on that street, and urging the protestors to head towards it. Melissa had no idea what she had in mind, but she added her voice to Kirsty's. To her relief, Wilson agreed, and finally the others capitulated and agreed to make this their destination.

"It's going to get rough," Wilson warned Melissa and Kirsty. "Stay together. Keep going."

"What's the plan?" Melissa yelled at Kirsty, slightly panicked.

"Federal building!" Kirsty yelled back, as if that answered anything. "Local police, no jurisdiction!"

Melissa got it. She was a fugitive to the local police, but in a building under Federal control she should be protected from them, and she had a better chance of them believing her about what happened to Tim. That was her assumption anyway. Maybe Kirsty had a grand plan to take over the building. The conspiracy theorist was no doubt pissed at Granger – how far would she go to seek revenge? Was her calm expression a mask for the crazy underneath? What was she capable of? Melissa didn't really know. She'd only met the woman a couple of times.

Wait, didn't Tim talk about two FBI agents who were under Granger's control? How far did Granger's influence reach? Perhaps Kirsty was betting on not all Federal agents based in Virginia being under Granger's control. Two of them certainly were, according to what Tim had told her. She struggled to recall their names but came up blank. Clark was one, possibly? The other she couldn't remember. She would probably run into them at their destination. Hopefully, agents not in league with Granger would outnumber those who were. Either way, this evening was not going to end well. She tried not to think about the fate awaiting her if they made it to the federal office, and instead focused on the increasingly unlikely chances of getting there at all.

More police rushed into position along the sides of the march. Melissa had no way to tell how much ground the entire protest covered, but she suspected the heaviest police presence was here at the front. She wasn't sure what they would do if the officers formed a barrier in front of them. They could attempt to switch course but that would lead them away from sanctuary.

Wilson's friends surrounded the trio now, and it was getting harder to see the police lining the sides of the street. Perhaps that was for the best. They knew where they were going, so they would make sure the three of them got there. Melissa was both thankful and a little intimidated. The people around her, mostly black, mostly young, were marching almost in unison. They waved their banners and shouted their chants, and Melissa was certainly grateful for these people putting themselves in harm's way for her benefit, or at least for Wilson's. A sudden feeling that she couldn't just run away suddenly gripped her and she missed a breath. Was this a panic attack? She'd never had one before. She forced herself to calm down, and to her relief her breathing came back under control.

Her protectors provided a distraction as the chanting fell silent. Rapid instructions flew from person to person around her. She looked around for the source of the distress and realized that the marchers ahead of her were slowing down. She was near the front but not close enough to see why.

"Roadblock," Wilson said.

Melissa assumed he meant police. What else could it mean? All she could see was protestors, but everyone near her was agitated and fearful.

"Keep moving!" Wilson bellowed, and others took up the call. The marchers picked up speed again. Melissa realized that the non-BLM people protesting with them had melted away. It could be because their allies had formed a ring around Melissa and Wilson, or it could be because they had gotten scared and were trying to leave the march. Melissa looked behind her but couldn't see beyond the defensive ring. She had no way to know if the rest of the protest had disbanded or still followed. She could certainly still hear chanting from back there, so maybe there were still brave people marching with them, or perhaps they were unaware of what was going on at the front. Either way, Melissa prayed nobody got hurt.

At first she thought it was her imagination, but the people around her really were closing in. Her personal space had disappeared, and now she found herself pressed in between Wilson, Kirsty and a couple strangers.

"Disperse immediately!" came a voice over a bullhorn. "Disperse immediately or be arrested."

That didn't sound good. Nobody around her ran, instead they kept moving on. Something flew over Melissa's head. She wasn't sure what it was at first, but then the unmistakable trail of smoke issued from the object like the tail of a kite, and Melissa knew things were going to get very bad.

"Keep your head down," Kirsty told her, bending low as the air started to thicken. Melissa joined her, but the feeling of claustrophobia worsened when all she could see were people's legs. It was getting hard to breathe, and not just because of the gas. The chanting around them disappeared, to be replaced by coughing and crying. But still the core of protestors held the line and moved forward. Melissa's knees hurt but she kept up with Kirsty, moving in bursts of speed to keep up. Someone to Melissa's left went down under a scrum of police officers, crushed under riot shields and pummeled by batons. Others immediately filled the break in the wall so that the fallen victim disappeared from sight very quickly. Melissa didn't know his name, and might never know what happened to him or if he was okay.

The shock of what she'd seen caused her to miss another breath, and with the gas closing in and her bandana doing little to protect her, every breath was vital. She staggered, but Wilson was there to hold her up. Like her and Kirsty he was crouching low, but his eyes were streaming and he was coughing.

Suddenly the back wall of their protective shield crumbled in a blast of water. People went down like bowling pins, struck with the full force of the water cannon mounted on top of one of the heavily armored tank-like vehicles. Melissa gaped at it through tear-filled eyes. The mist of water soaked her, making her clothes cling to her skin and causing her to shiver. She saw people running from the cannon, or knocked down by it. The water blast was not fun like a Super Soaker or a hosepipe in the summer. It was freezing and so powerful that nobody could stand against it.

"We need to abandon this!" Kirsty yelled, her voice hoarse from the gas.

"We're nearly there!" Wilson replied.

One benefit of the water cannon was that it pushed away the gas canisters and cleared the fumes from the air. Melissa had never felt so cold though, and she shivered so hard she felt her body might shake apart.

The cannon shut off abruptly and the police moved in. Some of them slipped on the slick pavement and went down, but most charged in to break up the protest once and for all.

Brave souls moved to close the huge gap wrought by the water cannon, but they could not move fast enough. Two officers reached Melissa and tried to grab her arms. Kirsty kicked one of them in the back, sending him sprawling into the other one. She gripped Melissa's arm and hauled her upright, then retreated into the wall of protestors in front of them, still marching presumably towards the federal building. This line too was thinning as it tried to break through a wall of officers. Chaos erupted, Melissa couldn't see what was going on and didn't know which way to go.

"Go get 'em," said Wilson in her ear, and he pushed her and Kirsty forward. Melissa turned in time to see him disappear in a mass of police officers, their batons swinging at his face and torso. She cried out but the sound was snatched away as a small band of protestors, some of the last still standing, surrounded her and Kirsty. All were soaked, all were coughing, all were barely standing, but somehow they built a defense around Melissa and Kirsty and kept on going, through the newly parted gap in the police wall in front of the building's entranceway. Melissa could see the lights inside, they were so close. One by one, the people around them fell away in a storm of riot shields and clubs. Every time a protestor disappeared in the melee, Melissa felt the impact like a punch in the stomach. Taking a deep breath, she pushed on forwards, Kirsty by her side, the lights of the building's foyer tantalizingly close.

And then they came to a crashing halt. City police officers moved in to block their access to the doors. Melissa looked around her to see the last two protestors taken down and put in handcuffs. She and Kirsty were the last ones standing, just a couple of feet from Federal territory. So close, yet it might as well have been three city blocks away.

The cops hesitated, as if waiting for instructions.

"Arrest them both!" yelled a voice. Melissa couldn't see who said it, but the effect was instant. The cops blocking their way stepped forward.

Melissa gasped as Kirsty stepped in behind her and placed an arm around her neck, the other pressing something metal into her back.

"Stand down or I kill her," Kirsty called. The advancing cops froze. "I have a gun. I will shoot her if you move." To illustrate her point, Kirsty pulled hard on Melissa's throat, causing her to cry out in pain.

"What are you doing?" Melissa rasped, trembling and struggling to keep her bladder from emptying.

"Trust me," Kirsty hissed.

The cops didn't seem to know what to do. They dropped their batons and shields and drew their guns, aiming them at the two women.

"Put the gun down," one of them said.

"Move aside or she dies," Kirsty repeated, again pulling hard on Melissa's neck.

Melissa was having problems breathing again. Panic was making her gasp for air. She felt dizzy and confused.

Very slowly, the cops moved aside. As she passed their line, Kirsty quickly spun around so her back was to the doors and she faced the cops again, Melissa between her and the guns. Carefully she backed into the building, passing through the automatic doors and into the bright lights of the federal building.

They passed through the security arch, which alarmed immediately, with flashing lights and a klaxon, to warn everyone that Kirsty was indeed armed. Federal guards now surrounded them, their weapons drawn.

"Put the weapon down, now!" someone screamed at them.

Melissa was still having trouble breathing. Kirsty's arm clamped around her neck didn't help, but the sight of all those guns pointed her way took her straight back to Howie's murder, and Tim's. She felt light-headed, like consciousness might slip away at any moment. She almost welcomed the fog entering her peripheral vision.

Then suddenly, Kirsty let her go. Melissa dropped to her knees, gasping for breath.

"It's okay," Kirsty said. "I'm not armed, look. It's just a cell phone. I was making a citizen's arrest of this wanted fugitive."

Melissa was aware of these words but she couldn't see if the metal object Kirsty jammed into her back had indeed been just a phone. She was on her hands and knees, the blackness around her vision now crowding into the foreground. Shouts and yells were very distant now, like she was hearing them from another room. She wondered if she would ever take another breath.

She struggled to raise her head, to try to stay conscious. The last face she saw before the blackness consumed her was that of a police officer standing just beyond the security arches, watching her with a cold detachment.

Officer Jason Hagley blinked, then turned away.

Voices… so distant now, and then…

chapter twenty-one

THEY: WANT YOU DEAD

Melissa opened her eyes to find a nurse standing beside her. She was middle-aged, white with blonde curly hair, and a kindly face somewhat ravaged by sun exposure and nicotine.

"Welcome back," the lady said with a smile. Her voice was deep and raspy, confirming Melissa's suspicion that she was a heavy smoker. Melissa tried to sit up but the nurse gently restrained her. "You had a panic attack and lost consciousness, but you're okay now. No harm done. Just lie still while you get yourself settled."

Melissa allowed her head to sink back into the pillow and she closed her eyes to clear the dizziness.

"I've never had a panic attack before," she said.

"No? Well it's not that unusual to start getting them in adulthood, especially if you've been through some trauma."

Melissa gave a short, humorless laugh. "Yeah you could say I've been through some trauma."

"Certainly sounds like it. I overheard the Feds talking about you."

"I didn't kill anyone," Melissa said instinctively. She knew it was a lie, assuming that rider had died when Wilson's helmet knocked him from his bike. But she hadn't killed who they said she'd killed.

"The Senator? Tim Barns? I voted him for him. Lovely man."

"Yes, he was. And I didn't kill him."

"Not my place to say one way or the other, my dear. Let's just say nothing about the news story makes much sense. No murder weapon recovered. No motive given. A police roadblock setup *before* the murder. The suspect a young Canadian woman previously rescued from the Senator's basement? Doesn't seem likely to me."

"You sound like a detective," Melissa said.

"Well," the nurse said as she slipped a blood pressure cuff around Melissa's arm, "you hang around these guys long enough, you start to think like them."

"Am I going to be arrested?"

"I think they want to hand you over to the city police. They say this is a State issue. You passed out in a Federal building, so we're obligated to make sure you're okay."

"I can't go to them. They helped set me up."

"You should tell the agents that. They'll be here in a moment. I buzzed them when you woke up."

"Where's Kirsty? Is she okay?"

"Is that the lady who brought you into the building? Yeah I've not seen her but apparently they're holding her somewhere nearby. They're discussing what to do with her."

Melissa relaxed slightly knowing Kirsty was fine. She felt a pang of anxiety over the fate of Wilson, and all the other protestors who fell before they reached the doors. The nurse meanwhile had pumped air into the cuff and was measuring the result.

"Do you know how many people got hurt?" Melissa asked after a moment.

"No idea, but there were a fair number of ambulances outside for some time after you got here. It's a mess outside, will take some time to clean up. You're safe in here anyway."

"It's not me I'm worried about."

Wilson had a son. Doubtless other protestors had young families too, all of whom must be worried sick about their fathers and mothers and unable to comprehend why they sacrificed so much for a couple of wanted killers. It was heartening to know there were people willing to take a stand and protect those under threat, even put themselves in harm's way. She resolved to make their sacrifice worth something. If they handed her over to the city police department, all this effort was for nothing and she'd be going to jail.

The nurse smiled again. "If you're feeling better I need to transfer you to an interview room. Is that okay?"

It wasn't, but what choice did she have? Melissa nodded.

The nurse went to the door and opened it, and waved in two armed officers. Melissa stood up a little shakily but was determined not to show weakness. They didn't put cuffs on her, but the two officers escorted her from the room without much regard for her comfort.

"Good luck," called the nurse.

"Thank you," Melissa replied, just before they whisked her away.

They took her to a featureless room with a mirror on one wall and a table with three simple wooden chairs. She knew the mirror was one-way glass – she'd seen enough police dramas to know that. She wondered if she faked fainting whether they would take her back to the nice nurse's office again. Tempting but no, she had to go through with this. The officers sat her in the single chair opposite the mirror and left her. Again there were no cuffs on her, but the slam of the door behind them made it clear she wasn't going anywhere until they allowed it.

Melissa had expected to wait an age, but only a few seconds later the door opened again.

The white older guy who entered first wore a stern expression and didn't smile at Melissa once. His partner, a pretty, younger Latina woman was considerably warmer, though Melissa was wise to this tactic too.

"This is Agent Clark, and I'm Agent Ortega," the woman said as she sat down. Clark remained standing, staring at Melissa like she was pond scum. Melissa knew immediately that this was the pair of agents Tim had dealt with, and as such she also knew they were in Granger's pocket.

"I'd like to speak to two different agents please," Melissa said.

"You don't get to make that choice, Miss Jones," Clark snapped unpleasantly.

"Well then I won't talk at all. Tim warned me about you two, he said that you've been compromised, so I won't talk to you."

"Compromised?" Ortega repeated, cocking her head slightly. The word clearly didn't sit well with her.

"You're in Granger's pocket. Tim told me you work for him, not your government. So why should I trust you to treat me fairly? On the other hand, you both know full well I didn't kill Tim and nor did Wilson, so why don't you just let me and my friends go?"

Clark tutted. "That's not going to happen."

"Why not? Why not do the right thing for a change instead of whatever Granger tells you to do?"

Ortega leaned forward, her earlier warmth fading fast.

"Nothing is as simple as you think it is. You're only nineteen. You couldn't possibly understand what drives people. You can't make assumptions about us, you have no idea."

"I'm not making any assumptions," Melissa shot back. "I'm going by what Tim told me, and I trusted him way more than I trust you. Neither of you batted an eyelid when I mentioned Granger's name, which means you weren't surprised to hear his name come up. I reckon that means you're in his pocket, just like Tim warned me. I want to talk to agents who haven't sold out to a millionaire Illuminati whack job who thinks he can shoot a US senator in the head in broad daylight and get away with it."

"Ah yes, about you murdering Barns," Clark said, leaning in closer and leering at her like a perverted uncle left alone with his teenage niece. "Where is this video you say proves you didn't kill him?"

Melissa blinked. "You have my phone. Do you need me to unlock it for you?"

"No, no need. We've been through your phone. There's no video of Barns's murder."

Melissa shook her head. "That's not possible. I shot that video. I…" She trailed off. Kirsty! She must have erased it when she took a copy. Why would she do that?

"What about on Kirsty's phone?" Melissa asked.

"Not there either."

Melissa was genuinely confused for a moment. And then she remembered something. These agents had not seen the video, so they had no clue that it didn't actually show Tim's death. That happened off-camera, but they must assume it did show the killing. Kirsty had simply maintained the mystery. By removing it from her phone, they couldn't see it and in their minds, it was still a threat. That meant Melissa had a bargaining chip. Damn, that Kirsty was pretty smart. Melissa had no idea where the video was now, presumably on Darkmice.com's servers somewhere. If Granger's people had stormed the building it was likely they had secured any servers on site. That meant Kirsty must have uploaded the video somewhere else. Either way, they didn't have it and that meant in their minds, it was still a threat to Granger.

Melissa smirked. "I guess you guys won't be seeing the

video until we release it to the internet."

"If you had the video, you would have released it already," Ortega countered.

"Maybe we want something in return," Melissa said. "Maybe we want to bargain with you."

Ortega sat back. Clark paced the room, scowling.

"Go on," Ortega said at last.

"If you let us all go and drop the charges against me and Wilson, we won't tell anyone that Granger shot Tim, and we won't release the video. We'll keep it, just in case Granger changes his mind, but we won't release it as long as Wilson and Kirsty stay free, and as long as Shania and I are allowed to return to Canada and come back whenever we want."

Clark and Ortega glanced at each other.

"Oh," Melissa said, sitting back in her chair. "That's disappointing. You don't have the authority to make that decision. Well, run along to Mr. Granger and ask him what he thinks. I'll wait."

Melissa's heart was pounding. She hadn't meant to be so sarcastic but she had to admit it was worth it for the looks on their faces. Clark seemed about to explode. Ortega sat quietly with a wry expression on her face. Was that appreciation? Was that acknowledgment that this nineteen-year old Canadian was not going to let them push her around or intimidate her?

Clark stormed from the room, throwing open the door and letting it bang against the wall. Ortega smiled at Melissa.

"I didn't expect you to have balls," she said. "You're quite impressive. I can see why Senator Barns liked you."

She left the room, closing the door behind her.

Melissa let all the air out of her lungs and sank her head down onto the desk. She hoped she wasn't going to have another panic attack, but she had surprised herself by standing up to them and the adrenalin rush was palpable.

Many people had been through a lot and sacrificed a lot to get her here. She would be damned if she was going to just bow down and do whatever they told her. She made a mental note to thank Kirsty for clearing the video off her phone. If the two agents had watched it already, she would have nothing to bargain with, and she'd probably be in the custody of the Richmond P.D. by now. What they couldn't see, they couldn't be sure about.

Or perhaps she'd overdone it. Maybe they were outside right now plotting to book her on federal charges, maybe anti-terrorism charges. Melissa wasn't any kind of expert on law, certainly not on US law, but she had a good idea of the kind of hell these people could put her through if they wanted to. She wiped away a tear that had sprung into being in her left eye. Would she ever see her parents again? Would her mother pass away while Melissa sat in prison in another country? She might never see her again.

The door opened and Melissa looked up, expecting to see federal officers pour in and drag her off to prison.

Instead, there was the man who had shot Tim Barns in the head, who had ordered Melissa's kidnapping and made her life hell these past few days.

Lionel Granger closed the door behind him and walked over to the table at which Melissa sat, staring back at him.

"Miss Jones, how nice to finally meet you."

Melissa did not feel it was nice at all, but she forced a smile. He reached out his hand to shake hers. She stared at it. She could smile hello but no way could she shake hands with a man who had shot dead a good man in cold blood in broad daylight. After a moment Granger shrugged and withdrew his hand.

"Miss Jones, you and your friends have led me a merry dance recently. I won't pretend I've enjoyed it, but it had provided something of a challenge. It's also given me an excuse to tear apart those sewer rats at Darkmice.com, so there's a bonus."

Melissa said nothing. She held his gaze but kept her expression neutral. Whatever happened, she must not let him get to her. If he did get to her, she must not show it.

"Coming to a federal building was smart," Granger continued, unfazed by her silence. "Believing I have less influence over federal authorities was naïve. The group I belong to has many strings to pull, all over the country and all over the world. Hiding from us will be tricky, but knowing who is on your side will be almost impossible until you've walked into the jaws of our trap. Oh dear, that didn't work as a metaphor at all, did it?" Granger chuckled to himself. "The jaws of our trap? Dear me."

"Why did you kill Tim?" Melissa asked suddenly, breaking her silence.

Granger stared at her for a moment then said, "I see, the direct approach. Well, at least you are talking to me. I wonder if perhaps you think I will incriminate myself and the Feds will arrest me. I assure you I am in no danger here. Usually we do this sort of thing… somewhere else, but here will do in a pinch. A few more hoops to jump through but nothing too strenuous. I can't torture you here of course. I'm kidding! I can absolutely torture you."

"Why did you kill Tim?"

"You want to satisfy your own curiosity. I see, well that's fair enough. I suppose, 'I had my reasons,' isn't going to suffice? No? Well, all right then."

"You talk way the fuck too much. Why did you kill Tim?"

Granger chuckled. "It's a failing of mine, certainly. I don't pretend to be perfect. So you want to know why I killed Tim? I killed him because of the kind of person he is. Was. I knew that whatever he told me, that he didn't copy the emails, that he wouldn't come after me even when you were safe, that he would capitulate to me and be my puppet in the senate, I didn't believe any of those things. He was telling me what I wanted to hear, and I knew that at the first opportunity he would stab me in the back. And when he did, I would have to kill him. Since it was inevitable that he would try to betray me, I figured why wait until he caused me actual trouble. He might ruin a key initiative at a vital moment, and that would certainly be upsetting to me, possibly catastrophic. So, I pre-empted his inevitable betrayal."

"You feared him," Melissa said. It wasn't a question.

"Feared him? Oh no, I didn't fear him. I am a practical man. He was a threat to my plans. To *our* plans. I couldn't have him pretending to be loyal and then causing me grief at a critical time. I considered breaking him, but what use would a broken man be to me? I have so many. It would take a considerable amount of time and resources to really break a man like Tim Barns, so why bother? There'll be someone else along soon to take his seat, and chances are good they'll be more… malleable."

"Is everyone in government in your pocket?"

"Oh goodness me, no. Just enough to influence, and to guide, and to course correct. It is not our time to be in power yet. We are building towards a glorious day when the peoples of the world will turn to us and *ask* us to lead them. They will beg us. And we will be ready. But that day has not arrived yet, so we wait, and we guide, and we influence. We put pressure in key places and we steer the ship where we want it to go.

"Tim was a good man, but like you his big failing was righteousness. It's very tiresome, to be honest. Righteous people can rarely be broken or negotiated with. They won't stop until they've torn down a perceived wrong and replaced it with… what? They never take time to consider the 'what'. They just tear it down, like terrorists but without the intentional killing. There are always deaths, but those are regrettable and 'for the greater good.'"

"And Tim's killing? Was that for the greater good?"

"No. It was to make my job easier. I am not a righteous person. I change my plans and my opinions based on the way the tide is turning. I am not a zealot who will stop at nothing to enact my vision of how things must be. I take my time and use more, indirect means of getting what we want. All true tyrants begin like Tim, and we must do what is necessary to cut them off before they become a real thorn in our side."

"So if Tim was like me, I guess that means you have to kill me too."

"Heaven's no! You are young, there is still plenty of time to steer you along the right path. You have a very promising career ahead of you in Hollywood, and so much potential. Unless of course, you give me a reason to kill you."

"The video."

"Yes, the video. I sincerely hope you're not planning to hold it against me."

"Of course I am. There are things I want, and you want the video. You still don't have it, do you?"

The merest flicker of a smile flashed in the corner of Granger's mouth.

"It is proving… elusive."

"And Kirsty hasn't given it to you?"

Granger's cool seemed to slip just a little. "Kirsty belongs to a group of people you would do well to avoid. They are insane, all of them. She doesn't care about you. She's decided she and her friends alone understand what we are all about and what's 'really' going on and she will use you until you are dried up and lifeless. Don't mistake her help for friendship. She and her kind are the worst of the worst."

"So let me get this straight. You, of all people, are

accusing someone else of using other people?"

"I don't use people! I guide people. Those who are loyal to me have control over their own destinies. It is not a one-sided relationship. I do not tell people what to do."

"No, you just threaten and coerce people and even kill to get what you want."

"I am nothing like Kirsty Frank!" Granger yelled, rising to his feet.

"No, you're not," Melissa agreed. "The difference is she wouldn't send her goons into your office firing machine guns and killing receptionists."

Granger fumed for a moment and then sat down. Tellingly, for the first time, he refused to make eye contact. "I did this city a favor. I only wish you'd been there during the day when all those scum had been in the office and we could have finished them all off in one go. I should have done it years ago."

"Interesting way to influence people," Melissa said.

Her opponent sat in silence for a moment, a look of fury making him look more like Mr. Burns than she had previously noticed.

"Darkmice are not people. They are peddlers of lies and ridiculous theories."

"They were right about you."

"They were not right about me!" Granger was on his feet again.

"Did I hit a nerve?" Melissa asked calmly.

"Give me the video!"

"I can't. Kirsty hid it somewhere on the net. I have no idea where it is, I just know how to access it."

"If you can access it, you know where it is!"

"I know where one copy is. There are three apparently, and I only know where one is. Nobody knows where all three are, not even Kirsty. It's a cool little program her friend came up with."

Granger stared at her. Clearly his understanding of technology was even sketchier than Melissa's.

"I want to see it."

"I'm not going to show it to you, and nor is Kirsty. We want it to eat at you."

Granger slammed a fist down on the table. It took everything Melissa could muster to prevent her from jumping out of her seat. Instead she merely blinked.

"You will show it to me, or…"

"Or nothing." Melissa kept her voice even and stayed seated, even as Granger stood in front of her with fury written on his face. "You're going to do as I say."

"Don't be ridiculous."

"Here are my demands."

"You are in no position to make demands!"

"Number one. I want all charges against me and Wilson dropped."

"And if I ignore your demands? What are you going to do? Release the video? I can say it was faked. I will avoid prosecution. You can't take me down."

"Number two. I want Shania and me to be able to go home to Canada and return to the States at any time without any issues."

"You think this is a game? You think I can't crush you and your little friends?"

"Number three. Anyone arrested at the protest today will be set free after receiving any necessary medical attention. That includes Trevor and Shania, Wilson and Kirsty."

"Even if you could take me down. What do you think would happen next? The Illuminati are bigger than any one person. It will be a setback in Virginia, but my fellow members of the order will step in to fill the gap, the plan will go ahead, you will have made *no difference.*"

"Number four. I want Officer Hagley to stand trial in a federal court and I want Howie's family to receive a substantial amount of compensation regardless of the outcome of the trial."

"You think I won't take the fall to preserve everything we have accomplished? You think I will put the plan in jeopardy just to meet the petty demands of a Canadian teenage Internet star?"

"Number five. I want senior police chiefs in Virginia to meet with Black Lives Matter and listen to what they're asking for. They deserve a fair hearing and to have their concerns addressed."

"Black Lives Matter is no better than Darkmice! They won't stop until white people bow to the black man. They are terrorists and troublemakers and I will not have my police department sit at the same table with that scum."

Melissa paused in her demands. She simply stared at Granger in silence for a moment. His true colors were shining now, and she just wanted to let his words hang in the air so he could have a chance to really hear what he'd said.

"Number six," she continued. "A trust fund will be set up in Tim's name to help kids in poverty get fed, sheltered and educated."

"Barns was a joke. He's better off dead. He had no idea what he was getting into and nor do you."

"Number seven. I never want to hear about the Illuminati, and I never want to hear from you, ever again. I want to pursue my dream in Hollywood without your influence or threats. You will never have anything to do with me ever again."

Granger sniffed. "Gladly, it would be a relief, quite frankly." He paused, waiting for the next demand. "What? That's it? You don't want me to lock myself in a box for the next one hundred years? You don't want the Illuminati to cease all activities and move to Iceland? You don't want the next US election to actually be decided by the will of the people? You dream so small, Melissa Jones."

"I'm being practical. I know what I can and can't control. You can carry on with your schemes and plans until you're in a wheelchair in a nursing home, for all I care. But you'll meet my demands or the world will see that video. And no, I don't believe releasing it will bring down the Illuminati, but I do believe it will bring down you, and I'm guessing that's something you won't be able to live with, even if your *order* survives. Break any of my demands and the video will go live. Do we have a deal?"

Granger scowled.

"Do we have a deal?" Melissa repeated, more firmly. Her heart was hammering, but she didn't feel any panic rising. This was exhilarating, life-affirming. After feeling thoroughly out of control for the past week she was now in the driving seat and it felt really good. Granger's range of facial expressions alone made it worth it, from rage to fake innocence to resignation, each one almost made up for the hell he'd put her through.

Almost.

Granger sat down. He smiled at Melissa, not in a condescending way, but rather with some measure of respect.

"I should never have had you kidnapped, Miss Jones. I should have let you return to Canada and have shot of you."

"You should never have had Howie killed," Melissa said. Now it was her turn to get angry.

Granger spread his hands wide. "Believe me, Miss Jones, I had nothing to do with Howie's death. You two were to be my power couple. I was grooming you both for great things."

"What?"

"Oh yes, Howie Do was already working for me. I ordered him to befriend you, bring you in to the fold. After you met his parents, you were supposed to come and meet me. Those were his instructions."

"That's not true."

"I'm afraid it is. But I can honestly say, having him shot by the police at a traffic stop was absolutely not part of the plan. I saw much potential in you, just as I had in Howie, and together you would be even more influential, unwittingly spreading my message and doing my work for me, just like so many other great artists before you. Howie saw your photo and was unsurprisingly eager to make your acquaintance when I suggested he get close to you."

"You're lying! Howie loved me!"

"Perhaps he really did fall in love with you, I don't really care. He was certainly on track to fulfil my plan to make you both great influencers to the younger generation."

Part of Melissa hated losing her cool. She had kept it together so well and was so close to achieving some kind of victory. But the rest of her was too angry, too blindsided by this new information to keep a lid on her temper. She realized she was on her feet, couldn't remember standing. She wanted to put her hands around Granger's throat and squeeze until he was dead.

"If it helps you to believe that Howie loved you, Melissa, then go ahead. It makes little difference to me. I knew you loved him, and I knew you could be turned into a weapon against me. I knew that Black Lives Matter would reach out to you, just like they reach out to everyone close to victims of police shootings, to recruit you, to make use of you. Not only had I lost Howie as one of my prime influencers, I was going to lose you too. That's why I had you kidnapped and placed in Tim's basement. It was a warning to him, that I could ruin his career if he didn't fall in line. It was also a warning to you, that you were way out of your depth, and you should run home to Toronto and stay the hell away from any kind of organized protest movement. When the dust had settled, I planned to have you brought back to Hollywood to continue your career, perhaps matchmake with another up-and-coming young rap star, and try again. Instead you had to get involved, and I had to kill Tim. So even that is your fault, in a way."

Granger's words crashed over Melissa in waves of revulsion and horror. She closed her eyes, trying to make it go away.

"Well that's disappointing," Granger continued, refusing to shut up. "I figured you'd worked all this out on your own already. Sorry if it's a bit of a shock."

He wasn't sorry at all. He knew exactly what he was doing. He had lost control of the confrontation and this bombshell was his way of gaining the upper hand. Melissa fought back tears, and forced her breathing into a regular rhythm. She would not pass out. She would not cry. She would not give him the satisfaction.

She sat down. She took a deep, deliberate breath and exhaled steadily.

"Those are my demands. Either you meet them, or the video goes viral and everyone knows you killed Tim. And you should know, if Kirsty and I don't walk out of here by dawn, the video will be released anyway."

This last warning was a bluff, but Melissa needed to gain the upper hand again. He knew he had gotten to her, that she was rattled, and the feeling of triumph when she was talking and he was the one losing his cool had completely dissipated.

Granger let out a deep sigh. "I can't guarantee you'll never see me again. Also, I'm not setting up a fucking trust fund for Barns, you can do that yourself. Thirdly, I'll ask the Richmond P.D. if they'll meet with Black Lives Matter, but I'm not going to tell them how to react to their demands. As for the rest, you and all your friends can go, and you're free to cross the border as you please. Officer Hagley will go away for a long time, don't worry. I was asked by Richmond P.D. to keep the feds out of the investigation, but quite honestly I'm pissed as hell at the moron for shooting my rising star, so I have little problem meeting that request. For your part, I'm assuming you'll be keeping the video somewhere I can't get to. Otherwise you lose your leverage. Fair enough. But if it ever sees the light of day, you'll find yourself in prison faster than you can add another demand for a fucking pony. I don't care if you're in the US, Canada or deepest, darkest Peru, I'll find you and I'll have you thrown in jail. Do we have a deal?"

Melissa was surprised she had won so much from him. He clearly wanted to cut his losses and stay in his current position of power and influence. That was fine with her. She was under no illusions about bringing him down or stopping his organization, but she wanted to make sure the damage he'd done to so many lives in the past few days was reversed as much as possible. Though nothing would ever bring back Howie and Tim, and from that perspective he was getting off extremely lightly. If Melissa could guarantee nobody else would get hurt on her account, then it was enough.

"One more thing, you leave Darkmice alone, okay? No more raids, no more shootings, and compensation to the families of the two victims."

Granger sighed again. "Oh fine. If they leave me alone, I'll leave them alone."

Melissa repressed her revulsion and reached out a hand. Granger shook it.

"I'd say it was a pleasure doing business with you," he said as he retrieved his hand. "But… yes, well…" He trailed off. Melissa felt much the same way. "You're free to go, Miss Jones. Enjoy your life and your career, and don't give me any reason to come after you."

Melissa stood up and walked to the door without a word. She opened it and was about to walk through when she paused and turned back.

"I'll take the pony too."

"Get out!"

chapter twenty-two

THEY: WANT YOU DEAD

Melissa and Kirsty stepped out into the morning sunshine, blinking and shielding their eyes. The street outside the federal building was strewn with garbage, abandoned clothes and signs, and in two cases, bodies.

Both lay under sheets but were unmistakable. Melissa's hand went to her mouth when she saw them. She couldn't help but stare, until she noticed the intermittent blood stains over the pavement too.

The police had closed the road to traffic and were busying themselves collecting evidence. Melissa highly doubted anyone would face prosecution for the two deaths and God-knows-how-many injuries, but the police had to be seen doing their duty, so here they were photographing and measuring.

Some officers glanced at Melissa but nobody moved to stop her as she wandered through the debris like the lone survivor of a plane crash picking her way through the wreckage. A tremendous feeling of guilt bit into her soul, not just for the two fallen but for all the people who had sacrificed to get her here. Now that she had "won", if you could call it that, her bargain with Granger suddenly seemed rather selfish. The good things she had wanted for other people, such as Tim's trust fund, or the Black Lives Matter negotiations, failed to materialize. Sure, anyone arrested or hurt at last night's protest would be taken care of and released, but other than that, all the conditions she had left in their contract had been for her and her immediate friends. She should have held out for more. Where was the compensation for the dead and wounded? Aside from Howie's family, there was no money for anyone else to help rebuild their lives. And the irony was Granger would be okaying compensation for the family of a man who was working for him anyway.

She should go back and renegotiate.

Of course, that wasn't an option. She had made her deal and walked free, and that in itself was an achievement.

Kirsty thought so too. "I'm proud of you," she said. "Granger's goons spent about five minutes with me while I explained what I'd done with the video. I don't know what you said to them, but here we are walking free."

"I made a deal with Granger," Melissa said, her voice hollow.

"You talked to Granger? Face to face?"

Melissa nodded.

"Well then I'm even more impressed. What did he agree to?"

"As long as the video never comes to light, Wilson and I get our charges dropped, everyone arrested last night goes free, Hagley is prosecuted by the Feds and he'll set up a meeting between Richmond P.D. and Black Lives Matter."

"That's not bad."

"I'm sorry it's not going to help you bring down Granger."

Kirsty shrugged. "I think we both know the video wouldn't have been enough for a conviction. It will do for now. Can you still cross the border?"

"As often as I want."

"That's great, congratulations!"

"It's not great for them," Melissa said, gesturing towards the two bodies, one of which they were now loading into the back of an ambulance. "It's not great for your guys who died. It's not great for Tim. It's not great for everyone who got hurt last night. Did you hear from Wilson? Is he okay?"

"I've no idea. I only just got my phone back."

Melissa took her phone from her pocket and saw that she had reception again. The block on her account was lifted. Small victories, she thought.

Kirsty was checking her phone now. "I don't see anything about Wilson. I'll get someone to come pick us up and we can go to the station."

They had reached the edge of the police cordon now. Life seemed pretty normal on the other side, with people headed to work and cars rushing by. There were a few jam ups as people tried to turn into the closed area and had to turn around. Aside from that life was continuing as normal. Most of these people had no clue how much of their government was in the pocket of a shadowy organization with nefarious plans for a New World Order.

A police car pulled up, its lights flashing but no siren blaring. Melissa halted abruptly. Was Granger already reneging on the deal?

The doors opened and to Melissa's huge relied, out climbed Shania, Trevor and Wilson. The car sped off, leaving the five of them to share hugs and laughs. Melissa had to be careful hugging Wilson as he had an arm in a sling and cuts and bruises covered his face. He was able to walk though, and seemed in good spirits.

"You got us out, baby girl!" he cried, high-fiving her with his good hand.

Melissa couldn't help but smile, despite her disappointment with the scope of the deal she had struck.

Shania hugged her again. "Thank you," she said. "Between you and me, I am fucking glad we're allowed to go home."

"The best news," Kirsty said, "is that Hagley's going to be prosecuted by the Feds."

This news raised a cheer from Trevor and Wilson especially.

"And there should be compensation coming your way," Melissa told the two of them. "It's not much and it doesn't begin to make up for Howie's death, but at least it's something for Curtis's future."

"Thank you," Wilson said.

"And, Black Lives Matter get to meet the Richmond PD chiefs."

"That's fantastic," said Wilson, smiling through his injuries. "Maybe they'll even listen to us."

"Miracles have happened before," Trevor agreed.

Shania hugged Melissa a third time. "Oh my God, you got this deal?"

Melissa nodded.

"That's amazing. You're amazing! Let's go home!"

They laughed. Trevor wanted to go home to make sure Jackie was okay, and Wilson said he would call Yolisa and have her and Curtis meet them all there. So they decided that the five of them would take Trevor's car back to his house for breakfast. It had been a very long night and they were all exhausted.

Trevor's car was thankfully where they had left it in a local parking lot. It had not been tagged or towed, and there was no ticket on the windshield. Trevor drove to where Wilson had left his car, and at that point they parted for the time being. They dropped Kirsty at the Darkmice.com offices too. She made sure they had her number, more hugs followed and they said goodbye to her.

Trevor drove Melissa and Shania to Tim Barns's house and hung back as they crossed the remnants of police tape surrounding the front doorway. Melissa took her key and opened the front door. They crossed the threshold with a silent reverence, a heavy feeling of despair settling on Melissa's shoulders. The place was just as they had left it that morning before Tim died. There were still breakfast plates in the sink to be washed. Tim's coffee mug was on the kitchen counter. Melissa placed it in the sink sadly. She wondered who would take ownership of the house now. Perhaps Tim's ex-wife? Whatever its fate, Melissa wanted to leave the house as she had found it, minus her things and Shania's of course.

The two of them retrieved their suitcases, which Wilson's friend had kindly brought from the airport. Ironically, they were now able to leave the country so they could have picked them up from the locker after all. Still, it was awesome to have a change of clothes and access to their own toiletries.

Enjoying some time to themselves, they each took showers and brushed plaque-encrusted teeth, and dressed in clean clothes, packing the dirty linens in their suitcases.

Once they were ready, Trevor helped take their suitcases to the car.

Considering the circumstances under which she'd come to be here, this house was, on balance, a place full of mostly positive memories. Tim was one of the good guys, and she missed him terribly. It was deeply sad that his life and career had been cut short in such a brutal and senseless way, and it nagged at Melissa's soul that they would probably never see justice for what happened.

They left and locked the door behind them, Melissa pushing her key through the mail slot before walking sadly to the car where Trevor and Shania now waited.

When Trevor pulled the car up in the driveway of his house,

there was a surprise waiting for them. Wilson came outside as they got out of the car, carrying a toddler in his good arm. Trevor lost his mind, grabbing the little boy and lifting him up high.

"Hi Curtis!" he crooned. "I'm your grandpa!"

Melissa and Shania couldn't help but smile. The kid was adorable, and Wilson was every inch the proud daddy. With a grin, Melissa saw that, yes, little Curtis did indeed have his daddy's ears. Jackie came out to join them and there was a tearful reunion as they all hugged and checked with each other to make sure they were all okay. Aside from Wilson's injuries, they had all come through relatively unscathed. Physically, at least. Melissa had not told anyone about what the nurse had said. The dead protestors still bothered her deeply too, although she didn't know them personally. She desperately wanted justice for them, for Tim, and for Howie. For now though, she was safe and there was little risk of her having a panic attack, so she relaxed and resolved to enjoy some time with these lovely people who had been so welcoming to her and Shania. Soon she would be going home, and that was something also to be thankful for.

Jackie had a beautiful breakfast set out ready for them, with bacon and sausages, fried tomatoes and beans, hash browns and eggs. Melissa was absolutely starving, so she devoured an entire plateful before Trevor had managed to feed Curtis more than a few spoonfuls of applesauce.

Finally she could hold onto her concerns no longer. "Are there any more folks in hospital, Wilson?" Melissa asked, her guilt rising to the surface again.

"Yeah," he said. "I'm going to stop by and see them this afternoon."

"How many?"

"Six I think. I'll check for sure. One of them is critical, she might not make it."

There was a moment of no talking as everyone absorbed this news. Only the noise of forks on plates continued.

Melissa was conscious of not ruining this time of healing, but she had to know. "And what about the two who died?" she asked Wilson.

He sighed, not out of irritation with her she hoped, but rather it seemed he too was sad to break away from this happy moment and return to unpleasant reality. "Jamal Harrison, who's a friend of mine, and a woman I didn't know. I will find out. I'll be at both their funerals."

"I can't believe they gave their lives for us."

"And I would have given my life for them. That's how this movement works. We don't just march around and shout things at the police. We put everything on the line."

"Well I'm deeply grateful," Melissa said.

"I'm sorry we can't stay for the funerals," Shania added.

"That's okay, I understand. You guys need to get home."

"My mother is sick," Melissa said. "I'm scared I may not get to see her alive if I don't go back soon. I'm sorry."

Wilson smiled understandingly. "It's fine. I'll pass on your condolences."

"It is an amazing movement," Melissa said. "If I lived here I would certainly be part of it. I promise to reach out to BLM in Toronto and see if I can help them in any way."

"I appreciate that," Wilson said.

"Maybe you should reconsider your involvement," Trevor said, nodding towards Curtis who was flinging applesauce around his highchair tray with a spoon.

"Jamal had two girls," Wilson said. "The rest of us will all be pitching in to help out his wife. But the struggle is for their future, so it's worth laying down our lives for. Dad, Curtis makes me more determined to fight. He's not gonna grow up with the same shit that I went through."

"Watch your language," Jackie scolded him.

"I mean it, Ma." Wilson was fired up now, his breakfast forgotten. "I don't want police in his school setting him up for prison when he leaves. I don't want cops on corners stopping him for walking or whatever innocent thing he's doing and planting drugs on him. I don't want no white guy deciding my kid's dangerous and shooting him dead in the street and saying he was just standing his ground so nobody can put him in jail. I don't want cops stopping him while he's driving and shooting him dead at the side of the road. I want better for him than what Howie and I got. Something's gotta change, ma. I can't lose my kid like I lost my brother."

There were tears in his eyes now. Jackie put down her plate and moved over to comfort him. Shania and Melissa exchanged sad glances. Curtis banged his spoon on the tray table and laughed, oblivious to his father's pain. Trevor shushed him and helped him spoon more sauce into his mouth. Wilson sobbed into his mother's shoulder while she comforted him.

Melissa was crying now too. Crying for Howie. Whatever his reasons for hooking up with her, whether Granger had lied or not, she had to believe he really did fall in love with her. She had not told anyone what Granger had told her, and nor did she intend to. It was between Melissa and Howie's memory, and she chose to believe he loved her. Granger might have been screwing with her but she doubted it. It was entirely plausible that Howie had sought her out and befriended her on Granger's instructions. But she did not believe there had been nothing there for him, that he was just fulfilling his obligations to his master. Their love had been more real than any relationship she'd had before. You couldn't fake that.

Could you?

Melissa had planned to load a second helping of food on her plate but suddenly she felt overfull and a little nauseous.

Should she tell Wilson the truth about Howie? Would it help anything if she did? If anything it would just make him feel worse to know that his brother worked for the man who had ruined all their lives. Or perhaps Wilson would do something stupid, try to take revenge on Granger, and end up landing himself straight back in jail, or worse.

Once they cleaned breakfast away, Jackie cleaned Curtis up and placed him on the carpet of the small living room to play freely. The others sat around watching, laughing when he did something silly, and interacting with him whenever the opportunity arose. Trevor and Jackie were doting grandparents, absolutely over the moon at this surprise addition to their family. Wilson sat back and let his parents enjoy their grandchild, shifting a few times in the armchair to try to get comfortable. His arm was bothering him, and Jackie paused to fetch some painkillers from the kitchen.

Melissa sat beside him, and their eyes met a few times. They shared smiles, and Melissa felt the urge to move closer to him. She resisted. He looked too much like Howie for any closeness between them to be anything but weird. Plus his parents and his kid were here.

The morning wore on and Melissa took advantage of her connected phone to call her parents to let them know she was okay and she was coming home. She texted Jasmine, her agent, to ask her to book a flight to Toronto for the following morning. Jackie insisted that the two girls stay the night and Trevor offered to drive them to the airport in the morning. Melissa even had time to record a quick video of herself on her phone and post it to her You Tube channel, assuring her fans that she was fine and she would be providing a full update in a day or two. She thanked people for their support and told them the charges against her were dropped. There had been a large number of comments coming in for days, but now responses to this latest video came in a deluge.

There were a few haters of course, but the overwhelming majority of comments were messages of support and relief.

Melissa felt normal again. It was nice here, laughing and joking with Shania and Howie's family, playing with Curtis and enjoying the little boy's innocence. Jackie found some old toys once belonging to Howie and Wilson, and she laid them out for Curtis to look through. He chose a stuffed rabbit and a number of toy cars, which he had terrific fun with racing them along the road-like pattern of Jackie and Trevor's carpet. Grandpa beamed as he raced cars with his grandson, and he kept looking over to Wilson and admonishing him for keeping Curtis a secret for so long. He was certainly making up for lost time now.

At last Wilson stood up.

"Mom, dad, can you watch Curtis for me? I'm going to the hospital to look in on Jamal."

"Of course, son," Jackie said. "Be careful, okay? Do you want your dad to drive you?"

"No, I'll be fine. The pill really helped."

"Okay, well go easy."

Wilson tried to bend down to kiss Curtis but it was too painful for him. Trevor lifted the boy up so he could give his dad a hug.

"Yolisa will be stopping by at four to pick him up. I should be back by then."

He grabbed his keys and left, waving to Melissa and Shania as he went.

Curtis watched him go with a curious look on his little face. He seemed quite happy to be with people who were, prior to just a few hours ago, total strangers.

The first indication that something might be wrong was the sound of an engine roaring and a car speeding by. It screeched to a halt a little way down the street, but from the angle through the living room window there were trees blocking their view. Was that where Wilson had parked his car?

A series of loud cracks followed, and then a bang so loud the windows rattled. Curtis started crying. Melissa stared at Shania in shock, unsure what to do.

Trevor was at the front door in moments. He didn't put any shoes on, just launched himself out onto his tiny driveway, squeezing by his car and out into the street. Melissa and Shania followed, and a moment later came Jackie carrying Curtis.

All four adults stood in the driveway gaping at what they were seeing.

Wilson's car was on fire. They could hear the screeching tires of the car that had committed the drive-by attack, out of sight now at the end of the street. Jackie hung back with Curtis while Trevor went inside the house at a run. Melissa and Shania approached Wilson's car, unable to process what they were seeing. They couldn't get near it – the heat drove them back. It was impossible to see if Wilson was in the front seat.

"Why isn't he trying to get out?" Jackie was calling, trying to shield Curtis's eyes from the blaze.

Melissa had no answer. She could not form words. She didn't know what to do.

Trevor came pounding past her carrying a fire extinguisher. He pulled out the pin as he ran and sprayed the fire with a jet of foam.

A neighbor came out to help, also carrying an extinguisher. Between them, the two men put out the fire in under a minute. Trevor approached the car, intending to open the driver's door. He stopped short and fell to his knees, the empty extinguisher dropping with a loud clank to the road. Trevor screamed, a terrible, soul-rending sound.

Melissa's legs went limp and she too collapsed to her

knees, not caring as the juddering pain of the impact shot up her thighs and hips. She stared in horror at Trevor's grief, knowing at once what it meant, what he was seeing. She didn't need to see it with her own eyes – didn't want to. Shania let out a loud, wracking cry. Jackie held Curtis tight and took him back into the house, sobbing loudly, almost hysterically. Trevor's neighbor took out his cell and dialed 9-1-1. Melissa wanted to tell him not to, tell him that the police couldn't help, but she couldn't move. Her knees were cemented to the ground, and her breathing was reduced to short gasps. The now-familiar fog of inkiness surrounded the periphery of her vision, and this time although she knew what it was, she didn't fight to stop it. She almost welcomed it.

Melissa pitched to the ground and lay there, dimly aware of wetness on her cheek. She felt no pain, she could see nothing but blackness.

chapter twenty-three

THEY WANT YOU DEAD

When Melissa woke, Shania was smiling at her.

"Welcome back," she said.

Melissa struggled to sit upright and Shania helped her up.

"What happened?"

"You had a panic attack, or at least the doctors think you did. Then you fell and hit your head."

Melissa reached out a hand and felt bandages on her cheek.

"Is it bad?"

"No, just some bruising. Nothing permanent. You don't even have a concussion."

"How long was I out for?"

"Not long, but you woke up in the ambulance screaming, so they sedated you. You've been in hospital about an hour."

"And Wilson?" Melissa asked, the terrible image of the burning car crashing back into her memory.

"He's… dead. I'm sorry."

"Oh my God," Melissa breathed, tears springing to her eyes. "Poor Curtis."

"Poor Jackie and Trevor. Losing both kids in one week. I can't imagine what they're going through."

"Did the police come?"

"Yeah, just before the ambulance."

Melissa's trepidation rose. "I don't trust the police. Whatever they say happened will be a lie. They'll probably try to pin it on me."

"Maybe. I called Kirsty and she said she would come straight over and I should go with you to the hospital. She said she would text us if she hears anything."

As if on cue, Shania's phone buzzed. She took it out and opened the text.

"Kirsty's talking with the police. They won't tell her much."

A pause, then another buzz.

"Oh God," Shania said.

"What?"

Shania's phone buzzed again.

"Kirsty says Wilson was shot three times before they threw a petrol bomb into his lap."

Melissa couldn't reply. An icy hand clasped around her heart and her breathing was causing her problems again. She closed her eyes and lay back, trying to regain control. She was suddenly aware of how much her knees hurt, and her throbbing cheek bone. She seized the pain and held on to it, bringing herself back from the fog of panic that threatened to overwhelm her.

"Oh God, are you okay? Mel? Shit!"

"I'll be fine," Melissa told her, without opening her eyes. "Well, I'm not fine but I'm not blacking out again."

She heard the relief in Shania's voice. "Sorry, I shouldn't have read you that last text."

"It's okay. I want to hear it. I want to know what happened."

There came another buzz, but this time it wasn't Shania's device.

"Where's my phone?" Melissa asked, looking around for it.

Shania reached over to her side table and retrieved it, handing it to her friend.

Melissa read the text that had just arrived from a restricted number. "You don't dictate terms to me." Melissa went cold. This was not some random attack, or even a gang revenge killing. There was real motive behind this. And she knew immediately who was to blame.

"Granger."

"What?" Shania looked confused. Melissa handed her the phone and she read the text. "You're sure?"

"I'm sure. This is his sick way of sending a message to me. The deal we made, I guess it's off? I don't know. Oh God, Shan, why did he have to kill Wilson?"

Shania put her arms around Melissa, being careful not to get caught up in her IV line.

"Because he's a sick twisted fuck and we should kill him."

Normally Melissa wouldn't approve of Shania's brutal honesty, but right now she was in full agreement. She felt like finding a gun, marching up to Granger and putting a bullet in his head.

Shania's phone buzzed again.

"Kirsty's telling us to sit tight. She's on her way to the hospital."

"I don't want to sit tight. I want to get out there and find Granger."

"You shouldn't go anywhere for now," Shania said. "At least until the doctors say you're okay to leave."

"Fuck that, I'm not sitting here waiting for permission. Three people I care about have died in one week. It's too much. I can't go back to Canada and pretend it didn't happen. I have to do something."

"What can we do?"

"I don't know, and I hate that I don't know."

"Then maybe we should just go home," Shania suggested,

sounding defeated.

"That's what he wants," Melissa said. "He wants me to leave with the knowledge that he beat me and I lost. He could have just told me we didn't have a deal. He didn't need to kill Wilson. Fuck..." She trailed off, more tears in her eyes. She couldn't believe this was happening. She couldn't believe people were still dying because of this vindictive bastard who couldn't let anything go, who refused to admit any kind of defeat, and couldn't bear to honor an agreement for which he did not come out on top. Well that was it. The gloves were off. "As soon as Kirsty gets here, we're releasing that video," she said. "I want everyone to know what this fucker did."

"Mel, I know you're angry. I am too, but I'm scared."

Melissa stared into her friend's eyes. She wasn't kidding, there was real fear there.

"We don't have the luxury of being scared. We can't let him get away with this *again*!"

"I know, but what if I lose you? What if he decides to kill me next, or go after our families?"

"But that's the point. We can't sit back and assume if we do nothing we'll all be okay. We did that and Wilson died anyway. We have to fight back to protect ourselves and the people we love. If we don't he'll just keep on hurting us until we completely crumble. Until there's no fight left in us. Until he controls every part of our lives."

"Maybe that's what we should do, bow down and give up. Anything to stop anyone else from dying."

They hugged again. Part of Melissa wanted to do the same thing, to tell Granger he had won, that they were returning to Canada and would never come back, or that she would work for him in Hollywood, whatever he wanted. Anything to keep her family and friends safe. But a bigger part of her knew Granger was too petty and impulsive for that. She had hurt his pride and he was going to make her pay for it. He would throw around his weight until he crushed her, until all the people she loved were hurt or dead. She was damned if she was going to let him do that.

"We have to fight, Shan. He could kill anyone at any time and the law won't touch him. We can really hurt him, show the world what he's capable of, and then no lawmaker will be able to turn a blind eye to him ever again."

"You hope. What if it just enrages him more? What if he takes it out on us?"

Melissa didn't get a chance to answer because at that moment Kirsty arrived. She hugged Melissa and Shania.

"Thank God you guys are okay. I'm so sorry about Wilson."

Melissa wasted no time getting to business. "I want to release the video."

Kirsty folded her arms. "No."

"What do you mean, no?"

"I mean no. I'm sorry, Melissa, I'm not going to take that risk right now."

"What else do we have to risk? Wilson is dead! We need to take Granger down."

"Two things. Firstly, I have a hell of a lot to risk. Two of my friends are dead, people I worked with and cared about. There are twenty more people who work for Darkmice, and Granger is just itching for an excuse to murder all of them. Secondly, the video proves Granger was there but not that he pulled the trigger. He's calling our bluff. He thinks that if the video was a smoking gun, excuse the term, then we would have released it already. He's realized that because we've not released it, it must not prove his guilt. He's pissed at us for playing him and he took it out on poor Wilson."

Melissa sat in stunned silence as Kirsty talked. It all made a horrible kind of sense.

"You're sure he didn't find the video?"

"I'm sure. If he'd seen it, Wilson wouldn't be dead and we'd all be under arrest again by now. This is his way of forcing our hand and getting us to release the video. For us to release it, it would have to be damning evidence and guaranteed to land him in prison. If we release it now, he'll see it and know for certain that it can't be used as evidence against him because it doesn't show the murder. If we don't release it now in retaliation for Wilson's murder, he knows we don't really have anything that could hold up in court. Either way, we're screwed."

Kirsty's logic was making Melissa's head spin.

"He's taking a heck of a gamble on us having nothing incriminating then."

"True, but as I said, he's weighed the options and decided if the video was worth releasing, we would have released it already. His ego is so immense that he can't stand to have you win. I guess he went away and thought about the deal you came to, and decided that our video wasn't all we were saying it was."

"What if we can link him to those emails sent to the attorney general?"

"Then the AG will lose his job and Granger might take a hit, but it's unlikely to put him behind bars or damage him in any lasting way."

"Fuck!" After all this, did they really have nothing left they could use to hurt him? Was he really going to get away with the deaths of Tim and Wilson? Would Granger force Melissa to return to Canada and wait for his permission to come back and serve him as an influential voice to the next generation on his behalf? She refused to be a puppet, but Granger could pull the plug on her career and ban her from the US any time he wanted. He was in control now. After all they had sacrificed, after those two protestors had died to get her to sanctuary last night.

"I want to see that bastard burn," Kirsty said with surprising steel in her voice. "But I didn't see this coming and we may be sunk as a result."

Melissa picked up her phone and read Granger's text again. It raised hot fury in her, the arrogance of it. And then something else, curiosity.

"Kirsty," Melissa began.

"Yes?"

"Do you have any way to find out the number this message was sent from?"

"Possibly. I have an expert on my staff. Give me your phone for a few hours and I'll let you know. How does that help you?"

"Can your expert also trace where this phone is, its location I mean?"

"Again, possibly. Where's this going?"

"Shania, remember when Bruce was chasing us around downtown Richmond and you were up on that roof?"

"Ugh, yeah," Shania said.

"Tim said he was taken somewhere and talked to by the two FBI agents, Clark and Ortega, and then by Granger. He said it was a place that wasn't official, so nobody would know where he was."

"Yeah, so?" Shania looked confused.

"Tim said he was walked there, not driven. So it must be somewhere close by to the internet café where we were looking at the emails we stole, before Bruce came in and you and I ran away."

"You think the text was sent from this building Tim was held in?" asked Kirsty.

"It's possible. If we could find out where that building is, we could try to break in and find some more evidence."

"That sounds like something that could land us in jail for good this time," Shania warned.

She had a point. Melissa was desperate to see her mother, and highly conscious that even a few days in prison here could mean never seeing her mom again if she took a turn for the worse.

"It's a very bad idea," Kirsty said. "There's no clear target, no exit plan, and if you're caught Granger will probably kill you both. What he's capable of… I mean, I know he's a killer but what he did to Wilson, just to make a point to you… It's insane. He might be insane. You can't predict what he'll do, or what he thinks he can get away with."

"Point taken. Can you at least see if it's possible to locate this place? We can go down and take a look this afternoon, at least see if there's a chance to get inside."

Kirsty nodded. "I'll do that, but I'm warning you now. This won't end well."

"Text Shania when you get an answer, okay?"

"Sure. Where are you going?"

"Downtown, to the area where Bruce chased us. Maybe we can find this place on our own."

"All right, but for God's sake be careful."

"We will."

Melissa showed Kirsty the code to unlock her phone then she and Shania gave her a hug and she left them.

"This is such a bad idea," Shania said.

"Shan, I can't let him get away with murdering Tim *and* Wilson. I just can't. If you want to get on that flight then I'll wait until you're safely away and then do it myself. I could use your help, no question, but it's your choice."

Shania sighed, long and loud.

"I'm in," she said at last.

chapter twenty-four

THEY: WANT YOU DEAD

Shania parked the car and she and Melissa were now on foot, retracing their steps from the day when they stole the Attorney General's emails and spent the afternoon trying to escape Bruce on the streets of downtown Richmond.

Melissa felt an air of determination. This was all or nothing. Either she would win today – and she had no real idea of how to achieve any kind of victory or what such a win might look like – or she would end up in prison or dead. She had no desire to die, but her aching, burning *need* to seek revenge on Granger was all-consuming – it outweighed all other considerations. People had died directly or indirectly because of her. If she'd stayed in Canada in the first place, all these people, from Howie, to Tim, to Wilson, to the protestors, they would all still be alive.

Good people were dead, but Granger still lived. This world wasn't just unfair, it was fucking evil.

The text from Kirsty arrived after half an hour of wandering around, trying aimlessly to find a suspicious building – which of course was impossible. Kirsty texted them an address and a map position.

"That's just a block away!" Shania said. She pointed east.

As they moved towards the place marked on her phone's

map, another text arrived.

"She's coming to meet us there," Melissa reported. She was not planning to wait a second longer than necessary. She was too enraged to be rational. Planning and calm negotiation had ended up with people she cared about dead. Her gut was telling her Granger expected her to run away in terror, and she was determined to do the exact opposite. She had some ideas of how to achieve her goals, but no clue if any of them would work, or if opportunities to put them into action would arise.

The building itself was in a side avenue, away from the main street with its bustle of shoppers and businesspeople, tramps and tourists. It was a four-story office building, with no sign above the doors, no directory of multiple business tenants stationed outside, and no obvious way to get to the lobby beyond the locked doors.

After a moment of searching, Melissa found a button set in the wall next to a mail slot. She pressed it, while the two women peered in through the glass door in an attempt to see any signs of movement inside.

Melissa pressed the bell again, and was considering finding a heavy object to use to smash the glass doors in when she saw someone approaching from the inside.

The figure unlocked the doors and opened one of them.

Shania took a step backwards in alarm, but Melissa held her ground.

"Bruce!" said Melissa, like she was greeting an old friend.

"The fuck do you want?" he said.

"We want to come in. Can we?"

"Fuck no!" Bruce slammed the door, locked it and went away.

"Well the good news is," Melissa commented to a spooked Shania, "he doesn't want to kidnap us any more."

"We should go," Shania said. "This was a bad idea."

"Bullshit. You can go, I'm staying."

Melissa pressed the bell again and held it.

Bruce appeared once more, unlocked and opened the door.

"Quit pressing that bell or I'll rip it out the wall and make you eat it."

But Melissa just pushed straight past him. Bruce was so shocked he didn't make any move to stop her. Instead he followed her into a modern lobby with a security desk and elevators, but again absolutely no signs of any actually businesses renting space in any of the building's suites. No floor directory, no logos, no people, nothing.

"You can't be in here," Bruce said.

Shania followed them in but looked ready to bolt any second if Bruce made a threatening move. Melissa sympathized after what Shania went through on that roof, but she could have used a solid backup right now. Her knees were shaking and her brain was screaming to run, but she was resolute. She wasn't leaving until she'd gotten results.

"Are you nuts?" Bruce said to her, frustrated he wasn't getting a reaction. "Get the fuck out of here!"

"How much does Granger pay you, Bruce?" Melissa asked.

"I ain't telling you that. Get out before I *put* you out."

"Because I'm betting, even though Granger is worth a fuck ton of money, he pays you shit. Am I right? You're replaceable, he probably barely talks to you, just orders you around, right?"

"Okay, I've had enough. Time to go, Missy."

Melissa backed away from him before he could grab her arm.

"I bet he treats you like dog shit on his shoe, am I right, Bruce?"

"You don't know anything about me, and I ain't gonna tell

you. Now stand still so I can throw you out."

But Melissa kept on ducking from his grasp and needling him with her words.

"What do you get, Bruce? A hundred bucks a day? Less than that."

"Lady, I do just fine." He reached into his jacket and pulled a gun. "Now don't make me shoot you or I'm going to be spending the rest of my day cleaning, and I fucking hate cleaning."

"Melissa," Shania said, her voice quavering.

"Look at my PR lady here, Shania." Bruce turned the gun on her, and Shania looked ready to bolt. Melissa held out a placating hand. "Guess how much she makes."

"I dunno. I don't care. Get the fuck out before I start putting holes in both of you!"

"I bet it's twice what you're making. And, she doesn't have to kill anyone, and there's no risk she'll go to jail. Do you want to go to jail, Bruce?"

"Nah I've done too much time already."

"So what, if the feds bust one of Granger's operations and you get left holding the bag, you think he's going to bail you out."

"I guess he will."

"Fuck no he won't," Melissa said. "He doesn't give a shit about you. You're replaceable because Granger pays you shit. If you're caught or you decide you're not going to do what he tells you to do, he'll dump you so fast your head will spin. Or he'll just have you shot and dumped in the river. You know he's capable of that."

Bruce's gun was still pointing at a near-panic stricken Shania, but his eyes were on Melissa.

"I bet Shania earns twice what you make."

"I doubt it."

"Tell the man how much you make, Shania," Melissa said.

Bruce's gaze swiveled to Shania, and Melissa took a moment to wink at her.

"Def… definitely double what Bruce makes," Shania stammered.

"What?" said Bruce. "That's bullshit. No way do you get paid two-hundred dollars a day for PR work."

Melissa laughed. "That's it? He pays you one-hundred a day? That sucks!"

"I get overtime, and weekends," Bruce insisted, his gun now pointing absently at a section of wall.

"Ooh, that's nice. How about you come work for me."

"What?"

"Bruce, I just signed a million-dollar contract with a major Hollywood studio to make a daytime talk show and produce a number of new television dramas. I have crazy fans out the wazoo, and I need a tough-talking no-nonsense bodyguard to work for me. I need someone who can plan security for my travel and ensure those fucking wingnuts don't put a finger on me. The hours will be great, you'll get overtime of course, you won't have to kill anyone or risk going to prison, and I'll pay you two-hundred a day. I might even feature you as a regular guest on my talk show, Bruce the Bodyguard. The fans will love it.

"This is nuts. I ain't working for you!"

Melissa's heart was hammering, but it was the good kind of tension, the triumphant kind like she'd felt negotiating with Granger. There was no panic-attack or fog in her vision, just a feeling of winning someone over to her cause.

"Three-hundred a day," she said.

"Dammit, Melissa, that's more than what I make!" Shania interjected, finally getting into the swing of the negotiation.

"I know Shania, but you don't put your life on the line for me. A man of Bruce's talents deserves proper compensation. And benefits."

Bruce actually seemed to be contemplating a defection.

"You're serious?"

"Completely." Melissa held out a hand, hardly daring to believe this was happening. "You're exactly what I've been looking for."

Bruce put his gun away and shook her hand.

"Okay, boss. Where do we start?"

Melissa tried not to make it too obvious that she was astonished and excited to have won him over. The bastard was complicit in multiple deaths, he may even have killed Wilson himself, and she had no intention of truly hiring him. But to win him over right now was exhilarating. Perhaps she really did have a chance to make a serious amount of damage in Granger's operations.

"Call Granger and tell him to come here. Don't let on that you're not working for him anymore."

"Sure thing."

Shania moved over to Melissa's side. As Bruce went to the security desk she leaned over and said, "You realize he's probably just going along with us for now, right? He's calling Granger and he still works for Granger."

"It's possible. It doesn't really matter. As long as he's not throwing us out or shooting us, I say it's a win."

"Okay well I hope you know what you're doing."

"No idea," Melissa replied.

"That doesn't fill me with confidence."

"He's on his way," Bruce reported.

Melissa flashed him a smile. "Awesome. So, what is this place?"

"This is Granger's unofficial office. He conducts a lot of off-the-books business here. The Illuminati meet here when Granger's hosting, and he brings people here he wants to… talk to. We run secret operations from here, and new recruits come here too."

"Was Howie here?" Melissa asked. She couldn't help herself.

"Howie Do? The rapper who got shot by the police? Yeah he was here. I got his autograph. I liked his stuff man, sucks that he died."

"Yeah it does," Melissa agreed in the understatement of the decade. "So he worked for Granger."

"Yup, Granger recruited him about a year ago."

Melissa glanced at Shania but tried to keep her emotions in check. This was not the time to lose it. She was not going to fall to pieces.

"How does Granger keep this place hidden from the city?"

"Bribes mostly. Also the suites are all listed at stupid high rental prices so they all stay available. We do a lot of work out of here that Granger doesn't want seen to be done at his regular office."

"Well that's very interesting, thanks Bruce!"

"You're welcome. Oh, do I get sick days?"

"Of course you do!"

"Awesome." Bruce seemed genuinely excited. He was either a much better actor than Melissa could have expected, or he truly was on board with this new arrangement. If it really was true, Melissa couldn't wait to see Granger's face.

There was a knock at the door.

Bruce took out his gun. "That's too soon to be Granger. Want me to get rid of them?" he asked.

Melissa and Shania turned to the door, which opened to reveal Kirsty.

"No, Bruce. She's with us." He put the gun away.

"What the hell is going on here?" Kirsty said irritably. "I said for you to meet me outside."

"We couldn't wait, right Shan?" Melissa said breezily. "Kirsty, this is Bruce. He used to work for Granger but now he works for me as my personal security specialist."

"Does he?" Kirsty said in disbelief, shaking Bruce's hand.

"Yes he does!"

"Well that's… great?" Kirsty didn't seem sure.

"Granger's on his way."

"Oh good. Melissa, can I have a word with you?"

"Not right now," she said. More people had arrived. It was Wilson's friends from Black Lives Matter. Over the next few minutes, several dozen of them filed into the lobby, greeting Melissa while Bruce, Shania and Kirsty gaped.

"They reached out to me and asked if they could help," Melissa explained. "I told them if they wanted to do something in Wilson's name, to come meet us here. And here they are!"

Melissa watched Bruce carefully as the lobby, which was a decent size, filled up with people, some of whose faces Melissa recognized from the protest.

More people started showing up. Some of them were more of the BLM people, but when a familiar, tall man entered the lobby wearing a brightly colored uniform, Melissa's heart soared.

"Amos!" she cried. She rushed to meet the big construction worker. He'd brought his crew, and then some. About forty workers in total, all in hard hats and high-visibility jackets. "I'm so glad you could come."

"Hey Melissa, we're happy to help. Heard what happened to your friend. So sorry."

"Thanks, and I truly appreciate it."

"Least we could do."

To Melissa's joy, more people showed up. A few more of Wilson's friends, and then some people who introduced themselves to her as fans. These were just average people. She made sure they realized that as per her posting, this situation could get dangerous. One guys said he didn't care, he was a big fan and what had happened to Melissa was just awful. Others agreed. They wanted to help too.

Melissa had put out a call on her channel and on social media sites to see who would show up. And show up they did. Despite the warnings about the risk involved, a few dozen followers of her channel arrived. Some of them were fans of Howie – she had put calls out on his fan groups too. She welcomed them all with open arms and ushered them into the building.

The lobby was now full of people, but there was plenty of room for more. Melissa felt energized. They were all here because she'd asked them to come. That felt good.

"You pay all these people?" Bruce asked her.

"Not all of them, no. Some are fans of mine."

He nodded appreciatively.

Amos approached Melissa. "So, what happens now?" he asked.

"Now we wait."

"Wait for what?"

"Not what," Melissa corrected him. "Who."

"What the fuck is all this?"

A hush fell throughout the crowd. Everyone turned to the man who had screamed his question from the doorway.

Lionel Granger strode into the lobby, causing a parting in the crowd as people moved out of his way. He wasn't alone; he had about four of his thugs with him. They were all armed, though none had drawn their weapons at this point. They kept hands near their guns and eyed the large crowd warily.

"Hi Lionel!" Melissa said, greeting him with artificial exuberance. "I'm so glad you could make it."

"Get the fuck out of my building, all of you. Bruce!"

Bruce stepped forward.

"Yeah?"

"Why did you let all these people in? And why didn't you

warn me when you asked us to come here. And why are you standing *next to Melissa Jones*?"

"Well, thing is." Bruce's demeanor resembled a schoolkid receiving a telling off from his grade one teacher. "I don't work for you anymore."

Granger stared at him. "You don't… you don't work for me?"

"Nope, that's right. I work for her now."

Sweet Jesus, it was coming true. He really had defected. Melissa could scarcely believe it.

Granger regarded him like something he'd just vomited onto the floor.

"I'm sorry, what?"

"I don't work for you. She outbid you."

"Out… bid… What?"

Melissa loved to see Granger squirm. Others in the room, mostly the BLM folks, were starting to realize who this man was. They moved forward to flank Melissa, nearly a hundred people, most of them black, staring at Granger, who didn't notice the crowd closing in because he was fixated on trying to comprehend what Bruce was telling him.

"Melissa made me an offer and I accepted. Oh, you should consider this my resignation."

Granger blinked. "You don't get to quit!" he screeched in fury. "I tell you when you're done. In fact, you are done." And with that, he reached for his gun.

It was at that moment that Granger realized he was outnumbered and that everyone was staring at him. He seemed slightly less sure of himself. Slowly, he took his hand away from his gun and took a step backwards, towards the door. Glancing behind him, he saw more of the BLM people blocking his way. Amos and his crew followed the lead of the protestors, moving to block Granger and his four cronies from leaving.

Granger gave a humorless smile in an attempt to placate the crowd.

"This is an… interesting turn of events," he said. Melissa could tell he only now fully comprehended the situation he had walked right into. He was not getting out in one piece. Wilson's friends were angry as hell – she could see it in their eyes. This man was the reason Wilson and the two protestors were dead. He was likely the reason for the attack on the protestors at two separate marches, and was maybe even an element behind the school to prison pipeline, the mass incarceration of minorities, and the militarization of police. Melissa had no evidence for any of this, but it seemed unlikely it was all happening just by chance. Looking at the faces of the protestors surrounding Granger, similar thoughts had occurred to them too. And Granger appeared extremely uncomfortable.

That made Melissa smile.

"See, your mistake, Mr. Granger," she said breezily, "is that you were so sure I'd run away to Canada after you had Wilson killed, that you didn't have my phone switched off again. So I was able to mobilize all these fine folks who were extremely gracious in coming out to defend me today. And now I have the advantage of numbers, and you Lionel Granger, the man who killed Tim Barns, the man who ordered the killing of Wilson Douglas, and the man responsible for the deaths of two protestors last night and countless other acts of aggression against average people…" She took a breath. "You are outnumbered and you're going to listen to us."

Melissa glanced around, happy to see that at least a dozen people, mostly her fans and the BLM protestors, had their phones out and were filming the proceedings. It was vital this was on camera, and she hoped many were also live broadcasting. If she'd planned this in more detail, she would have asked folks in advance. Never mind, things seemed to be going her way at last.

"You see," Melissa said, addressing the large crowd of people, all of them staring at Granger who was shifting from one leg to another and seemed to be contemplating going for his gun. "Mr. Granger here is a killer. He shot Senator Tim Barns in the head. I saw him do it. Wilson saw him too. Mr. Granger killed Tim Barns in broad daylight, down by the river, then blamed it on Wilson and me. When I finally convinced him to drop the charges or else I would release a video of him murdering Senator Barns, he did so. But then he decided to exact his revenge on Wilson Douglas, brother of murdered rapper Howie Do, shot by police a few days ago. Wilson died earlier today, shot and burned in his car while his infant son watched him die.

"So make no mistake, if you're looking for the source of many of Richmond's problems, if you're looking for one of the reasons why the people of this city are finding it so hard to stay out of jail and stay above the poverty line, well you're looking at him. Mr. Granger is happy to kill anyone who won't do as he says. Everyone's in his pocket. The police, Virginia's Attorney General, a bunch of state senators, enough so he can wield his control and influence over the laws that govern you all, without ever having to bother with running for office and those pesky elections."

"You have no evidence for any of your accusations," Granger said. His heavies had their hands on their guns now, but Granger indicated to them to keep their weapons holstered. He knew that shooting people here would draw in the police and the press, and result in some awkward questions. Plus he was so heavily outnumbered, his men couldn't possibly shoot everyone before he was set upon. He also knew he was on camera, broadcasting live to the internet, most likely. People all around the world could see what he was doing right now, and shooting unarmed people assembled to confront him would not put him in the best light.

A television screen set into the wall opposite the front desk sprang into life. Melissa turned to the desk to see Shania and Bruce at the computer. The assembled people parted to afford most people a view of the screen.

It was the video of Tim's death. It clearly showed Granger and Bruce, and his other thugs. All were present with Tim Barns, engaged in conversation with Granger about the USB drive. Although the shooting itself was not on camera, the sound of the gunshot made everyone jump.

"That's your video?" Granger scoffed. "I knew it wasn't conclusive. I knew you were bluffing."

Melissa cocked her head and regarded Granger almost with pity. "But Mr. Granger," she said. "If you didn't kill Tim, why would you need to see the video before you knew it didn't *show* you killing him?"

Granger's eyes widened. The assembled mass of people resonated with anger, all of it directed at him. Melissa couldn't believe this was happening. Granger was forced to face his crimes in front of a room full of witnesses. The man who loved to control everything from the sidelines was now thrust into the foreground for all to see, and he was squirming like a vampire in sunlight. Melissa half expected Granger to belch smoke from his suit sleeves before he spontaneously combusted.

The feed to the television switched over to a computer desktop. It showed a view of an email account's inbox, showing Granger's personal messages.

"Well look what we've found," Melissa said. She turned to Shania and Bruce, who were still behind the laptop at the security desk. "What have you got, Shania?"

Melissa's best friend sounded much more confident now.

She almost sounded like a game show voiceover. "Well Melissa, we've got a number of emails sent from Granger's account via a proxy to hide his address, sent to the Attorney General of Virginia telling him what to do and where to go, who to prosecute and who to let go."

"And do these emails match up with the ones we have from the AG's office?"

"It appears so, Melissa."

"Awesome. How did you access Granger's account?"

"Oh, that was me," said Bruce. "I know his password."

Melissa turned to Granger, who was now fuming openly.

"Tut tut, Mr. Granger," Melissa scolded him. "That's not exactly secure now is it?"

"Enough of this. Bruce, come here. We're leaving."

"Nuh uh," Bruce said. "I know when to leave the losing side."

Another video started playing, this one of a conversation between Granger and a man Melissa didn't recognize.

"Turn that off! Turn it off!" Granger said, his voice revealing something new, an edge of panic.

The Granger on screen was in a small window to the bottom left of the television, clearly in a live chat with the man whose face filled most of the screen. Many people around Melissa seemed to know who this was.

Amos whispered in Melissa's ear. "That's our mayor," he said.

Melissa turned to the security desk, her mouth open.

"Where did you get this?"

Shania smiled back. "Bruce here is proving well worth the money you're paying him," she replied.

"Harvey, I don't appreciate your delay in responding to my call," said Granger's small head inset on the screen.

"I'm sorry, Lionel. Truly I am. It's been a crazy day. Listen, about that contract you wanted my office to approve."

"It had better be done, Harvey, or you may find yourself losing the election next week, am I completely clear?"

There was uproar in the room. The conversation continued on screen but nobody could hear it over the din. Granger raised his hands for silence and eventually got it.

"This is all very clever, but I am being set up. This is a series of lies from the minds of conspiracy theorists. These are people who believe your water contains mind suppressants and your food contains drugs to make you comply with your government's instructions. They believe Prince was murdered and that the moon landings were faked. They think vaccines give you autism and that 9/11 was an inside job. They are crazy, they're full of shit, and you're all being suckered. I've never seen anything more ridiculous in my life, and I am sorry you've had your time wasted today."

There were murmurs throughout the crowd.

"As for you, Melissa Jones. I want you to stop this charade."

"I'm sure you do."

"I have a proposal for you."

"I'm not making any more deals with you, Lionel."

"Not even for your mother?"

Melissa struggled to prevent her legs from collapsing underneath her. "What? What about her?"

"The Virginia Cancer Institute is running a trial for a new drug that's seeing amazing results in breast cancer patients. Perhaps your mother could benefit from being enrolled."

Melissa was focused entirely on Granger now. Everyone else in the room melted away. Fog formed at the periphery of her vision. She was having trouble getting enough oxygen.

"Indeed," Granger continued. "Why don't we all walk out of here and go home, and I'll make some calls. We'd better hurry though, I hear she doesn't have much time left."

Melissa closed her eyes. She couldn't trust him. No deal would be honored. If she let him walk now, she would end up in jail or dead, so would Shania, and her mother would die without her. There was no trial. He was lying.

But what if he wasn't lying? What if there was even a small, tiny chance that there was a trial and it could help her mom.

Could she live with herself? If she told him to go fuck himself, could she go back to Toronto and sit at her mother's bedside while she wasted away, knowing there was something she *could have done*?

Melissa forced herself to breathe. The mist in her vision cleared. All eyes were on her. Everyone in the room was silent, watching to see what she would do next. If she told them to go home, would they listen? Would they let Granger walk out of here?

Granger was quiet now, his eyes fixed on her. There was a tiny smile on his lips. He knew he had her.

Except he didn't.

Melissa turned to Shania.

"Anything else you've found in Mr Granger's account?" she asked.

Shania spluttered, "Yeah but…"

"Then let's see it."

"Are you sure?"

Melissa turned back to Granger. She locked eyes with him again. The tiny smile was gone. He looked small. He looked frightened.

Sorry Mom…

"I'm sure," she said.

"What the fuck is that?" someone yelled, pointing at the TV. All eyes turned to the screen.

A series of drawings flashed by, image after image,

blueprints and development plans for buildings, like some future city from a science fiction movie.

Granger stammered, a look of panic on his face. "It's nothing, just drawings, just doodles, nothing at all!"

"Is that the General Lee Memorial?" Amos asked. "Where's the rest of Monument Avenue? What are all those buildings doing there?"

"What are we looking at?" Melissa asked, completely clueless.

Amos stood just a couple of feet from the TV now, staring at the images in stunned silence as they flashed by.

"My God! He wants to tear up the whole city. He wants to level Richmond and rebuild it as… as something else."

"It's pure speculation!" Granger insisted. "Just for fun." All his bravado was gone. Now he seemed like a small, old man who might be about to lose everything.

Melissa had no sympathy for him.

"This is Granger's master plan," Kirsty announced, stepping forward for the first time since Granger's arrival. She was probably making it up as she went, Melissa couldn't be sure, but the crowd seemed to be lapping it up. "He plans to level most of the city and rebuild it in his image. Approximately eighty-five percent of Richmond's residents are to be forced out of the city and placed into camps. They will eventually become slave labor to build this utopia for the remaining fifteen percent to enjoy. This is your future according to Lionel Granger, everyone. Until now we thought this was rumor, we had no way to prove it. But these are not just the doodles of a bored artist. These are detailed plans, and if we dig deeper I've no doubt we'll find incriminating details about how Granger intends to achieve his vision."

The murmurs were now turning murderous. Granger had played his final card and lost. He was barely holding it together. Now it was his turn to experience betrayal, to have the rules of the game changed underneath him, to have someone else be in control of his destiny.

"Fuck you, you Canadian *bitch!*"

Granger lost his cool. Melissa stared in shock as the man who had almost destroyed her life melted down in front of her.

"How dare you do this to me? How dare you, a woman, a teenager, a *foreigner*, how dare you? I will destroy you! I will tear you apart! I am the future of this city, it is dead without me. I will remake it just as we will remake America and the world, a New World Order. There will be no limit to how far I will go to achieve our plans. Tim Barns was in my way so I got rid of him, so what? He was nothing, an unworthy opponent. I run this town. I can shoot someone in the street and nothing happens to me. I control everyone in positions of power here, they all bow to me. That makes me more important than any of you. Any of you!"

Granger's four men backed away from him now, trying to melt into the crowd. The people wouldn't let them. They realized they were on the losing side here, and were looking to save their own skins.

But still Granger went on. He was ranting, raving like a lunatic.

"My city would be beautiful! You can't stop it. You can't stop any of it! Sure you can bring me down, well done, oh congratulations, but the vision will go on. There will be a new dawn over this world and we will be in control. One day, it will happen. Everything you hold dear will be swept away and we will have order!"

Granger stopped. He turned slowly towards the doors. A dozen police officers stood there with their mouths open. Beside them, a handful of federal agents. Leading the group were Clark and Ortega.

"Lionel Granger," Ortega said, stepping forward and removing handcuffs from her pocket. "You are under arrest for the murder of Tim Barns."

"No!" Granger cried, his control breaking apart like an iceberg in a heatwave. "Agent Ortega! Agent Clark! Officers, you can't turn on me! You can't arrest me. It's not possible. You work for me!"

Melissa watched in stunned silence as Ortega stepped forwards and grabbed Granger's arms. Pinning them behind his back, she placed the cuffs on his wrists as she read him his rights.

"I will be out in a day! You are making a huge mistake, all of you! You'll be killed for this. I'll kill every last one of you, and your families! Let me fucking go!"

Ortega handed Granger to the other agents who, led by Clark, escorted the furious millionaire from the building.

One agent was trying to arrest Bruce. Melissa rushed over.

"No no, please. He doesn't work for Granger, he works for me."

The agent looked confused, unsure what to do. Ortega came over.

"It's fine, let him go."

They let Bruce go, much to his obvious relief.

"Thank you," he said to Melissa.

"No problem."

Ortega addressed Melissa. "I can't speak for Agent Clark, but I'll be making a full confession as soon as I return to my office. I'm going to tell them I've been in Granger's pocket for four years now. I want it to end. You made it end. Thank you."

She reached out and took Melissa's hand. Melissa took it, but she was in such a state of shock she failed to take in what was happening.

Had they just won? Was it over? Really over?

The police arrested Granger's four men and took them from the building. Even inside, they could hear Granger screaming as he was placed in the back of Clark's car.

"What guarantee do I have you're not going to just let him go?" Melissa asked Ortega.

"I was just filmed arresting him by a dozen cameras. If he gets away it's on me. My career is over whether I take him in or let him go, so this is my chance. There's enough evidence here to make the charges stick, and if we can find a prosecutor who isn't already in his pocket, I think we can finally be rid of him. If it costs me my job, so be it."

"Maybe you can come work for me, Agent Ortega. I'm putting together an entourage."

"Maybe."

They shook hands again.

Ortega took a step backwards and addressed the crowd. "For what it's worth," she said, "I'm deeply sorry for all your losses. I should have had the guts to do something sooner to stop this. I will personally make sure Granger goes down for a long time before I hand in my badge."

"There's nothing you could have done," Melissa assured Ortega personally before she could leave.

"You say that, but… well, you did it. You're not even a trained agent. You're a teenager from Toronto, and you brought down the most powerful man in Virginia. That's no small feat. So, sincerely, thank you."

Ortega gave her a quick, loose salute and left the building.

Melissa, her heart still hammering, still in shock over what had just happened, turned to the crowd who were in a jubilant mood.

"Oh my God, you guys, we did it!" she cried. A huge cheer went up.

Shania rushed from the desk to wrap Melissa up in a big hug. Kirsty hugged them both, and Amos stepped in to embrace Melissa and lift her from her feet. The sense of release was palpable, and everyone in the room felt jubilation even if, Melissa suspected, they weren't entirely sure what they had just witnessed.

A chant of speech went up, imploring Melissa to say something.

She allowed Amos to help her up onto the security desk and a silent hush fell over the crowd.

"I want to thank you all for being here," she said, "most sincerely, from the bottom of my heart. My good friend, Tim Barns, would have loved to see so many people coming together to fight for this city. You've been part of an amazing thing today. You brought down a tyrant, not a flashy dictator dressed like a general with medals and human rights violations, but a shadowy operative who's been running things in this city for far too long without most people having a clue who he was. Nobody elected him, nobody asked him to run the city and nobody is holding him accountable. But from today that ends. I urge you to go out and spread the word. In the next few days, your mayor will fall, your attorney general will fall, and maybe countless other members of your government will collapse under the scandal that's about to go supernova. You all need to stand together and help your fellow citizens weather the storm. Hell, why not follow Tim's example and run for office! Congratulations everyone, today you took back your city!"

Everyone cheered and clapped, and Amos lifted Melissa onto his shoulders so everyone could shake her hands and thank her. In return she thanked them back. She could not have done this alone.

It was an amazing feeling, truly the best moment of Melissa's life. She tried to drink it all in, at the very least so she could talk about it on her channel later. But also so she could capture and remember this moment. She had won, or at least she thought she had. Maybe she'd find out she'd been duped in a day's time, but maybe not. This time it really felt like Granger had been utterly defeated. There was no deal, no bargain this time for him to renege on. Instead his former allies led him out in handcuffs. It had a finality to it. It had a triumph to it.

Melissa allowed the rapture of all these people to swallow her up.

chapter twenty-five

THEY: WANT YOU DEAD

"Are you sure this time? I've lost count of the number of times I've booked these tickets!"

Melissa was chatting to Jasmine over her phone.

"I'm sure," Melissa said. "We really are going home now."

"I'm glad to hear it. I'll make the arrangements and send you the details. And Melissa?"

"Yes?"

"Well done, hon. I'm seeing videos of you sticking it to that old bastard all over the internet. The TV news is running with it, they can't get enough."

"I know," Melissa said. "We're watching it here. And there's press camped outside. I guess I should go talk to them."

"Speaking as your agent, yes you should. It's excellent publicity. Have you seen the number of followers your channel has now? Plus I just got a call from your producer. He's concerned he may lose you to a rival network now that you're such hot property and is asking if there's anything else he can do to make sure you don't tear up your contract."

"Can I legally do that?"

"With the offers I'm seeing coming in, sure. You could afford the settlement I'd have to make with his lawyers."

"I'll stick with my current contract, but if you could ask him to make a few donations in my name I'd appreciate it." Melissa gave Jasmine the names of a couple of cancer charities who had done so much for her mother. "Oh and a donation to Black Lives Matter in Richmond would be great too."

"Sure, I'll mention it."

"Thanks, Jasmine."

"You're welcome, hon. And well done. I'm so glad you came through, and I'm really sorry to hear about Wilson."

"You know, if my producer is feeling extra generous, do you think he'd be willing to set up a trust fund for Wilson's kid?"

Jasmine made a note on a piece of paper off camera. "Sure, I'll see what I can do. Oh and Melissa?"

"Yeah?"

"Is this right? Did you hire security?"

"Oh, yeah. I hired one of Granger's guys. His name's Bruce. You'd like him. Well you probably wouldn't, but he's proved his loyalty and I could do with some protection in case Granger's friends decide to come after me."

"Gotcha. Well safe flight home and I'll see you soon."

"Thanks."

Melissa killed the call.

"I can't believe we're really going home!" Shania said, seeing Melissa was done.

"I know! I can't wait to see mom and dad again. I hope mom isn't too far gone."

There was a tear in Melissa's eye. Shania, knowing her friend so well, reached out and gathered Melissa into a big hug.

"I'm sure she's holding on to see you."

"I hope so."

Despite losing her second son, Jackie was in positive spirits.

She had provided food for Melissa, Shania and Kirsty, even with everything she must've been going through. Meanwhile, Trevor played with Curtis, a sad but hopeful look on his face. Both of them regarded Melissa with kindness and, something else. Was it gratitude? It was as if they were silently thanking her for taking a stand against the man who had taken their son from them, and helping to put him away. Perhaps they saw a brighter future for Curtis than they could provide for their two sons. Melissa didn't like to guess what was going on in their heads and she didn't wish to pry.

"I'm sorry we can't stay for the funeral," Melissa said. "But you should know my agent is arranging to pay the costs."

"Oh, my dear," Jackie said, her eyes filling with tears. "You don't have to do that."

"I wanted to. My contract is ridiculous. I don't need all that money. It makes me feel a little better to do some good with it. We're setting up a trust fund for Curtis too, to make sure he gets a good education."

Jackie hugged Melissa tightly.

"You've done so much for us. How can we ever thank you?"

The truth was, Melissa felt guilt more than anything else. It was her fault Howie was in Richmond when the cops pulled him over. It was her fault she had tried to strike a bargain with Granger that he ultimately took exception to, and Wilson had died as a result. If not for her, both of Jackie's boys would still be alive. If she'd never come to the States and started negotiations with this Hollywood producer, she would never have met Howie, and he might still be alive today. She knew obviously that she had not pulled the trigger of the gun that killed Howie, or the guns that killed Wilson or the firebomb that burned his body. Still she couldn't help but blame herself.

She thanked Jackie for being so gracious and promised she would visit again. She wanted to see Curtis grow up, and make sure he was provided for.

Melissa stepped outside. This might be one of the last sunny days of the year, so she appreciated the sun's warm rays. She felt immensely tired now. All the fight was gone from her and she just wanted to sleep. But first, she had to see her mother. The desperate sadness of the impending loss weighed heavily on her now that the distractions of the past week were gone. She had won, yes, but she had also lost so much, and wasn't done losing yet.

"I'm sorry, Melissa, but it's not over."

Kirsty approached from the house having followed her outside.

"Oh Kirsty, can't you let me have today?"

She drew level with Melissa and they stood together, looking out into the peaceful street.

"I wish I could. What you did today… was amazing. I've never seen anything like it. It's everything I've wanted to do since I first found out about Granger and who he really is. I've been trying to bring him down for years. Then you show up and destroy him in less than a week."

"Paid a heavy price though," Melissa said wistfully.

"Yes, you did. We all did."

"Oh," said Melissa, her guilt rising again, "I'm sorry, Kirsty. How are your people doing?"

"They're taking it hard. We're like a family and we've been through a lot together. Nothing like this though. I always knew going after people like Granger would be a risk, and that there was a chance it might end up with some of us dead, but until it happens it never feels like it really will…"

"I know what you mean."

"I know it hasn't been easy, any of it. You've endured more loss in just a few days than most people do in a lifetime, and under such horrific circumstances. That you're still standing is testament to your strength, Melissa. You really are a remarkable woman."

"Thanks. There's a 'but' coming, isn't there?"

Kirsty sighed. "Yeah. A big ol' but."

"It's not over because Granger is just part of a bigger organization, right?"

"The Illuminati are everywhere. Granger was a big player, no question. Taking him down will set them back and is a much needed kick in their collective rear ends. You've made yourself a target though, you realize that?"

"I get it. I'm not going to let it stop me though. I'll come back to the States after my mother… After…" Melissa couldn't finish that sentence. Kirsty put a consoling hand on her shoulder. "After," Melissa said, unable to be more specific but sure Kirsty knew what she meant. "I'm going to pursue my career and honor my contract."

"The man you'll be working for is one of them."

"I know, I figure rather than wait for them to come for me, I'm going to face him head on. I'm going to make him a lot of money. I'm going to make myself indispensable. I'm going to learn more about them, and I'm going to bring them all down."

"It's a worthy goal, and a completely impossible one."

"Maybe," Melissa said. "But I want to try. Maybe this is my purpose in life. Maybe this is the way I can continue to honor Howie, Tim and Wilson."

"You'll be putting yourself at risk. Your family too, and Shania."

"Shania is with me because she wants to help. It's her choice, she knows the risks. My family is in Canada, and I'm not naïve enough to think that makes them safe, but they are safer. I don't think Granger's organization will come after them."

"And what about you?"

"I'm ready for them. They're just bullies. I learned that if you stand up to bullies they usually have no idea how to react, and by the time they stop underestimating you it's too late."

"Don't count on it. They've seen you in action and they won't make Granger's mistakes again."

"Then I'll have to force them to make different mistakes."

Kirsty smiled.

"Do me a favor?" Melissa said after a moment of silence.

"Sure."

"Watch out for Trevor, Jackie and Curtis will you? Make sure they're okay. I can help them financially, but I can't watch over them."

"Sure, I'll keep an eye on them. I doubt the Illuminati will bother with them, since it's you causing them the headaches. But you can never be too careful."

"Thank you."

"Good luck to you, Melissa. I mean that."

The two women hugged, and then Kirsty walked to her car.

After Kirsty drove away and Melissa was alone, she told herself it was nearly time to go to the airport and fly back home. She wanted to sleep for a week but instead she would spend as much time with her mother as she could before the end. A pang of regret stabbed at her heart. She had done the right thing, she had little doubt, but she had passed up a possible opportunity to help her mother. Maybe she didn't have to die after all. Melissa would never know.

But she knew her mother would be proud of her. That was important too.

"I hope you're proud of me too, Tim," she said quietly, staring up into the cloudless sky. "I finished what you started. Maybe I'll even run for office one day."

It wasn't fair that Tim was dead. It wasn't fair that Howie and Wilson were dead. It wasn't fair that she might lose her mother any day now. None of it was fair. But as Melissa headed back inside to gather her things before flying home, she vowed she wasn't going to let their deaths be in vain.

Two figures approached the cell at a steady pace. One man and one woman halted in front of the bars and waited for the escorting officer to slide open the door. The stepped inside and the officer slammed the bars closed behind them.

Lionel Granger sat on the bunk, dressed in orange. He stood up as they entered, relief writ large on his face.

"Thank you for coming. I need to get out of here now. I could lose everything if I'm not there to save it."

The man and the woman regarded him for a moment. Granger's eyes shifted between their faces, imploring them silently to respond.

Eventually the woman said, "No."

"No?" Granger repeated. "What do you mean, 'no'?"

"She means no," said the man.

"You need to get me out!" Granger said, a note of desperation in his voice now.

"We think the best place for you is right here," the woman said.

"Don't be ridiculous. I'm one of you. We don't leave each other in jail. That's not how it works!"

"Consider the situation you've put yourself in," the woman explained. "You were broadcast to the internet admitting to killing a Virginia state Senator. You revealed our plans for the New World Order, which were to begin with the levelling of Richmond's poorer neighborhoods and the enslavement of its citizens. You were outwitted and outplayed by a *nineteen-year old You Tube star from Canada*! So, Lionel, please tell us, why should we risk revealing ourselves for you? What do you bring to the order that we have any need for?"

"I've made mistakes, but I have sworn my allegiance. Are you expelling me?"

The man responded this time. "Henceforth you are no longer a member of the Illuminati. You are a civilian, and will be treated as such when the time comes."

"When the time comes," the woman repeated.

"You are disavowed. Do not attempt to contact us. Do not look to us for help. You are done."

With that, the man and the woman left the cell, the officer clanging the door shut behind them.

Granger pressed himself up against the bars as the man and the woman walked away.

"No! You can't leave me here! You have to get me out. I can't go to jail. You can't leave me! I am one of you!"

They didn't respond. They didn't look back. They just kept on walking, Lionel Granger's cries echoing through the corridor as they left him behind.

Also Available From

VODKA & MILK

The Purple Don
Solomon

Revelations:
The New Scriptures
Solomon

They:
Want You Dead
Solomon

Trap Kitchen
Malachi Jenkins &
Roberto Smith
w/ Marisa Mendez

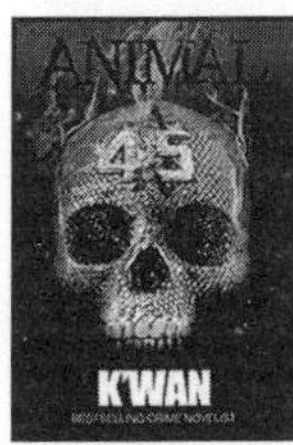

Animal 4.5
K'wan
Write 2 Eat Concepts

Captain Save-A-Hoe
iiKane

Cham-Pain
iiKane

Commissary Kitchen:
My Infamous Prison Cookbook
Albert "Prodigy" Johnson
w/ Kathy Iandoli

Hoodlum 2
The Good Son
K'wan
Write 2 Eat Concepts

All The Wrong Places
G.I.F.T.D

The Infamous
Solomon

Quantum Assassin
Chainworld
Matt Langley

MOVIE